To Kipp and Callie

Stone Wall

and

Other Stories

Bon voyage

Connie Claire

CONNIE CLAIRE SZARKE

NEWMAN SPRINGS PUBLISHING
320 Broad Street
Red Bank, NJ 07701

First originally published by Newman Springs Publishing 2020

This is a work of fiction based on true stories.
Names, characters, places, and incidents are the products
of the author's imagination. Resemblance to actual
events or persons, living or dead, is coincidental.

ISBN 978-1-64531-923-8 (Paperback)
ISBN 978-1-64531-924-5 (Digital)

Printed in the United States of America

Also by Connie Claire (Peterson) Szarke

Trilogy:

Delicate Armor
A Stone for Amer
Lady in the Moon, A Novel in Stories

"*Delicate Armor* is told by a young girl [Callie Lindstrom] growing up in a small town in Minnesota. She chants about her relationships with family and the town's people with their frequently odd behavior and characters... The author gives us truly beautiful descriptions of nature and the enduring relationship between the girl and her father..."

—Nike

"Grief and rage that didn't fade in seven decades drive the narrator [Will Lindstrom] of *A Stone for Amer* set in eastern Montana, 1919. The harsh realities of homesteading leave readers appreciative."
—Kristen Inbody

"Carrying her own psychic wounds with a feisty grace, [the narrator of *Lady in the Moon, A Novel in Stories*] expresses remarkable empathy and insight...This beautifully detailed, soulful work is a touch gritty and a touch angry over insensitivity and unfairness in the world it describes. And yet there is, as well, an underlying love for people and places in these stories, and a sort of joy emergent through the depth and honesty in Szarke's telling of them."
—Joe Paddock

Contents

Preface

Gloria Spencer loved to travel—sometimes with a friend, sometimes alone.

She hiked around Ireland, flew to France and Italy, boated over to Sicily, skied in Colorado, made it to Cape Cod, and finally searched for a fountain of youth, deep in the province of Brittany.

Once a person leaves home in order to travel, amazing, delightful, and shocking things can happen.

Stone Wall

After sailing from the west coast of Ireland to the wind-swept Aran Islands, Gloria Spencer, injured and alone, is prepared to spend her first night on Inishmaan propped against the stone wall of an ancient cemetery. That is, until Martin Faherty happens upon her.

Gloria Spencer never imagined finding herself on the island of Inishmaan with a man she'd just met kneeling at her feet. But there she was inside his thatched cottage, seated on a fainting couch with a soft, woolen blanket draped around her shoulders, her right leg bare to the knee. A pair of black and white sheepdogs, quiet after a robust welcoming, peered in through the door. Gloria winced at the pain in her ankle as Martin Faherty rubbed it dry with a coarse towel. A pan of Epsom saltwater, grown cold, sat on the floor next to her hiking shoe.

Martin scooped one dab of liniment from a jar pictured with a horse, spread the balm over his fingers, and massaged Gloria's leg. Beginning with the instep, he slowly worked his strong hands upward along the calf, as far as the knee, and back down again.

Gloria tried giving in to his soothing touch but stiffened when his fingers probed the area around her ankle.

A hint of recognition flickered in her mind as Martin looked up at her with a shy, sympathetic smile. His blue eyes seemed clouded by weariness.

"It's not broken, only sprained," he said, wrapping a wide bandage around her foot and ankle. "You'll be wanting to rest here for another day, I'm thinking."

"If only I had crutches or a cane, I could make it back to the pier."

"The last ferry left an hour ago, Miss."

"There must be another way back to the mainland."

"Fishing boats—but only in an emergency."

Gloria shrugged off the beige blanket and edged forward on the fainting couch. "This *is* an emergency. I need to get back to Rossaveal."

"As I see it, Miss, you're not dyin', nor are ya strugglin' to birth a baby."

Gloria laughed and sat back, waving a hand in resignation. "That's true. Well, then, I guess I'm on Inishmaan for the night."

"And it's welcome you are." Martin gathered his supplies and stood up. "Rest a bit while I find us something to eat."

He does look familiar, she thought, watching him cross the room. His build was slight but not delicate. His hair, the color of a pale carrot and flecked with gray, was neatly trimmed and parted on the right side.

Gloria was proud of her ability to read a person's eyes; she found no deception in Martin's—just that air of fatigue. Or was it practiced resignation? His smile, rather childlike for a middle-aged man, nudged her memory further. It *must* have been last week on the mainland, most likely in passing on a street in Doolin or Rossaveal.

She stretched and yawned, then nestled back against the curved couch, pondering the way he'd cared for her—for her ankle, that is—patiently, methodically, like a skilled doctor, but with laborer's hands, hands that worked with sheep and dogs and horses. She studied her own fingers, taking note of their grimy nails before plumping up her short auburn hair, unusually brittle to the touch—like the mossy turf she'd crawled through that afternoon.

A glance around the cottage left Gloria wondering where she'd sleep. Connected to this large room was a small bedroom just beyond the toilet. The only other space was the kitchen. How would she manage to spend the night here—or anywhere on the island—with only her camera, wallet, and a couple of books in her backpack? No toothbrush or makeup. No change of clothing.

The main room, although it had a fireplace, table, and chairs, plus the deep blue antique fainting couch where she reclined like Madame Récamier, seemed to be more a veterinary clinic than living quarters. Plastic shelves bolted to whitewashed walls were loaded with jars of liniment, medicines, syringes, shears, blades, combs, and brushes. Large gunnysacks, some empty, others bulky with fleeces, lay stacked in a corner. A large creamy-white sheepskin served as an area rug between the table and hearth.

"At least I'm safe," she murmured, "fortunate to be sitting next to this toasty fire, instead of on the cold, damp ground—all alone—propped against a stone wall, with only the dead for company."

Her hopes had risen like seabirds in the wind when Martin appeared on the narrow road near the old graveyard, standing erect in his horse-drawn cart, looking like an Irish charioteer.

Early that morning, Gloria had made the crossing—her final adventure before returning to the states. She'd chosen the island of Inishmaan, for it was small enough to bike around and had created stories that came out of this rugged middle Aran: her parents' stories and those written by John Millington Synge whose plays she'd grown to love.

Now in her mid-forties, Gloria felt fit once again. After a previous trip to Italy, she'd worked hard to lose the weight gained from platters of pasta with pork fat, custard, and daily scoops of *gelato*. Back at home, dancing around the living room to Sunday morning jazz on the radio, she began to feel like Ginger Rogers looked. Just in time, she had reclaimed the energy needed for this trip to Ireland and those long, steep hikes along the Cliffs of Moher and Slieve League, near Killybegs.

"Imagine," she'd told her friend, some time after returning home from Venice, "it's like cutting loose a five-pound bag of sugar from each hip and one from the belly."

"Well, good for you."

Back in Minnesota, Gloria had taken a brisk walk with her friend Pam around Lake of the Isles and stopped beneath the stone bridge to watch a pair of mallards paddling together. Clusters of maple leaves swirled in their wake.

"Be careful on this next trip," said Pam. "Have you forgotten that major incident in Venice? Are the police still trying to track you down for those parking violations?"

"No, I haven't received any more mail from them in the past month."

"Why would you go to Ireland in November? Won't it be cold and rainy? Dismal and dreary—just like here in Minnesota?"

"Ah, maybe, but not many tourists. I've done some home-work—mostly locals crossing over from the Galway coast. I'll have Ireland and the Aran Islands all to myself."

Sure enough, across from a roofless church, next to a heap of stones, Gloria prepared herself to spend the misty night alone, surrounded by massive moss-covered Gaelic crosses rising up gray against a darkening sky—and no sound, but for the rhythmic wash of the sea.

While wandering through the historic graveyard all alone, she fell down after twisting her ankle in one of those deep, narrow drain-age troughs that distinguish one burial plot from another. She lay there for several minutes before making an effort to stand. Bracing herself against the pain, she collapsed with a sharp reminder that her ankle might be broken.

"Thank God this didn't happen at the front end of my trip," she'd muttered to her company of stones.

The past eight days had been filled with green magnificence and a carefree wandering high above the ocean. Yet Slieve League, among the highest cliffs in Europe, had nearly been the death of her. Standing as close to the edge as she'd dared and peering straight down, Gloria felt suddenly dizzy and imagined herself free-falling into the North Atlantic—into those waves crashing far below, frothy white against the limestone. What if someone should come up behind me and…? She quickly stepped back.

"I managed to conquer my fear of heights," she printed on a postcard bound for Minneapolis. She drew an arrow on the edge of the cliff to show the exact spot where she'd dared to venture. "I figure if a sheep can lounge within a foot of death while munching grass, I should be able to grab a quick look." Certain that nobody else was close by, yet unnerved by the relentless wind, Gloria had sprawled on her stomach and inched forward. With her lips pressed against the turf, she peeked over the edge. "Just imagine!" she wrote on her card. "Two thousand feet straight down! A hell of a tumble! If there were tons of snow on a blue run, I could ski down!"

Farther up the coast, she'd ambled along the shores of Lough Gill toward Inishfree—"The Lake Isle of Inishfree," imitating the contemplative form and footsteps of her favorite poet. Afterward, she sat down on a boulder and fished Yeats from her backpack. While a pair of swans dawdled nearby, Gloria read in a loud voice: "I will arise and go now, for always night and day I hear lake water lapping with low sounds by the shore…" How she loved those words—and the water and woods.

And now she'd come to Aran—a harsh and beautiful end-of-the-world place.

Martin's sheepdogs barked outside the cottage. Gusts of wind rattled the windowpanes and bellowed down the chimney into the narrow fireplace. Hot coals glowed with the downdraft. Rolls of peat lay neatly stacked on the hearth. As pleasant and comforting as wood smoke, burning turf gave off the heady, earthy smell of dried roots and soil.

Martin returned from the kitchen carrying a large tray laden with steaming bowls of fish stew and thick slices of brown bread. He set the tray on the table and helped Gloria to a chair before sitting down across from her. For a time, the two ate in silence, as do people accustomed to living alone. Just as Martin broke off a piece of bread and dipped it into his soup, Gloria recalled precisely where she'd seen him. Nearly a week ago, she'd come upon two men standing together at the corner of Doolin's Main Street, then did what she always did while traveling—approached these locals and asked them to recommend a good place to eat.

"Right over there, inside the hotel," said the man who was Martin. He had smiled the same shy smile then, as he pointed out a building in the middle of the block: "O'Connell's Pub and Restaurant."

"And who might you be?" asked the second man.

"A visitor."

"That's nice," he said. "I could use a little visit."

Gloria simply smiled and thanked them before marching off toward O'Connell's.

Upon entering the hotel lobby, she realized why the men had been so friendly, especially the second one. They must have been taking a break from the clusters of middle-aged singles lounging on sofas and armchairs, and mingling near posters taped to the columns and walls:

November 16–18, 2007
The Matchmaking Weekend
Incorporating Blind Date,
Speed Dating & Matchmaking.
Music in all the pubs.
Top Bands including Robert Mizzel
and Patrick Feeney

While passing through the lobby, toward the restaurant, Gloria overheard bits of plaintive conversations, noticed resigned and disappointed looks stamped on the faces of those who hadn't found a

16

match. A few speed-dating sessions were still going on in the hallway where men and women sat across from each other at bare card tables. Some spoke with exaggerated animation and forced grins. Others seemed to have lost whatever enthusiasm they might have conjured up the first day. Deep, tired lines carved parentheses around their mouths. Dull eyes glazed over. It was November 18—the last day. Time had all but run out.

Midway through her meal, Gloria noticed the more timid man she'd seen outside. He was eating alone at a table on the far side of the dining room, picking at his food, and looking up with an eager smile each time a woman passed by. Several women stood chatting among themselves then moved on without so much as a glance in his direction. Each time, the man's bright look faded and he went back to his meal. Gloria sensed that slight, recalling a singles' dance she'd attended some years ago, allowing herself to feel invisible for too long, before finally leaving that hall.

Less vulnerable in his own home, Martin seemed somewhat detached, clearing the dishes, as if employed at a four-star restaurant. "Would you care for some tea, Miss?"

"Yes, I would. Thank you."

"I won't be but a minute."

While waiting for him to return from the kitchen, Gloria reflected on that Sunday afternoon in Doolin. She'd seen him one last time, just as she was leaving her tour of the woolen mill. He was walking down the opposite side of the street, toward the harbor, carrying his grip, wearing a black leather jacket over a mint-green shirt open at the neck. His blue jeans appeared as crisp, perhaps, as the day he'd arrived. He looked scrubbed and ready for town on a Saturday night. But the Matchmaking Weekend was over and the hopeful smile he'd worn inside the restaurant had disappeared. Instead, he passed a hand across his forehead and concentrated on the sidewalk as he made his way to the Aran Island Ferries.

Martin returned with their cups of tea.

"I don't know if you remember me," said Gloria, "but I saw you in Doolin last Sunday."

Martin sat down and fidgeted with his shirt collar. "I thought you looked familiar. You were there for the event?"

"No, just passing through."

"The women outnumbered the men," he said, pinching tiny nubs from the left sleeve of his wool sweater. "I might've got taken up that first night, but I didn't meet any ladies I cared about. Most of them were too forward or too hefty."

"I see," said Gloria.

Martin warmed his hands around the teacup. "And why might you have come here to Inishmaan?"

"I grew up hearing about these islands. My parents spent their honeymoon here, over fifty years ago. They're gone now, but I'll never forget what I learned from listening to them. I wanted to see the Arans for myself, visit the sights, especially Synge's cottage."

"Plenty of changes since then. We only got electricity in 1975."

"So now you have internet?"

"If you're interested in that sort of thing."

After a long pause, Martin continued. "And did you see it? The cottage?"

"I did. And I sat in his stone chair and read from *The Playboy of the Western World*. But I especially love *Riders to the Sea*."

"You truly care for these Irish writers, do you?"

"Oh, yes. My father taught literature and directed community theater—Synge and Yeats and Oscar Wilde." Gloria's eyes sparkled then narrowed as she sipped the steamy tea. "Are you familiar with them?"

"Not really. A little bit in school, but no—too busy making a living."

"Let me guess." Gloria pointed at the equipment on the shelves. "Sheep shearing."

"You know about that, do you?"

"Oh, yes. I have a cousin in Illinois who's a sheep shearer and a horse shoer. Hard work."

Martin got up to add more fuel to the fire. "Yes, very hard work." He moved his chair a little closer to Gloria's before sitting down again. "Yet I managed to finish with the fall shearing well before I went over to Doolin for the Matchmaking Weekend."

"You shear in the fall? How come?"

"To clean up the ewes for lambing in the spring. They fill out enough to stay warm during our winters."

Gloria flexed her bandaged foot. "That liniment must be doing some good. My ankle feels much better."

"Best to keep it fixed, Miss—and elevated."

Each time Martin spoke, a blush rose up from his neck, spread across his cheeks and forehead, then faded as soon as he left off with his part of the conversation. How different he was from several men she'd met back home—types who were not at all interested in what she thought or did, who could hardly wait for her to pause, so they could go on talking about their favorite subjects: themselves.

Encouraged by Martin's succinct questions, she described her bike ride around the island, the stone ruins on the way up to the highest point, the walled fort she'd climbed for a view of Connemara and the west coast. She wondered about the back-breaking labor and the number of years it took to create those myriad stone fences criss-crossing the treeless islands—like irregular quilt-work patterns that sectioned off fields and corrals for small flocks of sheep whose wool had indeed begun to thicken for winter and whose rumps stood out with blotches of red, green, or blue dye.

"A humane way of identification," said Martin. "Not like the hot poker branding done on the livestock in your country."

"Don't forget the human piercing of ears and noses."

Martin chuckled. "Lips and tongues. Sounds like some of the tourists we see here in summer."

Gloria laughed. "Oh, and the seal colonies in the shallows! I thought they were boulders until I saw them move."

"That's true. You must linger awhile in order to appreciate them, realize what they are."

Gloria described her impression of the heaps of fishnets that seemed impossible to untangle. And the stacks of old lobster traps in every color.

"They make for lovely photographs," she said. "And far from water, what about that old boat sitting at a tilt, in grass, where a boat doesn't belong?"

"That would be the last of the original *curraghs*. Hide and tar. They don't use them anymore. The old fishermen could tell you stories. Many from my father's generation drowned, never got a proper burial. But then, by dying that way, they saved on trees from the mainland."

"What do you mean?"

"A clean burial. No need for coffins. Wood is scarce here, you've noticed."

"Yes. I couldn't even find a stick for support after twisting my ankle in the cemetery. Not a twig to be found."

"Which is why we burn turf in these parts of Ireland. Nary a leaf nor a branch to bundle—no thanks to the English."

It seemed to please Martin that Gloria knew what he meant by that remark—how the English, under Cromwell, had swept the Irish Catholics westward, *to hell or Connacht*, across the sea to these wild, windswept islands where the limestone ruggedness hardly welcomed life. Their treacherous cliffs and the unpredictable Atlantic double-dared the desperate Irish.

"I grew up," said Martin, "hearing stories of how the English left our land barren. They clear-cut our trees for ship building and burned us out, pure and simple, starting in 1650 when Cromwell led his troops in the genocide of Irish Catholics."

Gloria shook her head. "Over four hundred years ago."

"And we'll never forget. Every generation knows what happened. We don't hold onto the bitter, but we never forget."

Quiet for a moment, Gloria gazed at the steady burn of turf in the fireplace.

"I don't think I could live in a place without trees," she said. "Trees are like people, milling about with birds on their branches, and the wind sounding through them: pines and maples, cottonwood trees. And willows! Oh, I used to spend hours climbing and reading books in our huge willow tree in the backyard when I was a kid."

Martin shrugged. "What we don't know, we don't miss. We have plenty of sea birds and all you can take of the wind. It just speaks a different language here."

He went on to explain how the survivors of long ago had to clear away boulders and layer sand and seaweed to create soil for planting. Now the old style of harsh living was replaced with modern conveniences: electricity, ferry boats, motorized fishing boats that made obsolete the hide- and tar-covered *curraghs*, which the fishermen used to row to the mainland or far into the Atlantic—small, ultimately frail boats that often capsized in heavy seas.

"Their crews," said Martin, "if they should turn up as far north as Donegal or found floating in the Bay of Gregory or snagged by an oar near the cliffs of Moher, were identified by the women folk, by the coded patterns they knitted into their men's sweaters. And if they weren't found, it was a clean burial they got in the north versus a deep grave here at home, tucked into the white boards of Connemara."

"You remembered! You're quoting *Riders to the Sea*!"

"No, Miss. That's just how it was when my father was a boy."

"'For when a man is nine days in the sea,'" she recited, "'and the wind blowing, it's hard set his own mother would be to say what man was it.'"

Martin nodded solemnly. "That's exactly how it was."

While the two sat quietly before the fire, Gloria returned in mind to the graveyard. How cold and lonely it had been for her crawling among the stones. Surrounded by crosses and heavy weathered slabs (heavy to keep the spirits in place), she'd come upon a triangular piece of limestone with obscure etchings. At one corner was a hole large enough for a hand to reach down. She'd read in her guidebook about this tomb-shrine, where pilgrims came to probe its cavity and touch the bones of a saint. Gloria had shuddered, imagining what horror could be inside. She might have dared to stick her fingers into the black hole if someone else had been at her side—and if she hadn't already injured herself.

In spite of the tea and warmth from the fire, she shivered for a moment, uncontrollably.

"Are you chilled then?" asked Martin.

"Oh, no. I was just thinking about my afternoon in the graveyard."

"Well, you're safe now. I'll get us some more hot tea."

"'And wasn't it a shame,'" she whispered to herself, repeating the lines she'd spoken while lying in that cemetery, "'I didn't bear you along with me…'"

The Playboy of the Western World, her father used to say, is a dickens of a play to memorize. But this part Gloria had remembered: "'And wasn't it a shame, I didn't bear you along with me to Kate Cassidy's wake, for you'd never see the match of it for flows of drink, the way when we sunk her bones at noonday in her narrow grave, there were five men, aye, and six men, stretched out retching speechless on the holy stones.'"

Maybe, she had imagined while lying among the tombs and whistling softly, *Just maybe I've crawled over Kate Cassidy's grave and the ghosts of these retching men are here with me, even now.* Propped against a slab, she raised an imaginary pint to Kate Cassidy, all the while wishing she'd had a shot of Jameson to warm her gizzard and chase away the dread.

Martin returned with fresh tea. "I'm out to feed the animals," he said. "You'll be all right then for a little while?"

"Oh yes, I'll be fine. This is so much better than where you found me."

Martin smiled warmly. "Drink your tea then, while it's hot."

Gloria was happy to be alone for a few minutes, to sit cozily before the fire. She watched the dance of yellow and blue flames, listened to the wind circling around the cottage and the dogs barking in their excitement to be fed. No matter how this day turned out, she was determined not to give up her adventures. In a way, she thought, *It's too bad I couldn't have met Martin at the beginning of my trip.*

At first, traveling solo had made her feel lonely, especially when she came upon boisterous families or nuzzling couples. Eventually, she found that being alone made her more gregarious, forced her to mingle with the locals and find out things she might never have otherwise learned. For example, that elderly man in the pub her first night in Galway—he'd spoken, not only of the extreme poverty endured by the Irish and their determination to survive Cromwell and the English, but also about his son, who had been so badly beaten in prison during The Troubles in Northern Ireland that he was never the same. Yet the old gentleman refused to remain bitter. (Just as Martin had said: "We don't hold onto the bitter.") If she'd been traveling with a friend, Gloria might never have had that conversation with that elderly man in the pub. And she might never have met Martin Faherty coming down the path in his horse-drawn trap.

How quickly the strong wind had started up from Galway Bay, blowing chilly and moist across the moors, bringing with it the damp odor of sheep's wool and the smell of burning peat. It was late afternoon. The lines of gray stones had grown dim and the far-reaching miles of stone fences were dissolving into a faded patchwork.

Sitting on the ground next to a stone wall, examining her ankle and the palms of her hands, which were scratched and dirty and dented by pebbles and thorns, Gloria felt like Pip's convict in the marsh—shackled, cold, and starving. Just as she'd determined to stand and try pedaling back to the harbor, that single horse came trotting toward her, leading this kind man.

Martin stepped back inside the cottage, carrying rolls of turf.

"Thank you, dear Martin, for saving me," said Gloria, more profusely than she'd intended. "If it hadn't been for you…"

Blushing at this unexpected outpouring, he set his armload of fuel on top of the existing pile and added a bit of turf to the steady fire. "Not a heartless soul hereabouts," he replied, glancing at Gloria.

At that moment, the door swung open and an elderly gentleman strode in as if pushed by a gust of wind. Brendan Faherty stopped in the middle of the room, looking like a sailor just in from the sea.

Unbeknownst to Gloria, Martin had called his father, and so it came as a surprise when this sturdy man appeared, wearing a seaman's cap and an ivory-colored woolen sweater, its thick turtleneck rising above the collar of a mariner's peacoat. Mr. Faherty carried himself with an air of authority and was exactly as he looked—purser, in charge of ferryboat passengers.

"Martin has many friends in Doolin," he said, greeting Gloria with cheerful eyes and handing her the cane he'd brought. "Finally, I have the privilege of meeting one. We like to tease him because we never get a look. You're the first to make the crossing."

Gloria hesitated, glancing from Mr. Faherty to Martin and back again. She stood up from the table and thanked him for the cane.

"You're welcome to it, Miss."

"I've been wanting to come to these islands for a long time," she said. "Martin rescued me this afternoon. Did he tell you?"

"He knows how to calm an injury. You're not from Ireland then?"

"No, the United States."

"Oho, the land of America's greatest failure. The once, we might understand. But twice, never. I hope you don't mind me saying that. You voted for him, did you?"

"Absolutely not."

"Well, then. I'll offer you a pint." He chuckled. "That is, if you're up to the ride."

With the help of Mr. Faherty's cane, Gloria hobbled to the bathroom to freshen up. Looking at herself in the mirror, she remembered an exchange she'd had with an acquaintance during a visit to Paris, prior to the second election in the USA. There was great concern, and Gloria had said at the house party, "If he gets in again, I'm really worried for our country." The French woman had pointed a finger at her and said in a foreboding voice, "*I'm* concerned for the *world*."

With Martin and his father on either side, she limped out of the cottage and climbed into Mr. Faherty's trap. Martin, carrying the woolen blanket, stepped up and settled next to Gloria on the little bench. He draped the blanket around her shoulders so tenderly that Gloria wondered if he might next slip his hand into hers. But off they went, keeping to themselves. Martin's father cradled the reins loosely in his large hands while the lively black mare trotted toward the pub.

After a brisk ride through the dark and the damp, Gloria was struck by the extreme warmth inside O'Brien's Pub. Rolls of turf burned hot in the narrow stone fireplace. A Saturday night crowd milled about, laughing and calling out to one another. Pints of ale, at varying levels of fullness, crowned the nicked wooden tables. Hurricane lamps, hanging from the ceiling, cast a warm glow over the dark walls and built-in shelves lined with tankards and clay jugs.

In one corner, an old man played concertina while another sawed at his fiddle. A young woman strummed her guitar and sang, "The lark in the morning, she rises up her nest, goes up in the air with the jewel on her breast..."

Voices rose in waves of greeting for Martin and his father, then fell in polite silence as Gloria stepped forward. Friends, glancing at her with sidelong curiosity, invited them to sit. Their eyes twinkled and their round and ruddy faces revealed an amused interest as Martin introduced his new friend, helped remove her jacket, got her seated, and made sure that her cane wouldn't slip to the floor.

"Like the jolly plowboy," sang the young woman with the guitar, "she whistles and she sings, comes home in the evening with the jewel on her wing."

After a time, the barmaid served Guiness all around as Mr. Faherty reintroduced Gloria each time someone new approached their table. "This is Martin's friend from America," he said at last. "They met in Doolin during the Matchmaking Weekend."

"Well, it's about time," said Seamus Molony, winking and slapping Martin on the back.

Gloria stared at Martin, who said nothing to correct the impression. Instead, he sat smiling like a boy on his first date. He seemed to be holding his breath, perhaps wondering if this American lady was going to set the facts to right or let them ride.

Gloria looked around at the open and expectant faces, at the hardworking hands now gripping raised pints of Guinness, and asked herself, *What would it hurt to play along? What would be the harm if I didn't?* And so she said to each one, "Pleased to meet you. I'm happy to be here." And the more she said it and the more hands she shook, the truer it became.

As the evening wore on, she found it pleasant to lean in a bit toward Martin, which, at first, caused him to sit up straight. Eventually, he began to edge closer to her, especially during the telling of a story and its resulting collective laughter. After a while, his hand found hers.

"America, eh?" said Seamus. "Say what you will about your previous president—he was a true diplomat. But the one you've got now…" Seamus tapped the side of his head with two fingers.

"I had no part in it," Gloria answered, wiping a bit of foam from her lips, "nor did over half of the voters. We'd like the world to know that."

"Suren we do know," replied Seamus, "so don't be fretting. Look what happened in Ireland. You'll get through your rough times, too, I'm thinking."

"We don't dwell on it, mind you," said Mr. Faherty, "but we never forget."

Soon the conversation turned to sheep and how quickly they were rounding out since the last shearing and how they would fare during the colder months in the highlands.

The highlands—Gloria recalled the huge ram she'd seen resting at the very edge of Slieve League and dozens of other sheep grazing on the mainland, atop the cliffs of Moher.

"Did you know, Miss," asked Sean Hogan, "that Martin Faherty here won the shearing contest again this year? That makes four years running."

"No, I didn't, but I'm not surprised."

Gloria remembered how he'd stripped away his gray sweater and rolled up his shirtsleeves in order to work on her ankle. She had seen the strength that lay in his arms—muscle and sinew and broad veins working their way down to thick fingers. It was easy to imagine Martin pinning a ewe and swiftly relieving her of her wool.

"Fifty ewes in one hour and ten," said Sean, clapping his friend on the shoulder.

"You came in a close second, though," said Martin. "Maybe next year, eh?"

He turned to Gloria, touched the back of her hand, and stood to excuse himself for a moment. Mr. Faherty wasted no time. He leaned in and whispered, "I think it's yourself he fancies, Miss. A fine chap he is, never married." He took a sip of ale. "Yes," he said, wiping his moist lips with the back of his hand, "it's yourself he fancies."

Smiling, Gloria raised her eyebrows and took a long drink from her own pint.

"Smooth, it is," said Brendan Faherty, leaning in closer, his eyes sparkling. "Like milk."

"That's true." Gloria smiled. "There's no bitterness at all. It goes down just like milk." And she took another healthy swallow after clinking glasses with Mr. Faherty.

As the evening wore on and friends left for their homes, it was decided that Gloria should stay the night at Ryan's Bed & Breakfast, a five-minute ride from the pub.

"We only have one other guest for the night," said Mr. Ryan, who was sitting across from Gloria at the dark wooden table. "You'll find Mary getting things in order for the morning breakfast. I'll call ahead to let her know you're coming."

Mr. Faherty drew his horse up in front of the B&B, a large white cottage with a red door. He and Martin helped Gloria to the ground.

"I'll leave you two alone then," he said, turning the horse and trap over to Martin. "The walk home will do me good." His eyes lively, he reached for Gloria's hand. "You like it here among us then, do you? Here on Inishmaan?"

"Very much, Mr. Faherty, but I can't stay. I have to catch a flight home Monday morning."

Mr. Faherty lost his bright look for a moment—a brief, nearly imperceptible moment.

"Then you'll be ferrying over to Rossaveal tomorrow?"

"I'm afraid so." She glanced back at Martin. "I've really enjoyed our time together."

Steadying herself with Mr. Faherty's cane, Gloria embraced the elderly man.

"Would you be going to mass with us in the morning?" he asked quickly.

"Yes, I'd like that. My ankle should be better by then."

"Best to keep it wrapped, I'm thinking," said Martin as he walked Gloria toward the door of the B&B. "That is, until you leave for home."

Gloria smiled and squeezed his arm.

Martin turned back to his father. "I'll come around for you in the morning," he said. "After I return her rental bicycle."

"Good night then," replied Mr. Faherty. He stood very still for a moment. Then, with a sad smile and a wave, he started down his path.

"Good night!" Gloria waved back.

It was nearly eleven o'clock when Mary Ryan, having heard their arrival, stepped outside to meet Martin and Gloria. Her face reflected the kind of humor one wears when anticipating the punch line of a long, clever joke.

"Martin," she smiled broadly, threading her arm through his. "'Tis good to see you. And Ms. Spencer, I have your room ready." Mrs. Ryan left Martin's side as soon as she saw Gloria's cane. "Why, what's happened to you, my dear? Don't tell me Brenden Faherty's horse stepped on your foot."

"No, no. Just a little clumsy."

Mrs. Ryan held the door open while Martin guided Gloria up the steps. She ushered them through the hallway and into the sitting room.

"You've had quite a day then. You'll likely be wanting to turn in soon, give that leg a rest."

Gloria settled back against the sofa's soft cushions and smiled up at Mary Ryan.

"It feels good just to sit here for a while, where it's quiet."

A quick look around the room gave her the sensation of lingering inside a block of amber. Lamp light, glowing through saffron-colored shades, blended with the buff-and-pomegranate hues of the carpet, the upholstered armchairs, and the gilded wood of tea tables and ecru doilies. Persimmon-colored walls held gold-framed prints of herding dogs among sheep pastured within stone enclosures. Books were lined up according to the colors of their spines: mauve, russet, forest green, indigo. Miniature porcelain dogs stood guard along the top shelves.

"Would you like a cup of tea?" asked Mrs. Ryan.

"Oh, yes. I'd love one." Gloria snuggled deeper into the cushions. Martin sat down next to her, but not too close.

"Martin? Tea?"

"Yes, please."

"Oh, before I forget, here's your room key, dear. Number three, first floor."

Mrs. Ryan left, soon to return with a silver tea service. After setting it on the low table, she walked behind the sofa, trailing her fingers along its back until they reached Martin's shoulder.

"Good night then, Ms. Spencer. Good night, Martin."

She moved slowly toward the door, stopping for a moment to glance back at her guests.

"I do hope that ankle doesn't give you too much trouble. Let me know if you'd like an ice pack."

"Thank you, Mrs. Ryan. I will."

Martin got up to make sure the door was closed then turned back to Gloria, flushed, as if he were too warm in his woolen sweater.

"She likes you," sang Gloria with an impish grin. "Mary Ryan likes you."

"I'd like to check the swelling on that ankle," said Martin. "Even with the cane, I'm afraid you've been exerting yourself."

He knelt down on the floor and carefully removed Gloria's shoe and stocking. His face had lost its timid look. Now he was taking charge with a confidence she hadn't anticipated. Nimble fingers rolled up the leg of her jeans and loosened the bandage clasp. Beginning at the back of her knee, he gradually worked his way down, massaging the calf muscles, then her ankle, and finally her foot—the arch, the ball, each toe—slowly, tenderly.

"Oh," said Gloria, "that feels so good."

Martin looked up at her with eyes energized, his shyness completely gone.

She reached out to touch his face. The instant her hand brushed his cheek, he edged forward. Gently spreading her blue-jeaned legs, he crept up between them to slip his arms around her waist. Gloria held his head against her breasts, inhaling the scent of damp wool, the musky heat from his skin, the faint sweetness of aftershave. With no sound to break the silence, they held each other for a long while, the warmth from one spreading over the other. Then, in a half crouch, Martin rose up for a kiss.

"Knock, knock," announced Mrs. Ryan, poking her head in. "Ms. Spencer, I forgot to… Oh, excuse me."

Martin quickly broke away and stood up, crimson flooding his neck and face.

"I do apologize for the intrusion," continued Mrs. Ryan, "but I forgot to ask if you'd like the full Irish breakfast in the morning, and at what hour."

Gloria sat for a second with her mouth open. Then she began to laugh and couldn't stop. Mrs. Ryan's joking face and her timing with the punchline notion of "a full Irish" breakfast' and recalling a movie she'd seen (*The Full Monty*) threw Gloria into such a spasm that she nearly rolled onto the floor.

Martin stood in the middle of the room with a mixed expression of shock, amusement, and embarrassment. Mrs. Ryan seemed to smile with the look of success.

Gloria quieted as quickly as she'd burst into laughter. "Martin," she asked with a final giggle, "what time is church?"

"Ten," he answered, his hands rigid in his pockets.

"Eight o'clock would be fine, Mrs. Ryan. The Irish breakfast, please."

"Very well," said their hostess, backing into the hallway, her eyes sparkling. "Good night then."

"I'd better go," said Martin as soon as Mrs. Ryan clicked the door shut. He helped Gloria up from the sofa.

"As I was saying," said Gloria, "Mary's keeping an eye on you."

"Well, Miss, it's you I'm partial to." Martin cupped her face between his hands and gave her a quick kiss. Then he picked up the cane and backpack, walked her to her room, took the key she handed him, unlocked the door, and followed her inside. Gloria wrapped her arms around him as he drew her close.

"I've spent a fine day with you," he said. "I'll be sorry to see you leave."

"And I," answered Gloria, soon feeling his soft lips, hesitant at first, then warm and full and tight against her own.

That night, she slept little. Not because of her ankle, which felt much better, but because of picturing her life on Inishmaan with Martin Faherty. Conflicting images elbowed one another through the channels of her mind: first she was helping Martin with the sheep and playing with the dogs, then she was missing her family and friends in Minnesota; next, she was bundled up to explore the barren ruggedness of the island, taking long walks on the cliffs above the sea, but then the lakes and woods back home beckoned her. She would miss the plays and the concerts and dancing around her living room on a Sunday morning to the sounds of Brazilian jazz. True, she marveled at the serpentine walls of stones on these islands that had taken decades and generations to build, but she couldn't imagine living without trees—the weeping of willows, the autumn colors of sugar maples, the white down of cottonwoods released to the wind.

Maybe Martin would come home with *her*. He was steps above a couple of men she'd dated long ago: one attached to his cell phone, picking at his teeth with the tine of a salad fork, indifferent to anything Gloria had to say; the other who slept with an apnea machine and ate his breakfast while smoking—a spoonful of oatmeal, then a drag off his Marlborough.

Martin Faherty, during this one day Gloria had known him, towered over the others.

She imagined the two of them traveling together. She'd introduce him to her friends who'd be thrilled that she, too, had finally found someone. Oh, there was so much to learn about this man. Perhaps he'd like to shear sheep out West, maybe Montana, Wyoming, or Colorado. They could ski together. She'd teach him if he didn't know how.

Sitting up in bed, Gloria hugged her drawn up knees and stared into the darkness. The wind had died down. No other sound replaced it.

She switched on the bedside lamp, got up to boil tea water in the small electric pot, and sifted through her backpack for something to read. Which should it be? Synge or Steinbeck?

The next morning, after church—a service attended by most of the locals who'd packed O'Brien's pub the night before—Martin and his father drove Gloria to the harbor where she offered to return the cane.

"My ankle is much better, thanks to the good doctor Martin."

"No, no," replied Mr. Faherty, "you'd best hold onto it. You might be needing it before the day is out."

The three stood as still and unassuming as dock posts, while crewmen hustled up and down the gangways. Several waved and called out in recognition.

"Are we on the same boat?" asked Gloria, breaking the silence.

"No, you'll go directly," said Mr. Faherty. "I sail first to Inisheer, then on to Rossaveal."

He took Gloria's hands in his. "You're welcome here, Miss," he said. "We'll be wanting to see you again."

"Some day, Mr. Faherty. I'm not sure when, but some day, I hope. Thank you for your kindness."

Brendan Faherty kissed the back of her hand, turned, and walked into the Island Ferry Office.

Just as Martin drew Gloria near to him, a crewman whistled from the boat's upper deck.

"That's where I'd like to ride," said Gloria, "in the open air."

Martin helped her across the gangplank and up the narrow iron staircase, which tolled a hollow, metallic sound with each syncopated step. No one else was above, except for the man who'd whistled at them.

"I'll thank you to mind your own business," said Martin, playfully punching his friend's shoulder.

"Five minutes, unless *you're* planning to sail to Rossaveal this morning." The crewman winked before scurrying down below.

Martin and Gloria stood together at the railing.

"I'm sorry to go," she whispered.

"And I." He reached into his jacket pocket and pulled out a small package.

"This is for you. To remember me by."

STONE WALL AND OTHER STORIES

Gloria accepted the gift and, like a schoolgirl, flung her arms around Martin. Keenly aware of the few moments left to them, they clung to each other, swaying forth and back as if at sea, until the ship's whistle signaled departure.

After a final kiss, Martin backed slowly away, then turned and disappeared down the metal steps. Gloria watched him leap off the gangway onto the cement wharf, where he spun around once and waved.

I'll bet he'd be a good skier, she thought, leaning over the railing.

"Goodbye!" she called out as the lines slipped from their moorings and the boat pulled away. Hot tears pooled in her eyes. "Goodbye, Martin!"

"Might you be writing?" he called out.

Gloria cupped her ear, trying to hear above the engine's roar. "What?"

"Might you be writing?"

"Yes," she answered, "I'll be all right!"

She quickly focused on the door of the Island Ferry Office, not wishing to see the look of disappointment on Martin's face.

As the boat surged away from land, the scent of peat fires gave over to the salt-sea air. Island buildings receded, colors melded together, and the once singular stone walls retreated into gray lines that soon blended with the moors. The growing distance dissolved Martin's precise features then reduced him to a tiny figure standing on the pier until he, in turn, disappeared.

Despite the cold, Gloria remained above decks all the way to Rossaveal, inhaling the chill damp air, watching sea birds manipulate the wind, now floating overhead, now veering off on a current with sharp skill. She leaned over the railing to study the powerful cut of the bow slicing through choppy seas. Enormous orange and white buoys, lashed to the lower deck, bounced above the churning wake, a frothy white trail as hypnotic as a fire's flame.

Holding the package Martin had given her, Gloria leaned against the bulkhead, untied the string, and peeled away the brown paper. Inside was a worn copy of *Riders to the Sea*. She opened it to the title page, read the inscription, and closed her eyes for a long moment.

Then, as the ferryboat sailed into Cashla Bay, Gloria looked back at the sea and gave a last little wave toward the Arans, now dots on the horizon.

"Remember me," he'd said at the last.

"Remember Martin Faherty" was what he had written in her book.

Amore in Italia

Gloria felt a tap on her shoulder as she bent over the sputtering lawnmower. In order to keep the engine running, she had to poke at the rubber button five times—long and slow, then short and staccato-like.

Feeling a heavier tap, she stood up straight, surprised to see her neighbor Mel.

"Your mower don't sound so good," he said after sipping from a pint jar filled with bourbon and an ice cube. "I could hear all those syncopated, grinding sounds from across the street."

Swarms of gnats gathered around in the heat, along with blossoms floating down from the overhead branches of an apple tree.

"Well, the motor's coughing, as usual, Mel, but at least it's running."

"For some time now, I've noticed you and this mower jumpin' around the yard like a couple a goats. Shut it down and I'll fix it."

With nicked fingers, he twisted and pulled out the cylinder, then held it up to the bright sky. "Hmm, made in Italy."

"Really! What a coincidence. I'm going back there pretty soon."

"I'll bet you've never changed this air filter. Oughta be able to see light through it. This one looks like a chunk of black lung disease."

"Ah, so that's the culprit," said Gloria. "Not the gas line."

"You got it. Go ahead and finish mowin' for now, but then get a new filter at the hardware store—another one just like it."

"Made in Italy?"

"Well, if you can—a few extra bucks, maybe."

"Thanks, Mel."

Swallowing the last bit of bourbon from his jar, he placed the cylinder inside the garage, waved, and took off down the street.

"By the way," he shouted, "enjoy your trip!"

"*Grazie*, Mel."

Gloria's smooth mowing made the yard clippings smell delicious, like a unique salad of pungent chives, Creeping Charlie from the mint family, volunteer ferns and daisies, patches of moss, and lemony dandelions nodding before the blade.

Brochures from chemical companies often appeared in her mailbox, but she tossed them into the recycling bin and held her crossed index fingers high in the air whenever white trucks drove by, with romping children and smiling dogs painted on the sides. If the drivers stopped to offer chemicals for her yard, Gloria would shake her head and suggest that they read *Silent Spring* by Rachel Carson.

Finally finished, she cleaned and tucked away her lawnmower, giving it an extra pat before closing the garage door.

Sweating, and pinching a gnat from her hair, she carried the old filter up the steps and inside her cottage, remembering those extreme sub-zero temperatures of last winter, along with piles of heavy snow and long icicles hanging from the edges of her roof.

"Winter and summer, whew!" she muttered. "Fall and spring, fall and spring—my favorite seasons."

Gloria set that old blackish filter down on the floor then relaxed for a moment in the hallway. Leaning against her antique commode, she glanced at the old wooden dish shaped like a pineapple; because it symbolized friendship, she'd included a small glass mortar and pestle set, hand-blown from clear flint glass—a gift from long ago, during her first trip to Italy.

At age twenty-two, Gloria had met Maurizio Palla. Now, during all these years later, she kept his gift in view, remembering their youthful energy and how they had spent their days together in *Firenze* and *Pisa*.

And soon, during her upcoming trip, she hoped to see him again.

Flopped on the living room floor next to her couch, Gloria turned on the fan, rummaged through several records, and found the

45s that dated back to the 1960s: Petula Clark singing "*Ciao Ciao*" to the tune of "Downtown," Jimmy Fontana crooning "*Il Mondo,*" and Emilio Pericoli making the girls swoon with "*Quando, Quando, Quando.*" "When, When, When?" The World. Greetings, Farewell.

Although the return address was missing, Maurizio's several cards and letters lay among the old records, reminding Gloria of the Italian beckoning wave of goodbye. This upcoming portion of the second trip to Italy began to take shape in her mind. *Di mi quando ti verrai.* "Tell me when I will see you—once more."

Several weeks ago, she had called Pam, one of her travel friends who said she'd love to visit Italy: "Rome, Venice, the Amalfi coast, Sorrento, Positano, Portofino."

"And then *Firenze* and *Pisa*," said Gloria, "so that we can locate Maurizio Palla, if he's still in that part of the country. It's been a long time."

"Oh, that's right. I remember hearing a little bit about him. Tell me more."

"Once we're on our way, Pam, I'll tell you the whole story."

Packed and lined up with a current passport, Gloria phoned her neighbor Mel, asking if he would keep an eye on her house and lawn for a couple of weeks.

"I bought that new air filter for the mower," she said. "And would you enjoy drinking *Chianti*?"

Finally, during their flight to Rome, Gloria told Pam all about her first trip to Italy and how she had met Maurizio.

Strolling around New York Harbor, three college friends and I, from small Midwestern towns, boarded the *Aurelia*, a student ship bound for Europe. After leaving the mouth of the Hudson River and New York Bay, we waved goodbye, as if the Statue of Liberty were watching us enter the ocean.

Heading into a fascinating part of the world, our first voyage took eight days and nights to cross the Atlantic on a boat loaded with youths seeking romance and adventures with "Three Coins in a Fountain" and play-acting "Charade." Not one of them was over twenty-five. Many couldn't wait to join the fashion parades on Carnaby Street in London, where businessmen hopped out of red double-decker buses and marched jauntily down the streets in flared suits and bowler hats, swinging their bumbershoots like fancy canes; where clothing in store windows and on young people along the *Avenue des Champs-Elysées* in Paris popped up as splashes of yellow and orange, green, and purple; the Vatican and Colosseum in Rome, ordering pasta and wine, and throwing coins into the Trevi Fountain.

The meals onboard, served by Italian waiters, took some getting used to. We learned how to eat as Europeans—fork in left hand, knife in right, and no switch. We had to keep them there, because if we laid our silver down, the waiters assumed that our meals were finished. So we learned that eating properly really meant business.

Wine was served with our evening meals of cheese, French bread, ox tongue, veal kidneys, calf brain, potatoes, cake, and apples. Back then I missed hamburgers, French fries, popcorn, homemade chocolate cake, and milk. Typical, I guess, of being twenty-two.

Many of the guys on board the *Aurelia* wore bellbottoms and styled their hair after the Beatles. We girls dressed in paisley A-line shifts, mini-skirts, and go-go boots, trying to look like Twiggy or Audrey Hepburn.

Every evening, we danced to live Italian music, sometimes tripping from side to side or scooting up and down, as the ship tipped back and forth, hit by high waves, especially during our fourth night out. A few of the girls swayed about, wiggled their hips, and stared at the four band members—talented, middle-aged men singing and playing "*Al di là*" ("Beyond"), among dozens and dozens of other beautiful love songs. At first, I was shocked, but then tried wiggling in front of Emilio Pericoli, who was singing "Return to Me" in both English and Italian. He smiled, chanting "*bambina*" and "My darling, my heart." *Oh!* I thought. *What a fabulous voice!* And he is so handsome!

During the daytime, from topside, we saw whales and terns. With long, forked tails and narrow wings, those seabirds never stopped flying. We watched them dive downward to eat scraps off the surface, poking into trails of it with their long bills. The ocean had become our ship's garbage disposal—down the fore hatchway, like a suddenly opened cesspool.

Throughout the evenings, odors of a normal ship, including smells from bilge water, machine grease, a few hides, and ocean brine popped in, while everybody danced, devoured heaps of ham and cheese sandwiches, and drank gallons of alcohol—no enforced drinking laws on the high seas. Quite a few students were lined up at the bars from morning 'til night. Eventually, they became low on funds, fell down sick, and went to bed.

Soon, with the pitch and yaw caused by monstrous waves slamming at the *Aurelia*, nearly everyone got seasick. Eventually, a few dancers drifted along in each other's arms, learning how to stumble and trip from one side of the ballroom to the other, each time those waves and troughs struck the ship. From below decks and on the dance floor, strident sounds of laughter and screams, moaning with hangovers, dancing and staggering from side to side, rose to a pitch. During lunch on the last day aboard, we were hit by an extra-large wave that sent the ship rocking, as if it wanted to tip over, along with dishes and people crashing to the floor.

In spite of all that, nearly everyone laughed and chatted and thought the trip was wonderful.

After spending several days in Rome, we arrived in Pisa, where my friends and I spilled out of our blue rental car—a Fiat that had been scratched and dented because one of the girls who loved to drive often backed into poles, fences, and signposts—accidentally.

Just as we started admiring the cathedral and inching toward the Leaning Tower of Pisa, described as "one of the world's most beloved architectural mistakes," two young men approached us; they were handsome, seemed friendly, and tried to speak English, explaining that they were self-appointed guides, named Max and Maurizio. I was mesmerized, having never experienced that kind of precocious male back home.

While skipping about with guitars hanging on their backs, they offered to take pictures and lead us girls around Pisa. To begin with,

Max and Maurizio charmed and posed each of us, one at a time, making sure that we stood some distance from the Leaning Tower and held out an arm and a hand just right for the photos. When I saw our pictures, they actually looked as though we were holding the Tower up, along its side, preventing it from tumbling down, along with its 294-step interior spiral staircase.

The following afternoon, we all met up next to the sea, with Maurizio and Max at *Marina di Pisa*, a beach not far from the Leaning Tower. We had so much fun wading and running through pebbles, lying in the sun, laughing, and chatting. The guys played their guitars and sang, then set up get-togethers for the next day.

Actually, during the next couple of days, Maurizio and his guitar ushered me all over *Pisa* and *Firenze*. I kept up with him as he leapt from bus to bench, darted into a nearby church for a quick dip of holy water and a ten-second prayer, went running along the parks, up and down more benches, scurried through museums, skipped along more beaches, inhaled saltwater smells, and stopped next to *Botticelli's* Birth of Venus, which reminded me of how she also had emerged fully grown from the sea, as I had practically been delivered by the ship *Aurelia*.

I love remembering the energy of being that age, and how, like an eager puppy, I had happily followed mercurial Maurizio who befriended me like a field-wise scamp.

We patted the stone feet of Michelangelo's *David*, that huge, brilliant sculpture, seventeen feet tall. Then I became highly impressed by *Leonardo da Vinci* who had been great at everything: architecture, sculpting, drawing, painting, science, mathematics, invention, history, literature, writing, engineering, anatomy, geology, botany, astronomy, cartography, music…WOW! I'd never before heard of such a human being like him. Finally, we stopped to eat.

During our last afternoon together, Maurizio took me to a picnic just outside of *Pisa*, which had been organized by several generations in his family: siblings, parents, aunts and uncles, cousins, nephews and nieces, grandparents. Being treated as if I were already a part of the family, I felt at home, amazed at how, under a blue sky, sunshine, and lovely trees, they'd set up long tables with richly colored cloths. I helped them place salads with olive oil, crusty loaves of bread that were soft inside, pasta with rich tomato and meat sauces, roasted chickens, and bottles of *Chianti*. And for dessert—double chocolate *biscotti*.

All afternoon, the children sang *a cappella*. The elderly joined in, and then Maurizio played his guitar and sang *Quando, Quando, Quando*.

Just before evening, there were hugs all around. Afterward, Maurizio led me back to the Cathedral Square. We sat down next to the Leaning Tower of Pisa, talked, held hands, admired one another, hugged, kissed, and like a young Emilio Pericoli, he began playing his guitar and singing "*Al di là*."

When Maurizio tried to sing "Strangers in the Night" in English, I shouted, "No, we're not!" He began to laugh and so did I. Then we danced our way along the avenue back to where my friends and I were staying until the next morning.

"*Ciao, ciao*," he whispered.

"What exactly does that mean?"

"Hello and goodbye. Or goodbye and hello."

"*Ciao, ciao*, Maurizio."

"I have something for you," he said, digging into his backpack and handing me a cloth bag. Inside was a small glass mortar and pestle he'd found for me at the university chemistry lab, where he was a student. Accepting his gift, I held it gently in my hands, determined that it would never break.

Maurizio bid me *arrivederci*, walked away backward, grinning, strumming his guitar and singing this one line: "exchanging glances, wondering in the night, what were the chances..." He waved the kind of wave that made me want to follow, instead of leave. We both stood still for a moment, then Maurizio ran back, hugged and kissed me goodbye, turned, and skipped off into the shadows of the night.

"That was the last you saw of him?" asked Pam, seated on the plane next to Gloria.

"Yes. So once we make it to *Pisa* and *Firenze*, toward the end of our trip, I hope to find him again."

"Me too. What a lovely time you had together."

Pam began playing solitaire on the pull-down tabletop.

Gloria settled back in the aisle seat, closed her eyes, and listened to Emilio Pericoli on the iPod, recalling how he'd sung *"Al di là"* on board the *Aurelia*. And then she remembered how Maurizio Palla sang it for her near the Leaning Tower of Pisa.

After landing in Rome, they rented a car, found a hotel, and went out for lunch.

Studying a phrase book, they practiced the pronunciation of various Italian words and names for the cities they'd planned to visit, including *Firenze and Venezia*. Of course, *Roma* and *Pisa* weren't as hard to pronounce.

They ambled among Roman monuments, marveled at the bright, cleaned paintings inside the Sistine Chapel, and found their way to Vatican Square, where they watched the Pope fall asleep while seated on his balcony, after waving and nodding at the massive crowd below.

Gloria and Pam spent the next several days along the *Amalfi* coast, taking long walks atop cliffs overlooking the Mediterranean Sea, valleys, fishing villages, lemon groves, and vineyards, from *Sorrento* to *Positano*, and *Portofino*.

Toward evening, the warm Mediterranean air blew in through their opened car windows, smelling of fresh saltwater and ruffling their hair as they wheeled around hairpin curves, heading north, eating fresh bread covered with *limoncello* jam, and singing along with Dean Martin's voice: "When the moon hits your eye like a bigga pizza pie, that's *amore*…"

After spending time in *Venezia*, a unique, watery, charming, and crowded city, Gloria and Pam drove their rental car out of the *Piazzali Roma* garage where it had been parked for two days. In order to avoid paying additional fees, they stopped close to a pedestrian bridge leading to the heart of Venice. Gloria was to wait while Pam rushed back to retrieve her passport from the hotel safe.

"Give me fifteen minutes," she said. "Twenty at the most."

Forty-five minutes went by and no Pam. *Perhaps*, thought Gloria, *her passport wasn't there. Or maybe she slipped and fell.*

As time ticked by, she wondered if abduction might be more likely, similar to what had happened years ago to a young American woman in Morocco—stolen and never seen again.

In order to search for her friend, Gloria ran inside a nearby shop and purchased a one-hour parking pass. It was noon, so she'd have to return by one o' clock in order to avoid a large fine.

After rushing into the *Hotel Guerrini*, she learned that Pam had retrieved her passport about an hour earlier. The receptionist didn't know which direction she'd gone after leaving the hotel. And no one else was with her.

Gloria rushed out, raced through the *vias* until twelve forty-five, revisiting in fast reverse the sections of Venice that they had taken hours to see, including *Piazza San Marco* and St. Mark's Basilica. She ran alongside clusters of pigeons, which took to the air, beating their wings and stirring up dust and feathers. She caught a whiff of cappuccino and glimpsed at diners feasting off forks twirled with pasta. Cocky gondolas bobbed up and down in the water, waiting for tourists. Gloria felt ill from panic and fear, regretting to say "*arrivederci*" in this way, and in such a rush, desperate to locate her travel friend.

"*Senora*," called out an elderly man seated on a bench. "*Lentamente.* You must savor *Venezia.*"

Sorry not to be able to slow down and enjoy this wonderful city any longer, she saw that it was ten minutes to one. Searching for her friend among all these streets and bridges and shops was like trying to find the longest noodle in a gigantic pile of spaghetti. She could only hope that Pam had already returned to their rental car.

As Gloria ran across the last bridge toward the parking lot, she saw two uniformed men standing next to the car. She checked her watch: one minute after one.

"I'm here!" she shouted. "Here I am!"

The younger of the two officers dressed in olive-drab military jackets, was writing a ticket on a large tablet with a dark metal cover flapped downward. The policemen were also dressed in tall black boots with tucked in pants that flared slightly at the hips. Their hats reminded Gloria of Gestapo pictures that she had seen in a history book, long ago. Strapped across their chests were shiny, leather holsters with pistols tucked off to one side.

"We are sorry, *senora*, it is past time."

"I've been searching for my friend, very worried about her. And it's only one minute after one."

"This is the law. It is past time."

"Please help me find her."

But they stood completely still and official, while Gloria informed them about what might have happened to Pam, feeling as if she were negotiating with a gondola instead of the gondolier.

"This ticket is written and cannot be changed," said the young officer.

He shoved the large piece of paper into Gloria's hand, said something about a police station nearby, fell silent, and walked away. The older officer hesitated, turned to look back at her for a moment, and then caught up with his partner.

Just then, she spotted Pam crossing the last bridge, raising a large *gelato* ice cream in each hand.

"Where have you been?" shouted Gloria. "I was so worried, tried to find you."

"Is that a rescue squad?" she asked, pointing at the two officers.

"No! I got back to our car one minute late, and they fined me 388,000 lira—two hundred dollars! Where were you?"

"I'm so sorry. I'll explain later, after we get going. Here, take your cone before it melts."

Pam hopped into the passenger side, finishing her *gelato*.

Still trembling, Gloria got behind the wheel and tried to relax for a moment before starting the engine. She checked her watery eyes and blushed cheeks in the rear view mirror, then sat back to take a large bite of her ice cream.

Suddenly, the older police officer came running up to their car and tapped at the driver's side.

"Oh my God, now what?" Gloria reluctantly rolled down the window.

The officer, looking back over his shoulder and carrying the large tablet with the dark metal cover, asked for the ticket sheet given to her a moment ago. With a pen, he replaced the 388,000 with 388,0 lira, the equivalent of two dollars, and asked her to pay right away, so he could mark it in the tablet and give her a receipt.

"No need to stop at police station," he said.

Shocked and grateful, Gloria set her ice cream down in a cup holder, pulled the 388.0 lira from her wallet and handed it to the officer.

"*Grazie*," she said, smiling at him. "*Molte grazie.*"

"*Prego.*" Then he gave her the receipt and rushed away.

Momentarily silent, and thinking about what had just happened, Gloria glanced back at a receding Venice as she drove slowly along the *Ponte della Liberta*.

"I'm sorry," said Pam. "I didn't mean to have you wait for so long. Amazing what that officer just did."

"For sure. We're very lucky because I've heard of other American travelers who received exorbitant parking charges in the mail, shortly after they returned home—envelopes from *Polizia de Italia, Venezia*. They had refused to stop at a police station to pay their tickets."

"Here's the station, on our right." Pam opened her window and pointed at the building. "Would you have stopped?"

"I didn't want to. Heck, a two-hundred-dollar fee for one minute over our time limit was ridiculous. From now on, we'll have wonderful memories about our days here in Venice. I'll never forget that older police officer and how he cared about our situation.

"Also, I am relieved, Pam—glad to know that you weren't abducted or hadn't fallen into the Grand Canal. You found your passport, so where were you all that time?"

"Well, I feel a bit guilty, even silly now. But I saw a marvelous man. Actually, the most radiant one I've ever seen.

"After I retrieved my passport from the hotel safe, I walked past a little glass shop that we hadn't visited before. You know how a store sometimes beckons you to come in. So I did. It was like stepping inside a jewel. The moment I entered and saw the glassmaker at his workbench, I just stood there, staring at him as he looked up and smiled. He reminded me of Tiepolo's exquisite drawings that I once saw inside the Minneapolis Art Museum: *The Head of Truth*. This was a pure, self-assured, most peaceful-looking man—beatific, as a Renaissance artist can create. Having met Salvatore—that's his name—made me forget what time it was and that you were waiting for me."

"Did you flirt with him?"

"No, no, it wasn't like that. I just felt an overwhelming calmness. Everything must have come together for that young man. And when he spoke—well, I'd never heard a voice quite like his: gentle and serene. Everyone who entered the shop seemed to bathe in his tranquility."

"I'm glad for you," said Gloria, "because some time ago, I met a musician who sang the most beautiful love songs. He had to have lived those words, I thought, in order to sing them like that. And so I trusted him. But I was wrong. Off stage, he insulted women and used every four-letter word out there."

"Well, at least we each met a kind man today—Salvatore and that police officer."

"Yup. And soon, I hope to see Maurizio once again."

After arriving in *Pisa*, Gloria checked the phone directory: Palla, Maurizio Palla. There were several Pallas listed, but when she called, the answers were all the same: "*Non ci Maurizio qui.*"

"Maybe he moved to Florence," said Pam. "You mentioned that he had a lot of family around there."

"Could be. Let's go."

They stopped to look at the Leaning Tower where Gloria and her college friends had first met Maurizio and Max. As usual, couples lounged on the grass, resting and eating picnic lunches. Tourists directed and photographed one another with strategically placed hands hovering in midair, as if to prevent the Tower from falling down.

Once they'd arrived in Florence, Gloria recalled just how beguiling it was, this birthplace of the Renaissance and capital city of Tuscany. Loaded with museums, art galleries, red-tiled roofs, and the Arno River, *Firenze*, she thought, is one of the most beautiful cities in the world. Its history of wealthy patrons and opulent churches, surrounded by squalid poverty, had all come together in its art.

And there was the singular *David*, sculpted in 1504 by Michelangelo, from a single block of marble. Gloria snapped pictures of him from every angle. "He is perfect, magnificent—a beautiful body created from stone."

"I'll probably have to censor my photo album once I'm home," said Pam. "That nudity might be too shocking for a few relatives. I can imagine their gasps and looks if they ever see a picture of this perfect seventeen-foot man."

Gloria had reserved her phone calls from a directory list of five Pallas until the third from her last day in Italy. Call too soon and a possible disappointment might color the rest of her visit—too late and there might not be enough time to renew the acquaintance. Besides, Gloria rather enjoyed the little flutter that came from anticipating their meeting. Would Maurizio remember her after all these years? What would he be like? She could still picture him as if it were yesterday: lean and laughing in the sunshine, slowing down just long enough to strum his guitar, then give her a hug and a kiss.

Gloria located him on the fourth try. A woman answered and said that she was *la madre*—his mother. Finally Maurizio's voice was on the line. Between her few words of Italian, a little bit of French, and his meager English, they managed to connect.

"Of co-course, I...re-remem-ber...you," he said with slurred speech. Gloria wondered if he'd been sipping from the Italian equivalent of her neighbor Mel's fruit jar.

Then Maurizio spoke a bit more clearly, inviting her and Pam to his apartment at *dieci Via Maggio*, eleven o'clock next morning. "I live with my mother," he said, "elderly, but she take good care of me."

That night, Gloria lay in bed wondering what had happened to Maurizio and why he was living with his mother. Had he ever married? Were there children? She remembered the picnic of long ago when everyone was so lively, singing, eating, welcoming, and enjoying one another's company. There seemed to be perpetual motion and good cheer where no one stopped to grow old or fall ill.

Heavy set with thick, white hair accented by streaks of black, *Senora Palla* stood waiting next to the opened door.

"*Buongiorno. Benvenuti. Vieni, vieni.*"

Gloria and Pam entered, welcomed by this warm-hearted woman with a flushed and smiling face. The scent of warm cake and coffee filled the apartment.

There, in the center of a narrow living room, was Maurizio, looking very elderly, and seated in a wheelchair that seemed too large and cumbersome for such small quarters. Except for a huge abdomen, he was very thin and his hair was mostly gone. If it hadn't been for his Roman nose and dark brown eyes, Gloria might never have recognized him out in public.

Shaking off her surprise, she walked over to Maurizio, leaned down, and gave him a hug. Then she introduced Pam.

Mrs. Palla, in her early eighties, stood next to them, nodding and wiping her hands over and over on her apron. Using a few descriptive words in English, she was able to explain that her son had been unable to walk for a long time, due to advanced multiple sclerosis.

"He is here for some years," she whispered, explaining that it had eventually become too difficult for him to live alone. He'd been engaged once, long ago, but never married.

Gloria knew a little more Italian and Maurizio tried to say a few words in English. His eyes moved rapidly, sometimes uncontrollably, and his hands couldn't always settle on the arms of his wheelchair, because of frequent muscle spasms. After he motioned, laughing at their memories, hearing Gloria talk about the wonderful times they'd spent together all those years ago, Maurizio experienced a mood swing with uncontrollable crying. His mother stepped over to calm him down, smiled at Gloria, and nodded with pleasure as soon as her son was able to shift back to some laughter.

Then she served her fresh cakes and coffee.

Of course, under the existing circumstances, theirs was as warm a visit as possible. Afterward, Gloria promised to write. And yes, of course, if she returned to Florence, she would call and stop by again.

Although embracing Maurizio felt like grasping the ends of a coat hanger, she held his shoulders for a moment, and then gave him a light kiss on each cheek.

After warm hugs with *Senora Palla*, and just before the door closed, Gloria glanced back one last time at Maurizio seated in his wheelchair. Looking exhausted, he was still trying to wave the Italian goodbye—that same beckoning wave of "come back again," which had almost made her return to him long ago.

During their long flight home, Gloria told Pam about a dream she'd had the night before they left Rome for the airport.

"It just seems to sum it all up," she said. "The way things worked out on more than one level."

"What was it about?"

"How everything changes during intermission."

"What on earth do you mean?"

"In my dream I was at a play, perfectly comfortable, sitting with friends. The actors were in the wings and, for some reason, in the aisles, rather than backstage, waiting to go on. Fans were rushing over to them and to my friends. They even approached me with their programs for autographs, dishing out compliments as if I were going on stage as well. Then the lights dimmed and the heavy, crimson curtain slowly parted. The footlights came up, gilding the actors who spoke in a way that I couldn't understand. Yet somehow it all felt right. And it was so exciting.

"At intermission, I went to the washroom. When I returned, my seat was taken. Another person, someone I didn't know, was in my place. In fact, the entire seating arrangement had changed and I couldn't recognize the new configuration. No one looked familiar anymore. No matter how hard I tried, I couldn't find my way. I saw a couple of friends up in the balcony, but they didn't seem to notice me. Mostly, everyone I knew had disappeared. The houselights were dimming again. A loud voice told me to sit down. The only empty seat left was wet and full of crumbs. That's when I realized that the second act was never going to be like the first."

Pam slowly nodded. "I think I know what you mean," she said. "It's also like you can never really go home again."

"Reminds me of Thomas Wolfe's novel," said Gloria. "The end of something, the beginning of something else. I know that returning to a place remembered from long ago won't ever be the same—there will be changes and the passing of time."

The day after Gloria returned home, her neighbor stopped by.

"I only had to mow once while you were gone," said Mel. "Didn't get any rain, pretty parched. Oh, and by the way, that new air filter is perfect on your mower—clears it all out."

After she handed him the gift bottle of *Chianti*, he held it up to the bright sky. "Ah, from Italy. Thanks. Welcome home."

"Glad to be back, Mel."

She went inside, closed the screen door, followed the path of sunlight into her living room, and glanced around at all of her things: stacks of books, records, and music; the piano she had bought instead of a new car; her favorite bronze lamp—a figure of Confucius holding an open book on his lap while seated on the back of a carp. How calm and settled he was there, reading while traveling on a fish. Some time ago, after reading several passages from the *Tao*, Gloria had sensed that she was much clearer in thought to a more balanced and unruffled existence.

Back in the hallway, she ran her fingers along the pineap-ple-shaped wooden bowl, and then picked up the glass mortar and pestle. Slowly moving the pestle in a circle, she chose to remember that long ago, lovely and clear day with Maurizio, when they were young and full of laughter:

> *Just before evening set in, Maurizio and his guitar led me back to the Cathedral. Sitting together on the grass, near The Leaning Tower of Pisa, he began to sing:*

50

STONE WALL AND OTHER STORIES

"Beyond the stars, there you are…Beyond the most beautiful things…Beyond the deepest sea… there you are for me."

Maurizio bid me arrivederci, waving the kind of wave that made me want to follow, instead of leave. Then he ran back, hugged and kissed me goodbye, turned, and skipped off into the shadows of the night.

"Ciao, ciao."

Salon de Beauté

Gloria Spencer enters a Beauty Salon and listens to her hair stylist, Candi, who does all the talking.

Hi, hon, haven't seen you before. New customer? I'm Candi. Pleased to meet you, Gloria. What'll it be? Cut and styling? Just sit yourself down at my station over there—the one with the red roses. Aren't they beautiful? From my boyfriend. He gave me these flowery Capri pants too—for my birthday. What a sweetie.

You're getting all spiffed up for a trip? Gay Paree! Well, lucky you. I hope it goes better than… Well, Roxy, one of my regulars, was supposed to be back a month ago, but she's still in Paris, not allowed to leave—detained by the police. Stella, her best friend, had to come home without her. Oh boy, was she upset. Naturally, she didn't want to leave Roxy behind, but what else could she do? Had to get back to work or lose her job. You know how that goes.

Hope you don't mind me crackin' my gum. I like to chew on account of these smells in here.

Anyhow, Stella couldn't wait to tell us all the details. If you ask me, I don't think Roxy would have done such a thing, but then I don't know her very well. She comes in every couple of weeks for a touch up. Doesn't talk much. The quiet type, you know?

Oh, listen to me going on about her as if she's still around.

My boyfriend says she shoulda stayed back here in the states. Would've had better luck hanging around the Quickie Mart produce section if she wanted to meet a guy. Instead, she traipses off to another country, lets herself get sweet-talked. Oh, those Frenchmen.

Sure as heck, she's in hot water now!

Stella says some of the men over there ain't all that great look-ing—kinda raw-boned. Chivalrous? Heck, not a one of 'em ever held a door open for her. Cut her off on the sidewalk, even—in a mad dash.

My, you have nice thick hair, dearie. I've got just the cut for you, unless you want a bouffant like mine. Let's go over to the sink, get away from these perm smells for a few minutes. You'll love my scalp massages—guaranteed to cure headaches.

A trip to Paris. Oh, they were going to have a great time! If you ask me, Roxy would have been better off, though, making eyes at some hunk from behind a stack of sweet, juicy, red, ripe water-malones. That's what Hal likes to say: *sweet, juicy, red, ripe water-malones.* Hal, that's my boyfriend. What a stitch.

Turn your head a little to the left, hon. Don't that warm water feel good? Let me know if it gets too hot.

Anyhow, it was one of those rebounds, you know, after her sec-ond divorce. Haven't we all been there these days! Roxy was on the prowl, looking sharp. I gave her one of those cute layered cuts—looked real good on her. Did a blunt cut for Stella. They looked like a couple of models, if I do say so myself. Stopped by to show off their new outfits the day before they left—just enough cleavage to fit in with those chic *Pareesiens.* Like, when in Rome, you know—

Stella said they went to some jazz club their first night. I can just picture her and Roxy sipping wine and cognac, ready to flirt and have a good time. A couple a guys edged over from their table to sit down with them. Well, then, one thing led to another and they ended up at an all-night sidewalk cafe—like those you see in the movies.

The guy next to Stella took off, had to go home. Just as well 'cause she could barely understand him anyways. Plus, he had BO so bad she nearly gagged. But the one that liked Roxy spoke pretty good English. Pascal, that was his name, I think. Yeah, Pascal—kinda different. Real foreign-sounding, wouldn't you say?

Anyway, this Pascal asked Roxy out for the next night, to a bal-let or some opera. I don't remember which. Not too shabby, huh? But she never seemed like the type to go in for that sort a thing. Now,

Stella, I can see, but Roxy? Oh, what the heck, I guess a little culture never hurt anyone.

Stella said she felt like a third wheel, told 'em she was tired, wanted to head back to the hotel and get some sleep. Roxy, of course, wouldn't let her go by herself. So before they split, she wrote her name and where they were staying on the back of a business card and gave it to Pascal.

From what I can remember, he lived on some island in the middle of the river. There's a river, you know, that runs through Paris. Said he had a nice apartment, but didn't offer his address or last name—just a cell phone number.

Stinko! Problem number 2. Pretty obvious, wouldn't you say?

Problem number 1: this guy should have escorted the women back to their hotel, especially that late at night.

Are you comfortable, Gloria? Everyone says they could just fall asleep when I massage their scalps. Is the back of your neck all right like this, propped on the sink?

Anyhow, Roxy ended up spending a lot of time with that guy. And Stella, well, she tried to be a good sport, going places all alone. But what fun is that? I'd have been pissed myself.

After the first week, they changed hotels 'cause they weren't getting any sleep: one couple screwing their brains out on the other side of the wall; another pair arguing every night; pots and pans banging around in the hotel kitchen at 4:00 a.m., tossing a bunch of noise up through windows above the air shaft.

So Roxy and Stella packed their bags, checked out of that first hotel, and got settled into a second one. Then they went shopping and out for dinner at the top of the Eiffel Tower. Doesn't that sound like fun? And what a view! Roxy paid for everything; I guess she felt guilty leaving Stella on her own during that first week.

Now, you're probably gonna fall out of your chair when I tell you what happened next.

Oh, here, let's wrap a towel around your head and go back to my station.

Don't those roses smell good? Hal—what a sweetheart.

Now where was I? Oh yeah, after they got back from the Eiffel Tower, around midnight, Stella happened to look out of their hotel window and couldn't believe her eyes. She grabbed her small binoculars, then told Roxy to quick turn off the lights and take a peek. You'll never guess what they saw down there on the street!

Oh, fudge, I dropped the comb. Just a sec, hon, I'll get a clean one.

Anyway, even if you've been around some city block a time or two, I'll bet you could never imagine what was going on down there. Stella told me everything.

Picture this: eight men in business suits, shuffling along in single file, spaced out, and lined up under a street light. Strange to see them dressed like that in the wee hours of the morning, acting as if they'd just left work, waiting for a bus. But all they did was inch along, without talking to one another, like a weird parade.

At that street corner, beneath the stop and go light sat a blue Renault—parked there through red and green, red and green—a compact car with two women inside: one behind the wheel and the other in the rear with her arms spread out against the seatback. And what do you think she was wearing?

You got that right. Not much. Nothing but big boobs!

Well, now, you think you've heard it all and then, boom! Or *voilà*!

Not that it matters, I guess, 'cause two people can screw around in smaller places than inside a little car. Heck, once my boyfriend and I did it in...well, pshh, that's another story.

Those men walked up to that car, one at a time, to stick their heads inside the rear window, while the others waited their turn, circling around with blank looks on their faces, lining up like pallbearers.

One of 'em stooped over to take a peek, then stepped back, turned around, and took off. The next guy leaned forward for a look, got in, and off they went for a five-minute ride around the block. Hah! Hah-hah! Five minutes?

All of a sudden, Stella dropped her binoculars. She called Roxy back over to the window and pointed out a single man standing beneath the streetlight. Dressed in a gray suit and lavender shirt, his shape looked awfully familiar. When he turned around, they caught his face. Sure enough, it was Pascal!

Just imagine how Roxy must have felt. She really liked this guy. I guess she took it awful hard, especially after talking about what an impression she'd make to all her friends and family by bringing that Frenchman home with her. Maybe even getting married one day.

Well, they watched to see if he would get inside the car or just take a peek and leave.

How many inches do you want cut off, dear? I think a short bob would be perfect for you.

Anyhow, they watched Pascal like a couple a hawks. And what do you think?

Yup! He crawls right into the back seat and off they go.

Roxy cried all night. Swore, too.

But now, here's where the story gets murky. We don't know if Roxy called Pascal the next day, or if someone at the first hotel told him where the girls were, or if there was even any more contact. Stella doesn't know 'cause Roxy just clammed up, said she didn't want to talk about him ever again. Early in the morning, she left on her own for most of the day. And so did Stella.

Two days later, the police found Pascal.

Just a sec, dear, while I untangle this hair dryer cord.

As I was saying, that man finally surfaced. Dead! Imagine— Pascal was dead and bloated, floating on the Seine River.

The officers found Roxy's business card in his pocket—wet, of course, but still readable. Didn't take 'em long to find *her*. Let me tell you, she's in real hot water.

They said it couldn't have been a suicide 'cause he'd taken some mean blows to the head. Of course, Pascal's wife is also a suspect. Can you believe it? A wife. Grown children. Grandkids.

So there you are, dearie. That's the scoop. It's all anyone talks about when they come into our beauty salon. We wonder how it's going to end. Poor Roxy—so desperate to find a man. I don't like to think she did him in, but you never know. She *was* kinda different.

There's one more thing that bothers me. A week ago, after Stella came in for her trim, I found a business card on the floor, wedged

56

beneath the counter; it was in a foreign language, but I could read the name Pascal Berliot, a Paris address, and phone number. That card must have fallen from Stella's purse. I wonder how and when she got it. And why?

Sweetie, you'd be better off traveling around the good old US of A, trolling for a sexy cowboy or linking up with some guy behind a pile of sweet, juicy, red, ripe watermalones. Or what the heck, go find yourself a big, burly longshoreman with anchors tattooed on his biceps—like my Hal.

Now *this* style is real cute on you, Gloria. Look in the mirror. What do you think?

Crème Brûlée

Having saved enough money for her first trip to Paris, Gloria Spencer planned to sightsee, shop, visit museums, practice French, and order a special dessert that she'd heard about, but never tasted; the creamy mixture topped with a golden brown crust made her mouth water as she pictured the ingredients coming together, served, and devoured.

Upon arrival, and leaving the Charles de Gaulle Airport, Gloria spotted her taxi driver, *Monsieur Mépris*, glaring from his rearview mirror. This, after telling him in her best *français*, that she wished to be dropped off at *l'Hôtel du Jeu de Paume, 54 rue Saint Louis*. She hadn't expected such a Gallic turn of events—issues relating to what? Her pronunciation? Fortunately, there was no war going on, as far as she knew. However, sensing that *Monsieur Mépris's* attitude was only the beginning, and some future experience might not go *très bien*, Gloria settled back to watch the gray industrial buildings flicker past, one after another, along the *autoroute, en route* to Paris.

At least her full flight from Chicago had been uneventful: no crying babies or screaming kids; no punching against the back of her seat; no flirtatious drunks (although a dab of flirtatiousness might have been fun); and her luggage was among the first to flop down the chute onto the carrousel.

Gloria's *raison d'être* in the City of Light for the next several days included the Louvre Museum, shopping at the *Galeries Lafayette*, and people-watching from *la terrasse d'un café*. At the top of her list, in bold print: a quest for that flamed dessert called *Crème Brûlée*.

At first, traveling on such whims had seemed foreign to her, decadent even. It wasn't easy letting go of her teacher habits: saving paper clips in empty Altoid tins, burgeoning files from years ago, collecting bric-a-brac for her high school Multicultural Literature classes, when she was supposed to be on vacation.

She'd finally decided to toss out useless files and replace them with travel brochures to exotic places: Ireland, Italy, Corsica, Sicily, *La Côte d'Azur*. She could now sip from a bottle of *Pastis de Marseilles* without saving the label.

As the taxi approached *l'Hôtel du Jeu de Paume*, Gloria spotted a bank where she could exchange a wad of one hundred dollar bills. She'd misplaced her ATM card and, after a last minute frantic search, had no choice but to write a check for cash, *en route* to the O'Hare International Airport.

"Ah," said Gloria, stepping out of the taxi, "*l'Hôtel du Jus de Pomme.*"

The driver frowned and shook his head. "*Jeu de Paume,*" he repeated slowly then growled.

"*Oui*, that's what I said."

Gloria's leftover *euros* from her trips to Ireland and Italy were enough to pay the driver, plus an additional charge per bag, plus tip. *Good Lord*, she thought, *the way the driver acted, it's a wonder he didn't bill me by the pound.* She had begun to feel like an overweight American (eager to start skiing again someday) with questionable language skills in a city of svelte, chic *Parisiennes* click-clacking down the cobblestones on tiny feet strapped in spikes.

The hotel porter wheeled her luggage inside, up the elevator to room 212, then quickly departed with the last of Gloria's *euros.*

She circled about the spacious room, sat with a bounce on the queen size bed, flung open those tall, narrow windows, and gazed down at the patio garden ablaze with potted bellflowers, marigolds, and bright red geraniums. She'd been eager to stay at this particular hotel after discovering on its website that the building was near the magnificent Louvre museum, once the king's palace, and had served as a seventeenth-century royal handball court—thus its name: *Jeu de Paume*: game of handball. Shoot. Dribble. Pass.

Standing in front of a large mirror, Gloria plumped up her bobbed hair, put on fresh lipstick, shouldered her handbag, and rushed off to find *la banque*.

Three people stood ahead of her at the teller window sectioned off by a daunting piece of plexi-glass with a tiny speaking hole carved in at cleavage level. When it was her turn, Gloria leaned down and asked, "May I speak English?"

"*Non!*" replied the stern-looking woman.

Gloria smiled, waiting for a chuckle that was sure to follow. But the clerk, like a sour actress with faulty timing, prolonged the silence until it screamed. Then, like a drill soldier, she turned with a click-clack and disappeared into the back room. Moments later, with great aplomb, another woman whose unnaturally black hair raked into a tight little bun and skewered with a long pencil, took her place behind the *guichet*.

"*Vous désirez, madame?*" she asked. "May I help you?"

"I would like to exchange this American money for *euros*, please." Gloria slipped her stack of bills into the dipped slot. Glancing back over her shoulder, she noticed a lengthy line of customers snaking toward the door.

The clerk's mouth puckered. "*Madame,*" she said, squaring her shoulders and shoving the bills back out of the slot, "I seemply cannot accept any of zees American beels wees dates before 1990. We must look at zem carefully, one by one. And please, where are you staying een Paree?"

Several customers hovered closely behind Gloria, murmuring with irritated interest.

She pressed her lips close to the speaker hole and whispered, "I am staying at the *Hôtel du Jus de Pomme*."

"*Pardon, madame.* I cannot hear you," called out the impatient woman, shrugging her shoulders and casting an exasperated look over Gloria's head, at the waiting crowd. "I cannot understand you!"

Beads of sweat trickled down Gloria's back. "*Au Jus de Pomme,*" she hissed, as if uttering the password for access into a Prohibition

Speakeasy. Her reading glasses slid down her nose as she began to check the tiny print on each bill.

One of the couples standing behind her started snickering.

"*Jus de pomme, jus de pomme,*" repeated a female. "Ha! Niles, this woman just said that she was staying in the apple juice! Hahahaha."

"*Merde, ah merde,*" someone muttered from halfway down the line.

Gloria knew that word: "Shit."

She turned to look back with a frown and saw several men shifting restlessly from one foot to the other.

"*Oh, la vâche,*" said one.

The cow? wondered Gloria. Why would he bring in a cow?

"*Ah, merde!*" shouted another.

After receiving some *euros,* finished at last, Gloria glanced up with tired eyes and a forced smile at the clerk who glared back at her through the plexi-glass. Then she turned to walk the gauntlet of disgruntled citizens who, with folded arms, silently scolded her out of the bank.

The summer air felt cool as it sifted through her drenched silk blouse. She clutched her handbag, sighed, and waited at the curb for a green pedestrian figure to light up on its post. Within inches of her toes, a motorbike zipped by, sounding like a chainsaw. A leashed Yorkie dog hopped up and down next to her, carrying on like a whiny gull.

Through clenched teeth, Gloria tested her own voice, simply speaking into the air: "I can't wait to get back to my hotel, whatever the hell it's called—*Pomme* or *Paume.* Gonna take a bath, then, yippee! Dinner and *crème brûlée!*"

These last words, loud and exciting, loosened her rigid jaw, causing several people at curbside to turn and stare at her.

After rushing back to her hotel room, Gloria filled the long, deep tub with tepid water, eased herself in, laid back, and thought about dinner—especially, what should become her favorite dessert:

those succulent flavors, the smooth creamy surprise beneath a burnt sugar crust that defies a spoon.

Gloria practiced the lovely, rounded vowels and soft consonants of the French language—*raison d'etre*—until they floated about the high ceiling and came together perfectly. Yes, this evening she would order *crème brûlée*, and for that her pronunciation was impeccable.

Wearing plenty of makeup and a lovely outfit, Gloria entered the elevator, *bien nippée* in black capri pants, high heels, and a sparkly pearl-gray spandex top that bared one shoulder and a touch of *décolletage*. Ready to step out among the fashionable *Parisiennes*, she pressed the main floor button, and then struck a pose in each of three mirrors. Paying little attention to the quivering flesh of her upper arms as she patted her hair, Gloria remembered the appointment back home, at *Salon de Beauté*. She lifted her chin and, with half-closed eyes, gazed at her lovely auburn hairstyle created by that talkative woman named Candi.

"*Bonne soirée*," sang the hotel doorman.

Happy to hear him wish her a good evening, Gloria smiled and took to the cobblestones, her high heels click clacking down the avenue.

Within minutes, she found an inviting little restaurant, a charming place called *Chez Victoire*, where a dozen tables shone like brightly scrubbed masks with white cloths and delicate vases filled with miniature lilies. Black and white prints of Paris in the fifties hung along golden walls. *Chez Victoire* exuded the delicious aromas of warm bread, buttery lemon and olive oil, braised lamb, broiled fish, sweets, and coffee.

The *maître d'hôtel* guided Gloria to a table for two. Noticing that other diners were directing their attention her way, she smiled and nodded at them as *monsieur* adjusted the chair beneath her.

Soon she was ordering *poisson*, without making the word for "fish" sound like "poison." *Salade* was no problem. She planned to eat lightly this evening, saving room for her *Crème Brûlée*. Oh, the very thought of it sent rivers of saliva trickling along the insides of her cheeks.

"*Et du vin blanc*," she added, athirst for white wine, and highly pleased with her growing ability to speak one of the most beautiful languages in the world. *"Sancerre, s'il vous plaît, monsieur."*

Dinner completed, Gloria leaned back against her comfortable chair and, with *savoir-faire*, practiced the ordering of her final course.

The waiter returned to clear the plates and sweep breadcrumbs from the tablecloth onto a small, gleaming silver shovel. Then he stood motionless before her.

"Vous désirez un dessert, madame?" he asked, tilting his head slightly.

Gloria sat up straight, her wrists resting properly at the table's edge. She gazed into the waiter's eyes—the same brown color as caramelized sugar.

A reprieve, the glorious finale to this long, frustrating day would be hers with the one utterance perfected through a lengthy repetition.

"Oui, monsieur. Je voudrais de la crème brûlée, s'il vous plaît."

"Oh, *madame*. I am very sorry, *madame*, but tonight zere ees no *crème brûlée*. For ze chef *s'est brûlé* as he was preparing eet. He ees een hospital wees, how you say, seconde degree burns to hees hands because of ze *chalumeau*—hees blowtorch. *Je regrette, madame*, but tonight and every night, zere weel be no *crème brûlée*."

In a flash, Gloria's blithe countenance gave way like a failed *soufflé*. Then, cocking her head, she murmured sweetly, *"Ah, monsieur*, but zere weel always be another *restaurant*."

A Dance with the Mountain

Late in the night, six inches of fluffy, snow-decorated trees, shrubs, roofs, and vehicles parked at the Snowmass ski resort near Aspen, Colorado. By morning, sunshine and a cool breeze shifted those silhouettes, guided birds among branches, and filled Gloria Spencer's lungs with fresh, clean air, bringing rosiness to her cheeks.

Still feeling a bit queasy about what she had decided to do this day, up on the mountaintop, Gloria, dressed in a glossy blue outfit and ski boots, hobbled over to her car and brushed away the last offerings of snow. Then she removed her mittens, opened the trunk, and reached for the plastic bag that had been riding around in there for several months—a medium-sized zip lock filled with ashes.

That Gloria should still be carrying human remains inside her car for such a long time seemed odd, if not reprehensible. But it no longer troubled her. The self-deception that believes lies in order to avoid confrontations got swept away.

Most days, as she drove to and from work, Gloria forgot that these ashes were in the trunk. Yet when the memory came back, she no longer fell apart. After all, her husband had turned out to be the opposite type of man she thought she'd married. It wasn't that she hadn't loved him. And he, perhaps, loved her in some fashion. But recalling what he had done during their two years together, and how he'd carried on prior to their marriage, Gloria whispered, "You deserve to stay in the trunk—*stay* in the trunk, Rob, until I can figure out what on earth to do with my half of your ashes."

And today was the day.

In 1999, during her mid-winter break from teaching, Gloria, still single, had flown to the Aspen/Pitkin County Airport in Colorado. She was eager to meet up with her friend Sarah, who had called to let her know that the Rocky Mountains had received massive amounts of snow, especially around Aspen and Snowmass.

Mid-morning of their first day out, eager as adolescents on vacation, they scooted up the snow-packed incline in front of Top of the Village condo, stepped into their bindings, and skied the short distance down to Fanny Hill lift where they'd catch the Coney Glade quad. Because it was crowded around this second lift, Gloria and Sarah slid into the singles' line, edging onboard with others for quicker rides up.

A middle-aged man eased himself onto the seat next to Gloria. During the five-minute ride from Fanny Hill, she learned that he, too, lived near the Twin Cities, and was an avid skier. Finding him attractive, she felt a pleasant vibe from the way he smiled and greeted her.

At mid-mountain, the Coney Glade lift dropped off its passengers.

"Enjoy," called out the man as he hopped down and skied off to the left.

"Have fun!" shouted Gloria.

He waved at her before gliding down the slope. His tall, trim form quickly disappeared over the first edge.

Sarah met up with Gloria, and together they raced down to Big Burn, which would take them up to deep, yet lighter snow at twelve thousand feet above sea level. The rarefied air would give way to a brilliant blue sky and sunshine, as if introducing springtime.

"This is the way to go," said Sarah, once again scooting along behind Gloria in a singles' line. "Besides, it's fun to meet new people. I last rode up with an elderly Japanese man who spoke little English."

"Did he give you a brief lesson in his language?"

"No, I'd be hopeless, even with a word or two. We just pointed at the mountain, and said stuff like *snow…beau-tee-ful…America*. Like that. Forces you to think about reducing language to essential elements, that's for sure."

"You sound like a writer, Sarah."

"Thanks. Anyway, you have to admire a guy like that, figuring out how to make it to Colorado all by himself."

"All for the love of skiing. Last year, at Red Lodge, Montana, I rode up with a woman who told me about her ninety-four-year-old mother who had driven out to the mountain by herself, skied a full day, went home, shoveled her driveway, and dropped dead."

"Wow! Not a bad way to go," said Sarah, "at that age."

Just as Gloria moved forward in the single line, she heard a familiar voice call out, "Hello, Minnesota!"

It was the man she'd ridden up with on the Coney Glade lift, approaching the gate to Big Burn at the same time.

Gloria laughed as she settled onto the seat next to him. "Hello, again."

"I do love fate," he said, holding out a gloved hand. "I'm Rob Graften."

"And I'm Gloria. Gloria Spencer."

"Pleased to meet you. What a great day." Rob lifted up his sunglasses, turned, and grinned at her. "You must be a good skier, heading up to the top."

"Not bad."

"Would you like to take a couple of runs with me?"

"Sure, that would be fun. I'll wait for my friend, though, and see if she'd like to join us."

Gloria turned to wave at Sarah, two lift-chairs back.

Settling forward, she took a longer look at Rob. Unlike most skiers, he wasn't wearing a helmet or even a stocking cap. She wondered how people could race around in cold air all day without covering their ears. He was handsome, like some European men Gloria had seen during her travels abroad: tan, a firm chin and straight nose, full lips, expensive wrap-around sunglasses. He had thick, silvery hair that stayed in place, unaffected by the wind. His black and red jacket made him look official, like a ski patrol.

Rob smiled. "No fair. Obviously, you can see more of me than I can of you."

Gloria tilted her goggles up and winked.

Reaching the top, they skied off to one side and waited for Sarah.

"I found another Minnesotan," said Gloria as soon as her friend joined them.

After introductions, the three took several runs together down Whispering Jesse and Dallas Freeway, before Sarah decided to head over to Alpine Springs.

"I want to ski a black diamond at High Alpine while I'm still feeling hardy," she said.

They agreed to meet for lunch at Café Suzanne, and then ski Elk Camp in the afternoon.

"You're welcome to join us, Rob."

"Thanks, Sarah, but I have some calls to make later on. Maybe tomorrow?"

After a few runs off Big Burn lift, Rob led Gloria along Sneaky's Glade where she stopped a couple of times to look for signs of animal life. Eventually, she spotted marten tracks in the snow under some lodge pole pines.

"What were you looking at?" asked Rob, waiting for her to catch up with him.

"I took a wildlife tour yesterday and now I'm in the habit of pulling over to see more. I learned all sorts of things."

"Okay, Ms. Magpie, let's hear one."

"Love that nickname! All right. Do you know how aspen trees grow?"

"I think so, but *you* tell me."

"Well, when a storm takes out a section of pines, it clears the ground for aspen roots to travel. They clone themselves by growing up from a single root system. You'll almost never see one all alone. What's more, they have photosynthesis in their bark."

"Aha, I didn't know about that last part. Now, here's one for you. Where does the term 'quaking aspen' come from?"

"The guide talked about that too. But let me hear *you* explain it."

"The leaves survive heavy winds on the mountains by whipping around in circles. That way they don't have to let go or get ripped off."

Gloria held her ski pole out to touch the closest branch. "I love these trees. They're so adaptable. Always in a pair—or a threesome."

"Yup, just like me," said Rob, turning downhill.

Gloria puzzled over that comment, but let it go and said nothing more.

Rob suggested stopping for a drink at the Ullrhof. They did one more run, this time down Mick's Gully. After speeding toward the bar/restaurant, they made slick stops next to the corral, clicked out of their bindings, propped their skis and poles against a railing, and clomped up the steps, onto the deck.

"I'll have some hot chocolate," said Gloria, removing her goggles.

"No cocktail? How about a beer?"

"Not until I'm done for the day. Otherwise, my legs turn into noodles."

She sat down at one of the tables, squinting up at the sunshine, while Rob went inside for refreshments. As soon as he brought out a tray of fries, a couple of donuts, and beverages, several magpies swooped in to land on a nearby railing. With long, tilting black tails and wings, and keen eyes, they danced along their perch, focusing on the tables.

Another woman, sitting nearby, got up to grab some napkins, leaving her tray for several seconds—long enough for one of the birds to hop down and swipe a chunk of bread.

"Did you see that?" remarked Gloria. "What an opportunist."

"Watch this," said Rob, holding a French fry over his head. The closest magpie rose up and plucked it off in mid-flight.

"Smart birds." Gloria extended her arm, holding a lengthy fry between her thumb and index finger. She barely felt it disappear, yet heard the faintest whisper of air from the bird's wings.

"Some people call them thieves," said Rob.

"Hmm, I guess they're just doing what magpies do to survive."

Beneath the warm sunshine, Gloria removed her stocking cap and shook out her shoulder-length auburn hair, remembering that Rob had called her Miss Magpie a half hour ago, while she edged along Sneaky's Glade to find more animals.

Gazing at her with soft brown eyes, Rob listened attentively as she revealed some of her background: a high school teacher, traveler, active in supporting environmental protection, living alone in a small cottage near Minneapolis.

"Several years ago," she said, patting her cheeks, "I'd come close to marrying a university professor who eventually dished out kindness and caring to everyone, except *moi*—Ms. Magpie."

"A total opposite," said Rob, shaking his head.

He seemed reluctant to go into much detail about himself, saying only that he was an attorney, worked for the Federal government, and traveled frequently from his mansion in North Oaks to New York and Washington, DC.

"I'm hardly ever home," he said. "People wonder why I don't move east—that's where most of my work and friends are—but I can't imagine leaving Minnesota. I *love* my house and our thousands of lakes. There's an easygoing pace around the Twin Cities and beyond—places where I can go to decompress."

"What exactly do you do?"

"I like to fish, occasionally. Some hiking. And *skiing*, obviously." He waved his red-jacketed arms at the treetops and slopes.

"I mean back east. What do you do as a lawyer for the federal government?"

"Let's just say that I provide legal representation of American interests overseas. Married once. Single for three years. No children.

"And by the way, Ms. Magpie, you have a beautiful smile. Lovely eyes." He reached across the table to touch her hand, saying that her blue eyes reminded him of sapphires.

Gloria grinned, lowered her head, and peered at him as though above reading glasses. "Not very original, Mr. Graften," she said in a silly voice. "Surely you can do…"

Rob laughed. "Hmm, I need new material, is that it? Let's see… I've got it! Your eyes contain the color of ice inside the glacier near Chamonix. How's that?"

"*Mer de Glace*. Now that's original. And by the *way*, I've been there."

"Really! When?"

"Two years ago. And you?"

"In the late eighties. I was in India on business and had a…"

"India—what did you do there?"

"Worked for a time on some corporate legal issues. Anyhow, I had a couple of weeks to travel anywhere I pleased afterward, so I chose France—a beautiful country, smaller than the state of Texas."

"*Très bien, Robert!* I had a fascinating trip to Paris—my first one. And finally found a restaurant that created my favorite dessert."

"What was that?"

"*Crème brûlée.* In fact, the color of your eyes reminds me of its golden brown crust."

"Delicious, Ms. Magpie."

"For sure. Speaking of delicious, let's do a couple more runs, then I'll meet Sarah for lunch."

Gloria turned to wave goodbye at the birds while they paced along the railing. Each one glanced back at her before zeroing in on the donut crumbs she'd left for them.

Rob, an excellent skier, showed Gloria how to plant her poles more aggressively and rhythmically in order to execute smarter, more fluid turns.

"Oh, I feel like a giant bird!" she called out.

"That's it, Ms. Magpie!" he shouted from behind. "Now you're dancing with the mountain!"

Before going their separate ways, they made dinner plans.

It was late when they left the Lobster Bar, midway up from Snowmass Village. A steady, gentle snowfall promised plenty of fresh powder for the next day.

After dinner, drinks, and getting to know one another, Rob walked Gloria to the door of her condo and wrapped his arms around her in a long, enveloping embrace. He gently rocked from side to side, as if in a slow dance, kissed her lightly, and then cupped her face in his hands.

"I really enjoyed our day together, Ms. Magpie."

"Me, too, Robby. And thanks for tonight."

"Let's make first runs in the morning. I'll meet you at eight thirty, bottom of Fanny Hill."

"Sounds great. Fresh snow. New tracks."

The entire next day, Rob's last before returning home, he spent with Gloria, sashaying together down the slopes, carving clean cuts along six inches of feathery snow. When they stopped to look back at their perfect linked-up S curves, Gloria said that their tracks resembled the arcs of dancing deer.

"Or corpulent snakes," said Rob, swinging his ski poles far apart, "racing each other."

During their last evening together, it seemed as if they'd known one another much longer than two days.

"Call me as soon as you get home," he said, tucking a personal card into her breast pocket.

Gloria and Rob dated over the next six months—an equivalent of three, since Rob's work took him back east for long periods. And then they celebrated the year 2000 with their wedding—a small ceremony and reception at the North Oaks Country Club. Her friend Sarah attended as bridesmaid, and Rob's close friend, Ralph Handy, as groomsman. Mr. Handy, a personal estate attorney, resembled Karl Rove, known as "The Man with the Plan." He had a similar oblong face and extra keen eyes.

Gloria rented out her cottage and moved into Rob's large home—a contemporary mansion with a distant lake view, next to woodsy acreage filled with maple trees, oaks, and pines.

"You can quit your job if you like," he said. "You really don't have to work—just help keep up our place while I'm away. All you have to do is oversee the cleaning staff and yard workers."

"Oh no, I love what I'm doing—teaching literature, working with teenagers. Besides, since you travel so much, I need something to keep me occupied. I'd like to join you in DC during my breaks or on a weekend."

"Possibly," said Rob, packing his bag. "I'm extremely busy, though, and wouldn't have much time to show you around."

An uneasy feeling entered Gloria's mind and began fiddling with her innards. But she took a deep breath and pushed it away, convincing herself that it was just her imagination. He's super busy. Don't go there anymore.

Although they were apart for long periods, Rob never failed to reserve some special times together, including another winter week at Snowmass—one of the few places where, except for his occasional, private phone calls, Gloria could have him all to herself.

One summer, they spent a couple of weekends along Lake Superior, wandering the rocky shorelines, collecting smooth stones, and daring each other to wade ever deeper into the clear, icy-cold water. One of their days had been unforgettable, hiking up to the Split Rock Lighthouse, stopping at Peterson's Fish Shack for smoked whitefish, and meandering along the shore in search of perfectly round stones.

Although she loved Lake Superior, Gloria had become aware of its incongruity: a hot summer sun, yet chilly winds blasting over steely waves. Even during the warmest months, the coldest of Great Lakes could take a person down within fifteen minutes.

Up north, Rob also received and made private calls. Once, he and Gloria left for home before noon on a Sunday, after his explanation about sudden work issues.

What he really did for a living was not completely clear to her during the first year of their marriage. Ever curious, she persisted until Rob got tired of telling her that he couldn't discuss details for security reasons. It had to do with certain legal affairs pertaining to Union Carbide, and that's all he would say.

What *she* was able to piece together during the second, and final year of their marriage, was that Rob had often traveled abroad to help resolve international disputes, that he'd been a key member of the legal team assembled in Bhopal, India, to deal with the 1984 toxic disaster, and that he was still working with the US State Department after problems resurfaced due to the Bhopal crisis.

Curiosity continually got the better of Gloria, especially when it came time to teach a literary/historical unit, which included India. She spent several hours researching details, focusing on events that had taken place within the last few decades. One evening, seated in front of her computer, she read the following paragraph:

On December 3, as they did every year since 1984, Bhopal, India survivors paraded through the streets with a burning effigy of Union Carbide's CEO, Warren Anderson. It was the fifteenth anniversary of their struggle since twenty-seven tons of methyl isocyanate exploded out of the Bhopal plant in the night, killing more than 22,000 people. There'd been no system in place to warn or evacuate the residents. Legal experts, gathering in Washington, DC, and India, worked for years to make sure that corporate officials never had to answer for their actions in a court of law.

Gloria reread the last sentence: *"Legal experts...worked for years to make sure that corporate officials never had to answer for their actions..."*

She looked down at her fingers, curved, still, hovering above the keyboard. Her wedding ring shimmered under the desk lamp. She felt herself go numb.

Surely he's there to work with both sides, she thought. Rob might be helping those poor people and can't discuss it. He likely has to be very careful, dealing with a sensitive situation.

Gloria closed the website window, logged off, and went to bed. Unable to sleep, she sensed that her lengthy efforts at self-deception were beginning to fade away, leaving her in limbo.

It was one of those rare weekends when Rob didn't have to be in Washington DC. Before preparing breakfast, Gloria leaned against the white kitchen counter, eager to tell her husband about the information she'd found on the internet.

"Why didn't Union Carbide help those people, Rob? After all, it was their responsibility."

"Because they have a good legal team. The best."

"Whoa! Who's looking out for the citizens? I can't stand the thought that more than twenty-two thousand people *died* and the rest were simply *abandoned*. Surely, you're aware of that."

Rob fell quiet for a moment.

"It's my job, Gloria. I'm just doing what I was hired to do."

"But aren't you there to help the people as well? You know what's right, don't you? Tell me there's someone representing those families."

"Yes, sweetie, I'm sure there is. But I have *my* job to do. All sides are entitled to legal representation."

"Mostly to the government—that's what I learned about this apocalyptic disaster. Almost *nothing* was given to the people who were affected. My God, there were corpses everywhere; many of them children—more than twenty-two thousand dead and then another one hundred thousand people suffering diseases of the lungs, eyes, and blood. Tons of dead animals!"

"You fret too much. You've got to relax."

"I need to know that you're not one of those working against the victims, that's all. You should be helping them."

"All right, if it'll make you feel better about the whole thing—yes, I'm helping."

"You know what I stand for, Rob."

"I hate to see you so stressed out about all this business—it happened a long time ago. It's over now."

"If it were over, why do you have to keep going back to DC? Why not work from here more often? On other things?"

From a large bowl on the counter, Gloria reached for one of the perfectly shaped, polished stones they'd collected from Lake Superior. "Beginning to wonder why you married me, since you're gone nearly all the time." She squeezed the stone, feeling it grow warmer in the palm of her hand.

"Sweetheart, you're one of the best things that's ever happened—smart, beautiful, and a *damn* good skier." Rob laughed and tickled Gloria's side until she shrieked and gasped for air.

"Besides," he added, giving her a quick kiss on the nose, "I love you, and it's nice to know there's someone keeping an eye on this place, waiting for me when I get home. Got to take my shower now and get ready to go."

"Go?" She dropped her stone back into the bowl. "Wait a minute! I thought you were staying home this weekend."

As soon as she heard the water running, Gloria rushed into Rob's office, clicked open his briefcase and flipped through the stack of papers. A newspaper clipping, dated March 4, 2005, was entitled "Proposed Deal Between Union Carbide's 100% owner Dow Chemical and Indian Oil Corp." She pulled the article and continued reading: "*Possible agreement to supply ethylene glycol technology for IOC's Panipat complex. Dow Chemical, Union Carbide's new corporate parent, has no legal obligations for the 1984 Bhopal disaster and may move forward as planned.*"

So that's how they got around it, thought Gloria. *A buyout.*

Then she spotted some of Rob's notes on a yellow legal pad: an outline of ideas on how to avoid court appearances by the CEOs and how, since Dow Chemical had stepped in, responsibility on the part of Union Carbide could finally be neutralized.

Gloria was shocked, not only at her findings, but at herself for having ignored these various signs for so long. She had been busy teaching, spending time with friends, managing the household, and wanting to trust Rob.

Now, the fact was no longer undeniable—what Rob had been doing all these years. He, as one of the lawyers, had helped to make sure that those responsible for the disaster never had to answer for it in a court of law. She hadn't wanted to know that about her husband. This was like looking at the first stage of a sunrise. You can stare at the smoky red disc for a few seconds, but once it rises above the trees and turns into a burning white ball, you have to look away.

Only now she couldn't turn away. Here were the facts: Dow Chemical would buy up Union Carbide in order to wipe out the past. Clever. No one would ever have to answer for what happened. This is what Rob had been involved with all along.

As soon as she heard her husband step out of the shower, Gloria quickly shut the briefcase and rushed back into the kitchen. Standing as still as possible, she reached toward the black granite countertop with trembling hands that reminded her of those aspen tree branches whose leaves fluttered in circles as soon as the wind came up.

Finally summoning the energy, she began the breakfast routine: cracking eggs into the frying pan, pouring orange juice and coffee, dropping slices of bread into the toaster. Every minor move felt like a major effort. Gloria took several long, deep breaths in order to calm down.

She would no longer ask why, because his answer would always be the same: "I need to prepare for Monday and that's the best place to do it, on site, meeting with other advisors."

Packed and ready to go, he sat down to breakfast. Seated opposite, Gloria watched Rob's every move. Funny, she thought, how, when your senses are bursting, ordinary actions become monumental: she stared at his well-manicured fingers as they curved just so to pick up a lump of sugar and drop it into his coffee; as he grasped the cream pitcher handle to pour out a measured white stream; as he slowly stirred the mix with a small spoon, while his little finger rose up slightly from the rest. She studied the fine hairs clustered below each knuckle, as Rob set the spoon down, raised the cup to his full lips, and peered at Gloria over the rim.

"What are you thinking, my little Ms. Magpie?" He set the cup down. "Concerned about…"

"I've always loved you, Rob."

"I love you, too, sweetheart. What's on your mind?"

"How about if I join you this time," she said in a cool voice, guessing his answer before she said these next words: "I have one final week off before school starts. Nothing much going on right now."

"Oh, sweetie, we've been through this before. I've got meetings every day, and a ton of work that popped up this weekend. Really, you'd be so bored."

"Are you kidding, Rob? Me bored? I *love* to travel, wander about on my own. It would be fun."

"I couldn't spend *any* time with you whatsoever, Gloria. I am booked solid."

"Couldn't we at least meet for dinner? Or a drink, if you're that busy. I could fly in on Monday."

"Those flights are most likely full, sweetheart. They're usually reserved way ahead."

Gloria dabbed a corner of toast into her egg yolk. Looking up quickly, she caught a strange shift in Rob's eyes as he took another sip of coffee. She knew it was no longer her imagination. His thoughts must have slipped to something or someone else.

"I have a hard time believing that, Rob, about flights."

"Well, that's one of the reasons I go on weekends. I wouldn't bother if I were you. Just take the week to relax, hon. Do a project, go for a hike, have lunch with your friends. I'll be home before you know it."

Gloria dropped her toast onto the plate and studied her husband's face. She remembered staring at him on the ski lift where they'd first met: handsome, confident, thick, silver hair perfectly trimmed, always in place, even in the wind. It had been a long time since his eyes had that same soft look for her, as the day when they fed French fries to the magpies. She'd fallen in love with him almost from the start. Now, in this last year, Rob had become distant, preoccupied, always in a hurry, very private, superficial in conversation. Even his lovemaking with her had turned semiautomatic.

Gloria had ignored so much, hadn't even really looked into his eyes for the longest time—not until this morning when she saw how they'd changed—open and lively one minute, veiled the next, especially when she persisted in bringing up her concerns, they were no longer a reminder of her favorite dessert: *crème brûlée*. When she wasn't asking questions, she was thinking them and Rob sensed that. Then he called her Ms. Magpie, as though they were back on the mountains, and she was "acting too pushy," as Rob stated, "more and more often."

One thing she'd learned, however, was not to challenge his skills as an attorney; she could never compete with his counter-questions, parries, or changes of subject. He'd fiddle with his briefcase and rifle through papers, and then, if Gloria pressed on, he'd become exasperated, forcing her to back off.

She remembered an evening when he'd inexplicably returned home late, dressed in a different outfit from the one he'd worn to work that morning, for some local meeting.

"My, you smell good," said Gloria as they sat down to dinner after a quick kiss, "as if you just showered. Did *you*?"

"Oh, I played handball after work with one of the guys," he said. "Got all sweaty."

"Really? I never knew you played handball, Rob."

He took a deep breath, began eating his dinner, and asked about her day.

His arsenal of comments had finally traveled far beyond Gloria's understanding.

On the last Saturday morning of his life, Rob Graften supposedly left for Washington, DC. As soon as he was gone, Gloria checked the internet for airline information; there were, indeed, several flights out each day with plenty of seats available. She decided to wait until Sunday to book a reservation—after she called her husband.

Waiting until morning seemed like an eternity.

"Hi, hon. Guess what?" Gloria tried to sound casual and cheery over the phone, but her strained voice came across as alien to her own ears; a pinched, small voice she'd hoped never to inherit.

"There are plenty of flights and seats open. I can join you after all."

A long pause steamed through from the other end. Then, in a very quiet voice, Rob said, "No. Don't."

"What? I don't understand. Why wouldn't you want to see me?"

"Don't come, Gloria. We'll talk when I get home."

That was all he said—his final words to her: "Don't come. We'll talk when I get home."

As soon as she heard the click on the other end, Gloria dropped the phone, then paced from room to room like a woman possessed. Growing more and more frantic, she began rummaging through Rob's closet, checking his coat pockets and shoe boxes, pulling out desk drawers and emptying their contents on the floor. She hauled boxes of files out of storage and, with a hammer and screwdriver, opened the locked filing cabinet. She found nothing that compromised him, until she pried open an old briefcase that had been tucked inside the closet, hidden against a dark corner. Inside, among various papers, was a birthday card from a woman named Ashley. There was a brief message—brief but romantic: "Happy birthday, sweetheart. All my love. See you soon!"

Gloria slipped to the floor. Propped against the bed, she examined the card and its envelope with the return address from New York City. *At least it's dated the year before we met*, she thought.

That night, she watched a couple of old movies, including *Charade*. She adored Audrey Hepburn, and somehow took up courage from her wonderfully unruffled demeanor, her elegance, and dignity. Throughout the night, unable to sleep, Gloria held on to Audrey Hepburn's character, Reggie Lampert, drawing strength from it—enough to keep from caving in.

Early Monday morning, she brewed a pot of coffee, worked on lesson plans for her literature and history classes, and then took a long walk in the woods. To counter the incessant repetition of frightening thoughts racing through her mind, she wandered among the trees, watched squirrels leap from branch to branch before hopping down to search for acorns along the ground.

That afternoon, she drove into the city and wandered through the Institute of Arts, making an effort to focus on paintings and sculptures. In the evening, she attended the Sheila Wellstone silent auction benefit for battered and abused women.

Around midnight, after tossing and turning, her tangled bedding flopping onto the floor, Gloria gave up trying to sleep. At three in the morning, she padded into the kitchen to eat chocolate chip cookies and sip green tea, wondering how she'd get through four more days, until Rob returned to verify what she already sensed— what she already knew.

Tuesday afternoon, Ralph Handy arrived at the house, carrying his briefcase and a legal-sized envelope tucked under one arm. Gloria opened the door and stepped back. Whenever she had met up with this man, Rob's close friend and personal estate attorney, he reminded her of a cocky, cutthroat lawyer. This time, he was quiet and somber-looking.

"What's wrong?" she whispered. "What's happened?"

"I need to come in, Gloria." He inhaled deeply from his cigarette before flicking it onto a shrub near the steps.

Standing in the foyer, he reached out to pat her shoulder. "Can we sit down?"

Gloria recoiled at his touch and cigarette smoke, then quickly turned back into the living room and stood next to the sofa.

Ralph Handy sat down in one of the armchairs. "I don't know exactly how to break this to you. It's about Rob."

Gloria felt her limbs go numb all the way to her toes and fingertips, as if tiny dams had been raised to block the flow of blood.

"He's all right though, isn't he?" It was as if she'd stepped away from herself in order to ask that question.

"No, he's not." Ralph Handy shook his head slowly. "It was a heart attack. It happened suddenly."

"Is he...? He'll come out of it, won't he?"

"It was massive."

Gloria's arms clamped tightly against her stomach as she lurched forward.

"When?"

"Late Sunday night."

"Sunday? And today is Tuesday!" Gloria began to tremble. Her head shook as if palsied. "Why did it take this long to let me know?" Then the dams broke as she stepped forward and shouted, "Where is Rob? I want to see him!"

Ralph Handy reached out to her. "Please calm down. Please. I know you're shocked and upset. We all are."

"What's going on? It's Tuesday. Where is he?"

"Still in New York City."

"But he was supposed to be in Washington DC. For his work."

"There's more that I hope you can handle. I'm reluctant to tell you everything all at once, but I think you have a right to know."

Gloria dropped down onto the sofa and grabbed a small pillow to clutch against her chest.

Ralph Handy went on to tell her that Rob had died in the apartment he'd shared for the past fifteen years with another woman.

"Ashley?"

"What did you say?"

"Her name is Ashley, isn't it?"

"How do you know?"

Gloria shrugged.

"I'm sorry. She called me first thing and I flew out."

"Ah, yes, lawyer to lawyer—sweeping up after the rich and secretive. You couldn't have let me know before flying off in your private jet?"

"That's uncalled for, Gloria."

"Like hell it is! I'm his wife! What's uncalled for is that you waited this long to contact me. I think you're lying. I want to know what's really going on there."

"This is how Rob asked me to handle it if anything should happen to him. I'm simply carrying out his wishes."

"His wishes? What do you mean? That should have been between *us*—Rob and me."

"I have here a copy of his will. He left instructions to be cremated. You are to receive half of his ashes."

"Half?" said Gloria, tossing her pillow onto the floor. "What kind of joke is this?"

"It's no joke. You will receive half. That's how Rob wanted it. After all, he was considering you."

Gloria emitted a shrill note of laughter. "What? I'm to be grateful that he was considering me—his wife?"

"Again, I'm sorry. I take it you never really knew about Ashley."

"How could I?" Gloria jumped up. "Who the hell do you people think you are, cheating, protecting each other's lies, ripping the world apart and making it all go your way! I want you out of here. Now!"

"Careful, Magpie, don't forget—he was my best friend. I know you're upset, but you need to hear all of it."

She felt like calling Ralph Handy every vulgar name she could think of, felt like giving him a punch in his potbelly paunch. She remembered how Reggie Lampert said that word in *Charade*: *Pun*-ch. So unruffled and cool—*pun*-ch.

"Gloria, did you hear me?"

"What?"

"You need to hear the rest."

"What more could there be? How do I even know Rob's dead if I can't see him?"

"Do not make trouble, Gloria."

"I don't believe you! I want to see him! I need to see my husband!"

"I'm warning you. Don't…make…trouble."

"Are you threatening me? Because if you are…"

Catching a nearly violent, then sinister and stony look from the man, Gloria fell suddenly quiet. His stare seemed to say, "Go no further, lady, or else."

Snapping her mouth shut, she thought of Audrey's aloof character in *Charade* when questioned by the French police. Consider how these guys operate. Be more like Reggie, self-contained, unflappable. Remember how she answered by simply saying the words "I don't know," in that sweet, innocent voice.

"Now, you are to keep Rob's Mercedes, his house and its contents, valued at around two million. He also wanted you to have one of his investment accounts in the amount of $250,000."

Ralph Handy went on to state that the remaining accounts, his Maryland and New York apartment buildings, and a vacation home in the Adirondacks, would go to Ashley, along with other investments.

"Everything has been arranged and is incontestable."

Gloria took a deep breath, remembering the lack of justice and aid for the people in Bhopal, and how so many of them died all those years ago.

"What about the funeral?" she asked quietly. Now it seemed as though she were discussing the death, not of her husband, but of a mere acquaintance.

"Naturally, the memorial service will take place in New York City, where most of his friends and colleagues live. Again, I'm sorry. I know all this comes as a complete shock. Will you be going to the service?"

Looking down at a spot on the white carpet where this man had just tracked in a trace of mud, she thought for a moment then looked up, her eyes meeting his.

"I don't know."

As soon as Ralph Handy left, Gloria barely made it to the bathroom. For the next couple of days, she ate almost nothing. Unfamiliar feelings took over, causing her to think how everything seemed surreal, like a prolonged death.

This time, it was a death, only much more. Now there were three things to mourn. Funny, she thought, how trouble often comes in threes.

Gloria flopped down on the bed, too exhausted even to call a friend. One thing was for certain; she had to set a time limit, must not let all this make her crazy. Age and a little experience, thank Providence for that. But first she had to figure out which of those three things was hitting her the hardest: his death, his betrayal, or that expanded and protected evil carried out in Bhopal, India.

Turning her head toward the open closet, Gloria glanced at Rob's dozens of shoes carefully arranged in cubbies, elegant suits hanging together, evenly spaced, and color-coded. His blue sweatshirt from Snowmass was still draped over the lounge chair next to their bed. She drew it close to her face, snuggled her nose against it, and smelled Rob's scent. Curled up on the bed, she began to weep, hugged the sweatshirt, and then, after a long while, fell asleep.

Later that day, Gloria's thoughts turned to her husband's work. Compared to the outcome of it all, she and Rob seemed like a couple of insignificant cogs in the relative scheme of things. It was never the first or last time people cheated and lied to others. But the fact that Rob had worked for years to protect a corporate power responsible for thousands of deaths was overwhelming and unforgivable. Far too long, she had tried to convince herself that her husband had had no part in that.

Suddenly, Gloria sat bolt upright and reached for the phone, gripped with a desire to call him. She could hurl some words at him: "How could you have done this to me—to them?"

Then she remembered that he had supposedly died...or had he? She was to receive some ashes, but would they be his? They could be from anything: a dead tree, ground up vermiculite, some kind of animal. How would she ever know for sure?

Lying back against the pillows, her racing mind began to imagine what Ashley might look like: a thin, faceless body with large breasts, cascading blond hair, and a butt that... She must have broken up Rob's first marriage, as well. He never wanted to discuss that either—his first marriage. "The past doesn't matter," he used to say, "just the present. Just us."

"Clever, philandering liar!" she shouted against her pillow. Then, as if a switch had been flicked, she thought of the fun, exciting times she'd spent with Rob, when he was generous, considerate, seemingly devoted, and loving.

Gloria dialed his cell phone number, but it had been deactivated. Then she phoned her friend Sarah and told her everything.

"This isn't about what you did or didn't do, Glo. It was obviously a pattern—he had that other woman on the string long before he met you."

"I'd hoped for the best in him, Sarah, but the truths just wouldn't fade away."

"Sometimes, *hope* can be a mean thing—keeping a wishful thinker in chains far too long."

"You're right. How are things going for you?"

"I've been out with several men in the past few months. With the last one, I knew our relationship was over the night I pointed out that lady in the moon. Her profile was so clear, like a lovely pencil portrait on a circle of golden paper high in the sky. But the guy I was with said that he couldn't see her and left it at that, eager to get back home to watch Monday night football. I'm actually enjoying time on my own now—eating meals over the sink, wandering about in my pajamas, without makeup, burping and farting just like some guys."

"Wow! That's a new side of you."

"True. And I'm wishing the best for you as well."

After hanging up, Gloria drifted into a nightmare where images ran like an old film out of control, and ribbons of celluloid piled up under a projector that spun and spun and wouldn't shut down—images of a shrine, a faceless Ashley, stripped from her Hindu sari, passing cocktails to Rob who is smiling and basking in a steamy, bubbling Jacuzzi. Suddenly, his face sags and he clutches his chest.

Two years together. Startling how quickly they passed. How the minutiae of living made up months that peeled away from each calendar. It was as if someone had opened a window, and a gust of wind tackled her carefully stacked reams of paper and their two calendars.

After slipping out of bed, Gloria wandered through the living room and reached, once again, into another bowl of smooth stones. *What did it take*, she wondered, *for a rock to become this flawless?* Centuries of tossing about in a Great Lake, rolling and bouncing along the sand, nuzzling against other rocks. Some were meant to be picked up and treasured. Others had to roll back and disappear, until the end of time.

The next morning, Ralph Handy delivered a decorative urn, placing it on the dining room table. Because Gloria just stood there and chose to say nothing, he turned and hurried away.

There it sat, right in the middle of the table—an expensive hardwood vase inlaid with white, pink, and yellow mother-of-pearl pieces shaped in little figures, hands linked, like tiny, ubiquitous women dancing along the rounded part of the vase—dancing around what was left of Rob.

These shapes reminded her of the beautiful birds prancing along the mountain railings, and how her husband used to wink and call her his "magpie." Although he'd described those birds as raucous and aggressive, Gloria chose to accept that nickname as a compliment; *magpies*, she told herself, *are social creatures, vocal, and gorgeous in their panda-like plumage.*

Funny, she thought, *the little things a person can remember.*

Then she recalled Rob's strong hands, long fingers stirring his coffee, reaching out to caress—another woman!

But try as she would, Gloria couldn't hate Rob for more than a few seconds at a time. Good thoughts sparred with the bad: the first warmth of their time together, growing comfortable with each other. She remembered how he'd once made pancakes and sausages for their breakfast in bed. They'd nibbled and cuddled, planned their next ski trip, and then made love.

How could he have put all that aside so easily the moment he stepped off the plane in DC? Or New York City? *For the life of me,* she muttered, *I'll never be able to understand a mind that works that way, shifting back and forth to this woman, then that woman.*

Gloria opened a utility drawer and pulled out a paring knife. Pointing it at one wall, then at the opposite wall, she shouted, "This woman, that woman! This woman, that woman!"

She grabbed a plastic bag from another drawer, then sat down at the dining table and drew the urn close to her. With the knife, she cut the seal, removed the top, dumped Rob's ashes into the zip lock bag, and, with thumb and finger, pinched it shut.

Unsure what to do next, she stared at the gray flecks and bone chips, wondering which half of Rob this was. The upper? The lower? A combination? *Or maybe it's not Rob at all,* she thought. Maybe it's just an animal.

Gloria jumped up so fast she felt light-headed racing out to the garage, while harsh thoughts ran through her mind: *I don't want these ashes in the house. No decoration along the fireplace mantel. No enshrining our bedroom dresser next to pictures of happy times together. I'll keep my photos, but not the ashes.*

Standing inside the garage, she'd thought of Lakeview Garden's mausoleum—an honorable place to rest. But then images of the thousands of dead and suffering in India fixed themselves in her mind, along with the imagined face of that other woman. Fifteen years of infidelity and denial. Twenty years of cunning and brutal law. No honor there.

Her thoughts alternated between burying Rob's ashes in the backyard under a favorite red maple tree, or flushing them down the toilet, or spreading them across the nearby field loaded with horse manure and cow-pies, or tossing them into Lake Superior.

Alone so often, Gloria had spent plenty of time each day after school driving around the countryside. Being surrounded by old oak trees, pasture land, and farm animals helped to clear her head. Once, she'd stopped along a back road where a herd of cattle began gathering next to the fence. They watched her every move as she got out of the car and walked toward them. They stared and stared all the while she muttered. It was as if they were friends standing close by, until she got all talked out. Maybe they would watch her sprinkle Rob's ashes nearby, as if attending a small funeral.

But that wasn't to happen.

After gazing around inside the garage, Gloria opened her car trunk and stuck the plastic bag in one corner, beneath a small gray towel. There the ashes would remain for the next few weeks.

Eventually, she put the North Oaks house on the market, furnishings and all, down to the empty mother-of-pearl vase. She found an attorney she could trust; he agreed to meet with state officials who, in turn, promised their help.

"I want this done with as little publicity as possible, until it's accomplished," she explained. "I want all proceeds from the sale to go to Bhopal survivors."

The attorney had looked at her wide-eyed, stunned. But Gloria went on.

"I want the money sent and tracked, to help clean up the ground water, which I understand is still contaminated, even after twenty years. I want the money to go toward medical expenses, to help children with birth defects. I want that money to do what Dow Chemical should have done."

"Gloria, there's not enough to do all of that," said the attorney. "It would take millions more."

"I don't care. Just do it. At least they'll know that my puny two million are out there facing off with their billions. And at the end, I want them to know that these dollars came from Rob Grafton's widow."

And that's just what happened.

Now, six months later and back in her small cottage, Gloria knew exactly where she would take Rob's ashes.

After Sarah had called to invite her for a ski week get-together at Snowmass, she packed up her car and drove to Colorado.

Gloria raised the trunk of her Outback, reached under the gray towel and found the plastic bag, which she tucked into the side pocket of her ski jacket.

Having arrived late in the season and feeling warm at the base, she removed her stocking cap and unzipped her jacket in order to cool down while riding by herself up the first and second lifts.

At the top of Big Burn, she slipped off to the right onto the Jack of Hearts run, skied part way down, and stopped next to a beautiful stand of tall aspens whose swollen buds were about to leaf out under the March sunshine. Higher up, small clusters of last year's leaves were still hooked to their branches, twisting slowly in the breeze. Deeper into the woods towered a stand of Lodge Pole pines, one of which had fallen part way down. Tipped at an angle and coated with a thin layer of snow, it was supported by the branches of its tall, upright neighbor.

Gloria removed the plastic bag from her pocket and raised it toward the sky for one last look before undoing the zip-lock. She slowly sprinkled Rob's ashes around the base of the nearest aspen tree whose leaves suddenly began to circle—faster and faster.

For several minutes, no longer shaking, she stared at the ashes, light and dark gray colors, small bone fragments, and tiny shards. Like coarse sand, some of them looked dirty on top of the snow. Others, however, sparkled against the pure white, and began tracking with the wind.

"You always loved a plurality," she whispered, tucking the empty bag back into her pocket. "Here's where we started, Rob. And here's where it ends."

She zipped up her jacket and put her cap and mittens back on, remembering his lessons and moments of love. Then, skiing as fast as she could the rest of the way down the slope, her tassel circling in the wind, Gloria poled each turn from crest to crest, feeling confident and free as a bird.

Suddenly, she heard his voice call out:

"There you go, Ms. Magpie, dancing with the mountain!"

French Roast

"Travel is fatal to prejudice, bigotry,
and narrow-mindedness."

—Mark Twain

THE MOMENT GLORIA SPENCER began studying advanced French, she dreamed of flying, once again, to Paris.

Among her to-do list: eat more *crème brûlée*; stretch out on the vast *Champs de Mars*, among those night lights that dress up *la Tour Eiffel*, where thousands of scintillating lights would soon festoon the tower, making it glow and dance into the year 2000, then of another evening, she would drape herself in a lovely gown and stride, like a queen, up and down those marble steps inside the *Opéra*. Gloria's language instructor, admired for her European flair, had shown several pictures to the students, including one where she was dancing along those golden steps.

Gloria also planned to wander through *la Malmaison*, several kilometers from Paris, where Empress Joséphine de Beauharnais spent the last years of her life after being dumped by Napoléon Bonaparte. Unable to produce an heir for her husband, she was forced to leave him. How on earth did Joséphine recover after being replaced by Marie Louise?

"Throughout history," said the professor, "there will often be another woman who does a man's laundry, cooks for him, gets pregnant, and weaves long strands of yarn around wire hangers."

Because Gloria was still rebounding after what had happened to her own marriage, she figured that it might be helpful to learn how

Joséphine had managed to live alone at *le Château de Malmaison*. And why was it called that? Looking up those words, she found that "*mal*" meant "evil, harm, pain, or hurt." And "*maison*" was the word for "house." House of "unhappiness," she guessed. But it was also described as a beautiful place surrounded by acres of pink flowers, including roses and carnations. So Gloria was eager to spend time there, in order to learn more about Joséphine.

And then there was *Madame Defarge*, the fictional character in Charles Dickens's *A Tale of Two Cities*. A servant's wife, she secretly encodes and registers marks for destruction in her knitting, using yarn to measure out the lives and killings of aristocratic men, including the Evrémonds who had destroyed her entire family.

Those three places—*l'Opéra*, *la Tour Eiffel*, and *la Malmaison*—could offer up magical moments, assuaging, soothing, helping Gloria's mind to shift and ease up, making new things possible.

Now, if only she could find a travel companion. Or might she go alone—once again?

At mid-evening of November 30, 1999, a voice crackled over her phone line: "Hey, sweetie, this is Preston. Remember me?"

Gloria thought she heard the words "Resilient me?"

A severe mid-western blizzard was dumping several feet of snow that clung to everything, including telephone wires that swung in the wind, pruning words that were traveling through them.

"I just…in…golf…famous actor…and…"

"You'll have to call back tomorrow," Gloria shouted, recognizing Preston Person's voice. "We're in the middle of a storm and I can't understand most of what you're saying."

Strange, she thought after hanging up. *I wonder what he wants.*

The two had met some years ago: Preston, a member of the Halcyon Ski Club; and Gloria, newly signed up for a trip to Vail. After that, they'd dated long enough for her to feel slightly encouraged, even daring to consider the possibility of a future together. But then Preston decided that a move to Los Angeles would better suit his upcoming career. Gloria pined away for several days before realizing that he probably wasn't the man for her; at parties and various gatherings, he'd say, "Well, Gloria and I think thus and so, don't we, sugar?" Then he'd rub her neck, expecting agreement. When she replied, "No, I really don't see it that way," his eyelids would flutter and his cheeks turned florid.

As soon as Preston had moved away, they'd lost touch with one another.

The next day, after that blizzard, he called again. Hanging on the phone for twenty minutes, Gloria listened while Preston elaborated about his life as a stockbroker with a large and successful new firm. This time, it was just fine to do all of the listening, because she had no desire to talk about her own personal issues, especially about the man *she* had recently met, skied with, married, and...

"I've made and lost oodles of money," he said. "Could have been a millionaire twice over if things had worked out right. Now, even though I haven't reached the million mark yet, I've decided to continue traveling the world, including Mexico and South America— been there several times. So now I've got all these frequent flier miles and I thought it would be fun to go to Paris for New Year's Eve. If I remember correctly, you used to be interested in traveling there, so how about it?"

"Hmm, it's tempting, because I was hoping to make it back there a second time."

Wandering from room to room while chatting on the phone, Gloria stopped in front of her full-length mirror, which seemed to have grown narrower and acquired wrinkles that reflected back onto her face and arms.

"Why me?" she asked. "We haven't been in touch for such a long time. Don't you know anybody in LA who might go with you?"

"Everybody's busy. I'm feeling a little burned out and kind of lonesome. Besides, I could use a break for the holidays, especially this one. You say you're learning advanced French? You could be my translator. Also, I'd like to see you again, Glo. So how about it?"

"I'll give it some thought, Pres. If I do go, I'll pay for my own flight."

"Sure, sure, of course. Whatever you say. You're a good sport. Isn't it fun to be spontaneous once in a while?"

"I said I'd think about it. By the way, would you like to hear what else I've been doing in my spare time? Besides learning French?"

"Shoot!"

"Well, I recently went to an interesting shop called *Salon de Beauté*, where my hairdresser told me a weird story about something strange that had happened in Paris."

"What on earth was that?"

"A man got killed, possibly murdered by an American woman who'd gone out with him a few times."

"Yikes! That's a scary story. What else have *you* been up to?"

"I just bought some fleece at a sheep farm, and I've been washing, teasing, carding, and spinning, ready to start knitting another sweater. No weaving strands of yarn around wire hangers for me! My new sweater's going to be beautiful—a fisherman knit pattern."

"Uh, I hope you don't plan to knit on this trip. There won't be time for that."

"I might bring it along on the plane. Unless they consider knitting needles as weapons these days, it would be something for me to do on a long flight. But no, I don't plan on knitting in Paris, especially *à la Place de la Concorde*."

"What do you mean?"

"That's where Madame Lafarge used to knit—below the guillotine."

"Who the hell is that? Oh, never mind! Whatever. Gotta run. I'm golfing in an hour with a very important client. Talk to you in a couple of days to firm things up. If it's a go, we should meet at Chicago's O'Hare on the twenty-sixth of December, inside the Admiral's Club—they all know me there. Actually, we should decide by tomorrow morning, so I can make our reservations."

"Woops! I'll have to check my passport. What if it's expired?"

"Hope not! So long."

The first time Gloria had traveled to Paris wasn't as pleasant as she thought it would be. Her French wasn't quite up to par, although she had made a hobby of practicing, in her estimation, the most beautiful language in the world—repeating catchy phrases like *Champs-Elysées* and Dahling, *je vous aime beaucoup*. After deciding to take a class at the *Alliance Française*, she met people from faraway places like Morocco, *Sénégal*, and *Québec*. Back at home, she practiced reading aloud—even her local newspaper, in English with a French accent.

Yes, she thought, *for my second trip to Paris I should feel more seasoned. This time, going with a long-ago friend is tempting. The price might be right. Since I'm no longer in love with anyone, I can pay total attention to all of the sites, instead of focusing on a man by my side. And, I'll definitely order some more* crème brûlée.

Gloria remembered how her friend Kathy had talked about meeting a cool guy in Paris and hanging out with him for a week. Even though they'd visited the *Louvre* museum, *Notre Dame* Cathedral, and the *Opéra*, Kathy said that she hadn't observed much of anything other than her Frenchman's slender figure, handsome face, kissing lips, and long arms and fingers wrapped around her shoulders while strolling up and down the streets and inside those buildings.

Because it had been some time since Gloria had gone on her first trip, she was feeling housebound. *A second journey to Paris*, she thought, *should make me feel more seasoned. And when you travel, Kathy had once said, everything balances out.*

But would it be the right decision to go with Preston who seemed to be experiencing some rough days and feeling a bit lonely?

He called back the next morning.

"Did you find your passport, Glo?"

"I did."

"Is it current?"

"Yes, it is."

"All right! Great! The day after Christmas, meet me inside the Admiral's Club at Chicago's O'Hare. Just ask for me at the desk—everyone there knows who I am. The girl will call me down from the lounge as soon as you arrive."

"Sounds good, Preston. I'm looking forward to some *joie de vivre* once again."

"What does that mean?"

"Joy of living."

"Yah. Okay. See you soon."

The afternoon of December 26, having flown from Minneapolis/ St. Paul to Chicago, Gloria tugged her luggage through the executive-style door of the Admiral's Club. Her small suitcase, strapped onto a collapsible tote with bungee cords, tipped over sideways as she approached the desk. A young woman, chic and well-coiffed, pointed at the elevator and said, "Go right on up. Third level."

After hoisting the backpack onto one shoulder, Gloria trailed her up-righted tote into and out of the elevator.

Preston, dressed in faded blue jeans and a black leather jacket that parenthetically framed his stomach, was leaning against the lounge bar, drinking a pink cocktail. Surprised, Gloria sensed that he seemed shorter and a bit heavier than she remembered. In fact, she thought, he looks a lot like Mickey Rooney.

Preston slowly turned around, checked his cell phone, and watched Gloria trail her bag toward him.

"How come that woman didn't call me? I thought she'd page me as soon as you arrived."

"Well, hello to you too. How was your flight from LA? Did you enjoy Christmas?"

He gave Gloria a quick hug. "Okay. So-so. Glad to get together, again. It's been a long time."

Then he turned back to the bar.

"You want a cocktail?" he asked. "I could use another Chivas. That's all I ever drink—the best: Chivas Regal Extra. Let's sit down in that booth over there—relax for a while. We've got an hour before our flight. Hell, I should have been paged by that young woman as soon as you arrived."

"I brought along some chips," said Gloria, rummaging through her backpack, amazed by Preston's strange greeting. "Oh, and I've got orange slices and nuts, in case we get hungry on the plane."

"Geez, immigrant food, huh? I've got a large smoked salmon in the kitchen here. Don't let me forget it before we leave. I had the waitress put it in the fridge. They all like to wait on me, you know, because I'm…"

"Oh, knock it off, Preston. No need to impress everyone around here, including me."

"I don't know what you're talking about. Wha'd I say? Hey, I'm just contributing to the larder. Hmm, you know, Gloria, you've really changed."

"Thanks, I'm glad you noticed," she said, smiling at his frown.

She'd been practicing yoga during the last few weeks, and the effects of it had begun to show, not only along her body, but in her confident blue eyes and relaxed mouth. After removing her red beret, she patted the French braid along the back of her head, glad that it was still intact.

"By the way," said Preston, "I'm gonna try upgrading to business class when we arrive at the gate. They owe me that. I fly with them all the time. They're getting to know me around here."

As he grew impatient, Gloria slowly sipped her vodka gimlet, feeling a flick of negative travel tapping into her, along with the tug of home. She could still back out of this trip. But then she imagined strolling down the *Champs-Elysées* to the *Arc de Triomphe*, and feeling wonderfully mesmerized by promenading over to the Eiffel Tower that would sparkle at night with its glittering lights. She bolted the rest of her gimlet and felt the immediate rush of alcohol flowing into her system, helping her relax.

She followed Preston as he rushed over to the departure gate, approached the desk, and demanded an upgrade.

"I'm sorry, sir, what's your name?"

"Persons. Preston Persons."

"I'll do my best, sir, but I can't promise anything until we see if coach fills to capacity."

Perspiring, he stood still for a moment, and then sat down next to Gloria, crossing and uncrossing his legs. "Oh, geez, I nearly forgot my fish." He jumped up and dashed back to the bar.

When he returned with his package, filled with dry ice, he opened another small bag so that Gloria could see the large lemons he had brought: "Aren't they beauties?"

"Yes, they are. Good ole California lemons."

"God, I really shouldn't be doing this trip right now," he said, looking glum. "I just took a ten-thousand-dollar hit back home. Had to sell some stock on margin. Figured I'd better take care of it before I left or it could get a whole lot worse. I have a feeling it's not gonna be worth shit by the time I get back."

"Okay, if that's what you need to do, go home and deal with it. I'll hang out in Paris by myself. I did that once before."

He shot her a look, then slouched in the waiting room chair, stretched his legs, and sighed while gazing at his spotless white tennis shoes.

"My God, Pres, we're supposed to be having some fun together. We haven't seen each other or been in contact for such a long time. What's bugging you?"

"It's the job. I know that I've got to let it go for a few days. I'll try."

"That's the spirit. Lighten up." She reached into her backpack for some cashews. "Anything else?"

"Well, yes. I recently broke up with a woman, and…" He quickly turned to hug Gloria and give her a kiss. Then he tucked his face against her neck for a moment.

"Now you tell me," she said, leaning back and patting him on the shoulder as he tried kissing her again. "I'm not up to doing a rebound, Pres."

"Got it. Can't blame me for holding out a little hope, though, can you, Glo?" He tried to smile then pulled out a monogrammed handkerchief and wiped his eyes. "Naw, we're just gonna have fun, see some sights, celebrate the big New Year 2000."

Gloria handed him an envelope. "Here's the money for my share of this flight. Thanks for setting it up."

"Oh—I guess that's how it's gonna go, huh?" He gazed at Gloria, then, once again, at the woman behind the departure desk.

Preston's sagging double chin tucked itself in and out of his shirt collar all the while he talked about the stock market and his performance record with the firm. He spoke nonstop, looking straight ahead, as if no one sat next to him. While Gloria listened, she saw his face turn various colors: cherry red, a bleached honeydew melon, and gray. Rather sad-looking, his eyes, small and porcine, blinked over and over. He scratched an ear, then ran his short fingers through wisps of white hair at the back of his head.

Finally, the airline employee motioned for him to approach the desk.

Preston hopped up, reached into his breast pocket for the tickets, and strode over double time. After several minutes, he turned and flashed a happy grin.

"I can do this," Gloria whispered to herself, while leaning over to replace her snacks inside the backpack. "Just make the best of it, girl."

Among the last line of passengers, Gloria and Preston boarded the plane. Fresh, bright attendants welcomed and directed them to their business class lounge seats. They trailed their carry-on luggage through first class where several travelers were already settled, legs and noses elevated, blasé glances taking in the struggles of overburdened souls on their way to the rear.

"Now, isn't this great?" said Preston, plopping down in his seat. "Even though we couldn't get into first class, at least we're away from the rubes in coach."

"Something tells me that I wouldn't mind being among your so-called 'rubes.' Here, how about a little immigrant food." Gloria held out several orange slices brought from her own refrigerator.

"Miss, could I get a copy of the *Wall Street Journal*?" Preston asked one of the attendants. "Geez, I should have phoned my secretary before boarding. Gotta give her directions constantly. She's been with us for fifteen years, but she wouldn't know what to do, even if it bit her in the bippy. She's been such a…well, probably has PMS, 'cause all she does is crab. Wonder how many more thousands of bucks I'm losing." His protruding lower lip made him look as though he were about to weep.

"Preston, I'm sick of this. I'd like to tell you to shut it down, but my good upbringing prevents me from saying that. I'm heading for

Paris with you, paying my share, hoping to have a good time. I can't believe how you've changed."

"I'm sorry. Shouldn't talk shop. After all, we're on vacation, right?"

"Right! And don't forget, you're the one who planned this trip."

"It's just that I need to stay on top of things and I've got all these numbers reeling through my mind. I have some very important clients, you know." He peered at Gloria over half glasses as if expecting a sympathetic nod.

Gloria sighed, shook her head, and busied herself with a sleek, zippered kit tucked into the aircraft pocket on the bulkhead wall. The dark blue pouch was filled with a tiny toothbrush and paste, mouthwash, lotion, warm socks, earplugs, and a sleep mask. She took out the earplugs, poked them into her ears, and reclined her seat while the pilots tested their engines, and stragglers settled in coach. Then she closed her eyes and pronounced, with delight, the places she'd planned to visit: *Montmartre, Notre Dame de Paris, Le Louvre, L'Opéra, Le Château Malmaison, La Tour Eiffel.*

Preston struggled out of his jacket and fidgeted with the seat belt, causing several things to fall out of his carry-on bag.

A woman seated behind tapped him on the shoulder. "You dropped this," she said, raising a bottle of tiny blue pills.

Preston scowled and grabbed the vial. "Thanks," he said, tucking it back into his bag. "Can't get along without these little babies—Mycoxafailin."

"What are they?" asked Gloria, removing one of her earplugs.

"Never mind," he muttered with a giggle.

The flight attendants prepared for takeoff by explaining, in English and fractured French, how to attach a seat belt and, if need be, how to slide into the Atlantic Ocean before inflating their life vests.

"Hah," said Gloria, "can't you just picture a hundred and fifty pumped up passengers bouncing off each other through the exits and into the waves? What an image."

"They don't allow smoking on these flights anymore." Preston held up two fingers. "I used to be a heavy smoker—at least two packs a day. How about you?"

"No. But you might try a French cigarette when we get to Paris. I've heard about the *Gauloise* brand. Read about them once in a story. By the way, have you been reading any good books lately?" she asked while pulling a volume from her backpack.

"I don't read. No time after all the newspapers I have to go through—business and finance. It's all I can do to keep up with those and the market sections. I might pick up a murder mystery, but that's rare. After hours, I don't like to have to think."

"Any good films lately? Concerts? Plays?"

"No time."

Gloria sighed and stared at him for a moment. "What's happened, Preston? You used to laugh, have fun, bring me flowers, and listen to music. Remember when we skied Vail together?"

"Vaguely. That was a long time ago. What about it?"

"After the last run, our whole group clomped into that big two-story bar and the waitress spilled a pitcher of beer all over my new red sweater. Remember?"

"Oh, yeah. I couldn't believe it when you jumped up, raised your arms, and shouted something about winning the Super Bowl."

"So what, Pres? You guys started licking the beer off the back of my hand-knitted sweater."

"Total lack of class how those men started doing that."

"So did you—lick some off. You laughed and laughed—just silly, carefree fun."

"Pshh, it took a long time to get those wool fibers off my tongue."

"Well, I felt as if I'd just been baptized for winning the Giant Slalom—or the Super Bowl. Or for knitting that gorgeous sweater."

"Joke, joke. Didn't you hear me? Those wool fibers got stuck in my tongue."

"Yeah." Smiling, Gloria leaned back against her seat. "I can still hear the applause and whistling from that balcony." She sat forward for a minute and looked at Preston. "Far as I'm concerned, there can be worse barbs on a tongue than tiny wool fibers."

"Well, you did look good in red—I will say that."

"Thanks. And you were an excellent skier."

"Did you bring more knitting along with you?"

"Nope. Had to leave my new project at home this time. No more knitting needles allowed on board the planes."

After smacking his lips a few times, Preston opened a second vial of pills and chucked a couple of them into his mouth.

"Let's see," said Gloria. "How's your tongue now?"

"This world is a serious place, Glo. Not much room for silliness and games anymore. People need to have plenty of money to get along these days. And money means vigilance. I have to stay on top of it 24-7. By the way, how's your portfolio?"

"Ho-hum, yawn, yawn…there's my answer with just a *soupçon* of *insouciance*—that, by the way is a new phrase I picked up in French class last week."

Preston frowned and shook his head. "What does that mean?"

"A dash of unconcern."

Nibbling another orange slice, Gloria turned to the page in *A Tale of Two Cities*, bookmarked by a Langston Hughes photo and the line from one of his poems: "My soul has grown deep like the rivers."

Before drifting into her novel, she chuckled, recalling how Kathy had warned her about this trip to Paris: "Well, my dear Gloria," she'd said, "now that you've buttered your bread, you must lie on it."

"Well," she'd replied, laughing, "maybe it will float me along the Seine River like a big, buttery *bateau mouche*."

Deep in the quiet time, before the flight attendants began shoving heavy carts down the aisle, Gloria's lids lowered over her pale blue eyes. Dark lashes brushed the fragile skin that had received its daily application of anti-aging cream just before leaving home that morning. The lines at either side of her mouth had deepened, a bit like those joints on the face of Ventriloquist Dummy Charlie McCarthy. Before leaving for the airport, she had tweezed several hairs from her chin, and evened up her eyebrows. All of this grooming made her think about the story of *Le Petit Prince* and how he took care of his lovely flower, watered plants, and plucked the weeds on his planet before gallivanting around the universe.

While sleeping, she dreamed about "Funny Face" and dancing in a Paris park with Fred Astaire; he swept her along through exquisite turns and delicate bends until her long hair brushed the grass. Fred's shiny patent leather shoes moved gracefully along the ground while his satin-striped pants blended in among the folds of Gloria's pale blue taffeta skirt.

Awakening inside the airplane, she noticed that her French braid had come undone, leaving a wad of hair hanging in her face. She brushed it aside, stretched her arms and legs, and peeked out through a slit in the window, squinting at the fresh daylight and shimmering water far below. According to her watch, it was 2:00 a.m. back home, in the upper Midwest. Gloria shifted herself up from the aircraft recliner that was propelling her into a prolonged new day, and forwarded her watch to 9:00 a.m.

"Mmm, that coffee smells delicious," she said, looking at the cart. "Like French Roast—which I love."

"I could go for a cup." Preston smacked his lips and stared at Gloria. "You sure as hell flopped around during your nap."

"Yup, it was a fun one, dancing with Fred Astaire."

In spite of a warm leather coat, wool slacks, and sweater, Gloria shivered while standing next to her luggage outside the Charles DeGaulle airport terminal. Her red wool scarf floated about as she began shuffling her feet, waving her arms, and doing a little dance toward Preston.

"You look like a tourist," he said, eyeing Gloria's outfit and her red beret tipped at a jaunty angle.

She grinned. "And you don't look at all wilted after eight cramped hours aboard the plane. Or are you?"

"You see," he continued, hitching up his blue jeans and rocking back and forth on smudged white tennis shoes, "the trick is to appear local." He tugged and tugged at the zipper of his snug black leather jacket, then stopped, unable to draw it up against the battle of his bulge.

"I see," replied Gloria, glancing at Preston's protruding stomach. "Wouldn't you like to fit in at the Ritz?"

"Oh, shut it down, Glo."

In silence, they waited for a shuttle, which would take them into the heart of Paris.

Before boarding the transfer bus from the airport to *La Gare du Nord* train station, Gloria danced a little soft shoe then turned to stare at the horizon and seemingly endless rows of leafless trees, whose branches reached up to claw at the edges of a gray and ochre sky—a typical winter's day in northern France.

"You're acting like a tourist," said Preston.

"To the Ritz!" shouted Gloria as they boarded the bus. Preston grinned and snorted. Everyone else looked up to stare. She smiled at them, and several smiled back.

Outside the train station, they joined a convoluted line of people waiting for taxis.

"Let's get this show on the road," said Preston. "I came here to be among the French and dine well. Oh, by the way, did I tell you, Gloria, that I know of a perfect restaurant for tomorrow night? The *maître d'* will likely have heard of me."

"How so, if you've never been here before?"

Just then a woman at one bend of the curling line turned to Gloria and said, "You look so cute in your beret—very French."

"Thank you. So do you," she replied, noticing the woman's purple tam. "Where are you from?"

"California."

"Really! So is…" She turned to include Preston in the conversation, but he had stepped away, out of line.

"How long will you be here?" asked the woman.

"Until the second of January. I'm eager to visit a bunch of places, and then see the Eiffel Tower on New Year's Eve."

The woman smiled and nodded. "Me too. Have fun."

A herd of taxis arrived, one after another, swallowing up the tourists for delivery to various parts of the city.

Once inside their taxi, Gloria couldn't wait to practice French, as she had tried to do some time ago. After announcing *31, avenue de Friedland, s'il vous plaît*, she began chatting with the driver about the Upper Midwest's snow and cold weather. As she proudly exaggerated what it took to endure that climate, it seemed she was reaffirming how tough and resilient she had become in a variety of ways.

She learned that the driver was from Tunisia, that he had a wife and three children, and they were Muslim. He smiled through the rearview mirror, which pleased Gloria, after remembering how another taxi driver had flashed dirty looks at her during that first trip to Paris.

"What are you talking to him for?" asked Preston. "Just say where we want to go; that's enough. Oh, and tell him that I need to find an ATM before we get to our hotel. I don't have enough French money to pay taxi fare. No time to exchange dollars before I left home."

"It should be euros, Pres." Gloria opened her handbag. "Here, I've got some. Then we can take a walk later and find a cash machine. I'm sure there's one near the hotel."

"No. I want to stop now."

The driver pulled over next to a curb and swept his right arm across the seat back to point at a machine.

Preston got out and stabbed at the buttons. After punching them over and over again, he shot his fist into the air. "This damned thing just ate my credit card!"

Gloria got out of the taxi and looked at the screen where all of the words were in German. She started to giggle after seeing the taxi driver place his hand over a grin that shook the corners of his mouth.

"C'mon, Pres, just relax. We'll get it figured out."

But Preston looked as if he had just sucked on one of his lemons after learning that he wouldn't be able to retrieve his card until the next day.

The banker, eager to lock up for the evening, quickly explained the only option: "Zat ees when ze secret code ees applied daily to open up ze machine. *Je regrette, monsieur, vous devez revenir demain à dix heures.*"

"What did he just say, Gloria? What the hell is he talking about?"

"We'll have to come back tomorrow morning, at ten o'clock."

It was still a mile to their hotel, and of course, the taxi's meter had been running all the while.

A brisk U-turn on Friedland brought them to their canopied entrance. Gloria paid the driver and wished him a Happy New Year.

"*Et bonne année à vous, madame,*" he replied.

The Friedland was a charming hotel just down the street from a breath-taking view of the *Arc de Triomphe*, which, when illuminating against a cloudy or darkening sky, come evening, would seem like a megalith that had lowered itself from another world, in order to set down on this spot.

"Oh, look," exclaimed Gloria, "isn't it stunning? I can't wait to see the lights!"

"Yeah, yeah, grab that bag, would ya? Let's go inside and get our room figured out."

Preston introduced himself to the *concierge*.

Upon hearing that there was only one room available, Gloria asked, "*S'il vous plaît, est-ce une chambre à deux lits?*"

She wondered if she'd have to say it twice—a room with two beds? But she caught the receptionist's glance, along with a nod, and knew that she had made herself clear.

"What did you just say?" asked Preston as they rode up the elevator. "What were you talking about?"

"I wanted to make sure there would be two beds—I'll need my own."

"Are you serious, Gloria? After all, we do have a history together."

"What'd I tell you from the beginning? I thought I made myself clear."

"I thought you were just joking," said Preston, unzipping his luggage next to one of the beds.

"Nope. I don't joke about things like that."

"Whatever. First order of business: get my smoked salmon into this mini-fridge."

Preston removed cans of water, soda, and beer, and lined them up on the dresser. Then he lifted the long Styrofoam package filled with dry ice and fish from his suitcase, and jammed it into the small refrigerator.

"I don't mean to be ungrateful, Pres, but do you realize that we're in a country surrounded on three sides by water and criss-crossed by rivers? You could toss a line into the Seine River and catch a fish if you wanted to. Wouldn't that be fun? Fishing in Paris!" She began singing that line to the tune of "April in Paris," over and over, dancing around the room.

Preston shrugged and set his lemons next to the TV.

"Oh, God," he cried out suddenly. "I've got to call my secretary right away. Where's my phone?"

He rifled through his suitcase, bags, and jacket pockets. Although he had just entered the room, he also looked under the beds and inside the closets and drawers.

"I can't find my cell phone. Shit, I must have lost it on the plane when my blue pills fell out. I don't feel well. Where are my other pills?"

"Here," said Gloria, "let me help you look."

After another search through all of their belongings, even her own, Gloria sat down on the edge of her bed.

"Oh, Pres, I'm sorry. This just isn't your day."

"I can't function without my phone. Or my pills. Or my credit card! Everything's gone to hell! I need a hug."

Gloria walked over to Preston and lightly wrapped her arms around his shoulders.

"Now, if you'll excuse me," she said, "I'm going to take a long, hot shower. Or bath. We'll get the phone and pills thing figured out later. And then tomorrow, maybe we could go to the *Louvre* museum, after we get your credit card back."

"Aren't you hungry?" asked Preston, eating a portion of his salmon and several snacks from Gloria's bag.

"No. Just tired. Thirsty and tired."

After drinking a can of sparkling water, Gloria locked herself in the bathroom and soaked in the tall tub, zapping her face with a cool spray from the showerhead hooked to a long, metal cord. Afterward, wrapped in an oversized terry robe, she stepped back into the drained tub, leaned out of the square window, and looked down onto the street, staring at the solid form of the illuminated *Arc*, spotting it from an angle that she'd never seen before, even in a picture book. She memorized its shape and noted how those massive arches anchored a straightforward, powerful presence.

The early evening air cooled her flushed face and ruffled her damp hair. Noisy traffic circled the *Arc* then peeled off from the rotary in a dozen directions. Some headlights came her way along the avenue three floors below. A large black dog loped along, sniffing in the gutters, occasionally glancing back at his master.

Gloria whistled loudly through her front teeth and quickly ducked her head back in. Then she slowly peeked out and saw the man looking up at her, while his dog barked. She laughed, waved, and closed the window.

Gloire. After learning how to pronounce her name in French, she grew to love the sound of the Gl followed by *wa* and a soft *r*. *Gloire. Bonjour, je m'appelle Gloire.* Her name was also part of the French national anthem: *Le jour de gloire est arriveé*—the day of glory has arrived.

Preston was lying in bed with linked fingers tucked under his head. His stomach sloped up and down beneath the sheet, like a snowy foothill. He turned to face Gloria, looking suggestively at her as she stepped out of the bathroom, wearing her pajamas. With a forced smile and slow shifting of hips, he patted the available side of his mattress.

"I don't suppose you'd…"

"No, Preston. Sorry. Good night now. Hope you'll feel better in the morning."

She climbed into her own bed and turned out the lamplight, shifting her thoughts to those outstanding places that she and her friend would visit during the next few days.

Within several minutes, Preston got up to go to the bathroom. Just before he staggered back out, there came a strange, loud noise—like something dropped or tossed away.

Remaining silent, Gloria briefly remembered a few of their past times together and how much Preston had changed since then. Finally, she fell asleep after visualizing the Mona Lisa painting and the Winged Victory statue waiting to be seen inside the *Louvre* museum.

And then she had a crazy dream: in some small tank swam a beautiful pearl gray and white fish with yellow markings. His eyes seemed to speak to her as he wriggled and played, sliding along her arms and hands with his silky skin. *How could anyone kill such a fish?* she thought. Somehow, a heat register wound up near the tank making the water extremely hot. Soon, the fish, lying upon the surface, diminished in size and turned dark. After she touched him, a great swirl of blood and tissue flowed away from his lovely shape, slowly dissolved, and became parts of the water.

Among dreams—like this one triggered by a fish—some really do come true; sensitivity and closeness longed for in life might dissolve. For Gloria, this dream, like a wild card in the deck, played out the passing of attachment and hope.

Early the next morning, Preston hoisted himself up on one elbow and announced, "I've decided to go home. I don't feel well. Lost stuff. Too much on my mind. And by the way, Glo, you're not a lot of fun anymore."

Gloria hadn't expected this. She was ready for more complaints and anguish, but not prepared for such criticism and abandonment.

"Aren't you overreacting, Pres? It's not as if you can just hail the next cab home. You haven't even had time to recover from jet lag. And here we are, in one of the world's most beautiful cities. I thought we could have some fun together."

"I'm worried about my work, everything that's lost. Hope I don't end up like my uncle."

"Who's he?"

"A hardworking farmer."

"What happened to him?"

"A long time ago, he had to put his wife in a nursing home. I stopped by to visit her and there was Uncle Earl, just in from picking corn. We talked about how long my aunt had been in there, which cost him nearly everything. He said, 'I used to be a rich man. Now all I have left is my name.' So with all that in my head, I just want to get back home, because nothing is going right. I thought that maybe you and I could...you know," he said, stroking his mattress.

"Oh, for God's sake, Pres. Maybe I should just knit you into a sweater, along with my..."

"That's not funny! All that guillotine crap with Madame Defarge."

"Woops—I didn't think you knew about her."

"While you were sleeping on the plane, I read a couple of pages in your notebook. Sick!"

Gloria took a deep breath. "I'm sorry. I don't mean to turn into a Madame Defarge. It's all history, events to learn from. And that's what I'm trying to do at this stage in my life."

"Thank God, lady!"

Now, when she looked at Preston, he seemed to be a stranger lacking *joie de vivre*—like someone she'd never *really* known before. And then, the memory of her strange husband—that man she'd met while skiing in Colorado—crept back into her mind.

"If you need to go home, Pres, go."

"I'll pick up my credit card this morning," he said, "and reschedule a flight for as soon as possible. Stay if you want. You've got this room until the second of January."

"Fine. Probably for the better."

Preston sneezed and coughed into his same monogrammed handkerchief.

Gloria felt disappointed, a bit nervous, and somewhat jubilant all at the same time. Because she'd traveled by herself during that first trip, it took only several moments adjusting to the idea of being alone once again. Eventually, an itinerary for one began to take shape in her mind, as she remembered that a person should only get upset about someone who truly cares and is cared for. Then, when *Gloire* realized that she could explore and fawn over this city just as she wished, unencumbered, her spirit began to soar like the tall spire atop Notre Dame Cathedral.

Because Preston needed to spend time searching for lost items and planning his return flight home, off Gloria went to the *Louvre* museum.

She loved all her hours spent surrounded by the world of art, surprised at how small the Mona Lisa painting was, as it came into view, and amazed to be welcomed by the Winged Victory of Samothrace; at the far end of the grand hallway and staircase, there stood that headless woman on a ship's prow. Although this goddess no longer had arms or a head, her huge and beautiful wings welcomed all who entered the museum, and waved goodbye as they left.

At five o'clock the next morning, Preston Persons packed his bags and slammed shut the closet doors.

"Are you awake, Glo?"

"Uh-uh."

"I'll call you after I get home."

"No need."

Lying perfectly still with one eye barely opened, Gloria watched Preston drag his luggage into the hallway and clap the door shut, while groaning his way out of her world.

She remembered a quotation from Ernest Hemingway: "Never go on trips with anyone you do not love."

Sitting up in bed, Gloria wondered if Preston had left the rest of his smoked salmon inside the refrigerator. If he had, she would feed it to those stray cats she'd seen in a nearby park.

Up to check, she spotted his lemons still next to the television. But the salmon was gone.

Gloire flipped on some music and searched the backpack for her Girl Scout knife and sugar cubes saved from on board the plane. She carried the lemons into the bathroom, washed them, and peeled off the plastic wrap from one of the glasses next to the sink.

Juice ran through her fingers as she cut the perfect skin and creamy flesh of the first lemon. Saliva began to drizzle down the insides of her cheeks and over her tongue.

She squeezed each half until liquid, seeds, and pulp gushed into her glass—squeezed until the rind turned nearly dry.

While Gloria held the next lemon up toward the heat lamp to admire her favorite color, a bit of juice from the first trickled down her arm and dripped from her elbow, reminding her of a scene with Sally, played by Susan Sarandon, in the 1981 movie *Atlantic City.*

Gloria cut and squeezed the second one, turning the glistening half globes around in her hand, crushing them until juiceless bits of pulp hung limp from their edges.

She fished out big seeds from the glass and tossed them away. There, at the bottom of the wastebasket, lay Preston's pill bottle, completely shattered—Viagra, the little blue pills that he'd called *Mycoxafailin* in the airplane, and *Ibepokin* in their hotel room.

While the tap water flowed to icy cold, Gloria peeled away the pulp lining from one of the lemon rinds, then scored the pungent flesh to release oils, which she rubbed over the backs of her hands and arms, shoulders and breasts, just as Sally did in the movie, using lemon as a cleansing agent, to remove bad smells, and to keep her skin supple and sexy.

Gloria held each hand to her nose and inhaled long and deep, holding in the fragrance as if it were perfume, watched the sugar cubes dissolve in the sour juice, then added some cold water and slowly stirred the mixture with the blade of her knife.

"Moonlight Serenade" began playing on the radio. *Gloire* carried her lemonade in an outstretched hand and danced into the room like Kim Novak swaying on the beach with William Holden in that scene from *Picnic.* She circled and hip hopped to another version, extending her arms between sips of exquisite lemonade.

Catching her own smiling image in the mirror, Gloria raised her glass, let Pres slip away from her mind, refused to enter ground zero, and crooned to the tune of "Moonlight Serenade," singing "Misogyny Marinade."

After finishing her juice, she smacked her lips, got dressed, and slipped out for another glorious day in the city of Paris.

While wandering through the narrow streets along the hill of *Montmartre,* Gloria waved at an old woman draping her blanket over a third floor window casing, then watched a skinny mutt hold up traffic while he deposited his steaming pile in the middle of a street near the *Sacré Coeur* basilica. Finally, she smelled fresh, warm bread, croissants, and strong coffee—French Roast—that made the early gray chill of these last December mornings less penetrating.

During the afternoon, between the *Arc de Triomphe* and *La Place de la Concorde,* Gloria strolled up and down the *Champs-Elysées.* Tiny human images lined the high top of the Arc, viewing the long, festive avenue connecting the square of harmony. Among a sea of coats and hats sauntering beneath the bare chestnut trees festooned with strings of white lights, she spotted an elegant clothing store and went inside.

"*Bonjour, madame.*"

Gloria returned the clerk's greeting, bought a lovely dress, and left with the gentle sweep of rounded vowels and soft *r*'s: *Merci, madame. Au revoir, madame.*

That evening, wearing her new golden yellow gown, she stood in front of the *Palais Garnier* opera house, studied the sculptures, and waved at the two gilt copper statues atop the façade: *L'Harmonie et La Poésie,* high above the row of comic and tragic antique masks. Then she entered, purchased a ticket, and approached the Grand Stairway, surrounded by luxurious rings of lights and colored marble. Gloria slowly dance-stepped up the sweeping staircase, pretending to be Belle in *Beauty and the Beast.* Once seated, she remembered watching *The Phantom of the Opera,* and glanced at the chandelier hanging from the ceiling, glad to know that she wasn't seated directly beneath it.

The next day, she traveled by bus to *Le Château Malmaison* where Empress Joséphine, during the last five years of her life, had lived alone after Napoléon Bonaparte had traded her in for a more fertile woman: Empress Marie Louise.

From a large portrait, Joséphine locked eyes with Gloria in a direct, confident gaze. Wearing a gauzy white empire dress in that picture, and draping her pale arm along the back of a settee, she appeared lithe and calm, forever self-possessed.

If she'd had two children with her first husband, Alexandre de Beauharnais, who was guillotined during the Reign of Terror, why wasn't she able to produce an heir for Napoléon Bonaparte?

"Josie, my dear," she whispered at the photo, "why didn't you cut your hair, dress like a soldier, and go along with your hubby on his campaigns? But then, you're not like Joan of Arc, are you? You might have done needlepoint in his tent, waiting for him to return from the front. Or maybe not. I guess you were better off alone, living out your remaining years here at *Malmaison*."

Gloria was relieved to learn that the "evil house" was first used as a hideout for Norman invaders in the mid-1200s. "That name had less to do with you, Joséphine."

On New Year's Eve, after finding a restaurant that created the most delicious *crème brûlée*, Gloria dashed over to the Eiffel Tower with the sweet, creamy taste of her favorite dessert running through her mouth. There she stood, looking around at thousands of people, awestruck by the upcoming celebration, feeling confident and soon ready to step back into life at home, eager to knit the shapes of a *fleur de lis*, the *Arc de Triomphe*, and a *crème brûlée* into her new sweater pattern.

At midnight, the Eiffel Tower called out *Bonne Année* 2000, and danced with strobe lights from peak to base. Music, shouting, applause, barking dogs, dancing children, fireworks, and those wild blue strobe lights carried Gloria into the next millennium.

Wakan Tanka

(Great Spirit—Great Mystery)

Inside his darkened den, Tyler Burrell slouched in a favorite wing-back chair, surrounded by books, mindlessly watching a wildlife documentary on television. Halfway around the globe from Los Angeles, chimpanzees swung on branches and big cats drank from the same watering hole as their prey. Then a scene shift made Tyler shudder; grazing zebras snapped their heads up, galloped *en masse*, and fled danger, their exquisite stripes blurring in the stampede. One large animal, running along the outside of the herd, stumbled and rolled, struggling for a brief moment to survive the razor claws and teeth of a lion.

"Gotta keep up the pace, fella," Tyler called out to the big screen, "or Lauper's gonna get you."

Somehow, the big zebra recovered and got back onto his galloping hooves just in time to avoid becoming a feast for the lion's pride.

On Sundays, Tyler tried to relax after long workweeks at the corporate law firm of T. Campbell, Pritchard & Longley. But even on weekends CEO Bob Lauper often called him. "Tyler, my man. We've got a big account to go over. I want you here stat."

Tyler had become used to dressing for the possibility of hustling back to the office when called—soft gray flannel slacks, black Gucci loafers, and a light cashmere sweater. At thirty-five, he had, with a touch of uncertainty, nearly perfected imitating the studied elegance of his sixty-year-old boss who assured him that within the company's stable of young, ambitious future execs, Tyler was the one he had his eye on.

Bob Lauper, silver-haired, tall, and fit, struck a regal pose, whether in an Armani three-piece or Bermuda shorts and a barbecue apron. His neck ties, sporting golf, polo, or hunting scenes woven into silk, held perfect Windsor knots checked often by long, tan fingers whose manicured nails shone with a clear coat of polish. He might have been a handsome man were it not for those thin lips pressed together in a hard line. Although Lauper moved with the confidence of a man who'd lost no battles, those determined lips countered any sensuality he might have exuded.

He'd had his eye on Tyler for the better part of a year and never failed to remind him. "You, my man, are going places. That is, if you don't blow it."

Impressed with this young man's style, résumés, and portfolio of earlier accomplishments while working for a small law firm, Lauper had welcomed him into the fold and immediately became his mentor.

"We can use a man with your solid background, Ty. You've got the looks, brains, and a modicum of panache. That's what it takes. Step on a few toes if you have to. Just follow my lead."

For weeks, Tyler had fed off those words, looked up "modicum of panache," and was thrilled to have what it meant: a flamboyant manner. With English and Accounting, Ty had gone on to earn another degree in corporate law. In September of 1995, he'd married his pretty college sweetheart, Tiffany, the girl with long, strawberry-blond hair and deep blue eyes.

Before working with Bob Lauper, Tyler and Tiffany, with her unpretentious personality, had enjoyed three fun-loving and adventuresome years of simple pleasures: barefoot walks along the ocean front, picnics, playing Frisbee on the beach, chasing each other until they fell down on the sand, laughing, hugging, and kissing.

When had all that changed? Tyler pondered how the end of their happiness had sneaked up on them, taking him by surprise. More often than not, he felt very much alone.

An only child, orphaned at fifteen, he'd thrived on the attention and encouragement of Bob Lauper: the golf dates, the generous gifts of cuff-links and a Rolex watch, the frequent invitations to the Lauper home in the Hills, where crystal high-ball glasses were filled with Glenfiddich Special Reserve over clear ice cubes.

There'd been troubling moments, however, that Tyler had tried to ignore for the first couple of years in order not to jeopardize his position with the firm. There was that evening when Lauper insisted the men take their after-dinner cognacs into his wild game trophy room, the size of a small auditorium. Tyler feigned interest in the retelling of those kills, the display of powerful guns and ammunition, the stuffed lynx and elk, cougar and water buffalo, grizzly bear and antelope arranged among fake boulders and brittle grasses. Each was illuminated, one at a time, as Lauper flipped the switches rigged to spotlight them. Eventually, Tyler found ways to avoid that room whenever the other male guests gathered there after dinner.

But wherever they were, whatever they did, Lauper edged over to Tyler's side reminding him not to screw up.

"Don't blow it this time!" he'd shout as Tyler positioned himself for their weekly tee-off at the country club. That was typical of Bob's style, trying to throw the guys off to measure their "*sang-froid*"—coolness, composure. Tyler found it increasingly difficult to muster up his good-sport grin. He broke his stance while running fingers through his hair. Then, with face averted, re-positioned his feet as though he were tamping down a divot before swinging a golf club.

Not bad, he thought, watching his golf ball arc against a gray-blue sky etched in smog.

II

But Lauper wouldn't be calling him today. Maybe later. Maybe tomorrow.

Tyler turned off the television and went upstairs to his bathroom where he rearranged a set of after-shave bottles, cradling one of the flasks in the palm of his hand; it had been a gift from Tiffany—a truce gift—and he loved how she'd pronounced the name: "'Lolita Lempicka,' darling," she'd purred, "this is the latest manly scent…for my man on his way up."

Tyler thought about how Tiffany had encircled his neck with her arms, careful not to smudge her makeup against his face. He removed the cap from his "Lolita Lempicka," shook a few drops onto his palm, rubbed his hands together, and smoothed the clean scent onto his face. He inhaled deeply. Leaning toward the leather-framed mirror, Tyler sighed after checking his skin and eyes. Dark circles and sallow tones were still there. Resting his forehead against the mirror, he watched his breath create fog along the lower part.

"I thought she'd be home by now," he muttered, "but who am I kidding?"

Tyler wandered into his bedroom and picked up one of the books from a tall stack on the nightstand. He opened the cover of *The Last Tycoon* and read its foreword: "Scott Fitzgerald died suddenly of a heart attack (December 21, 1940) the day after he had written the first episode of chapter 6 for this novel."

Only forty-four. Nine years older than me, thought Tyler, sitting on the edge of the bed with his book—an unfinished novel published posthumously.

Bob Lauper's reading list for Tyler included the company financial reports and account portfolios, the *New York Times* business section and the *Los Angeles Times*.

"Whatever else you read," he'd said after noticing a novel on the lunchroom table, is on your own time, away from the office."

Problem was, even at home, Tyler never had time to read what he loved, what kept him alive. Steinbeck helped him understand relationships. Dickens brought him to his knees. Dana and Hemingway gave him adventure. Fitzgerald's story included a suicide by a failed Hollywood producer.

"You don't need a shrink," a friend had told him. "Just read great literature—that'll provide all the answers you're looking for, give you everything you need to get through life."

Now that he had all the time in the world, Tyler was too preoccupied about his future, unable to absorb more than a paragraph or two from any book.

I have to settle my mind, he thought. *Make some decisions so that I can stay with these pages.*

III

A year ago, nothing seemed impossible: coveted connections, the palpable promise of financial success, perfect bodies. Both Tyler and Tiffany had worked out at the club, jogged, and loved to swim. It was when Tiffany decided to connect with the busiest, most reputable plastic surgeons in Los Angeles that Tyler first became concerned. He hardly recognized her anymore; her nose was different—tiny—and the skin above her eyes had been tightened. Her lips were constantly swollen and pouty-looking.

"My God, Tiffany," he'd cried. "What are you doing to yourself?"

"We have to have the look, Ty honey." She leaned into him with her pursed thick lips painted a bright red. "You want to be proud of me, don't you, sweetie?"

Tyler had tried to see her new persona as an asset, while making the required effort to run alongside the pack with all his stripes intact: his Mercedes, her Jaguar, their townhouse in Beverly Hills, the condo at Tahoe, the promised position, his beautiful wife, the parties. All that was supposed to matter. But after a while, the plastic could no longer buy the fun. Tiffany, bored, with nothing more to want in terms of material gain, began looking elsewhere for excitement, partying in penthouses, and flirting with other men.

"We're top-shelving alongside the 'right people,'" she'd say to her husband, trying to convince him that these were the greatest men who were introducing them to the best caviar, the most beautiful illegal ivory *objets d'art* and any number of yaks' chin-hair scarves secreted in from a remote Afghan village—"only five hundred dollars apiece, darling."

Tyler thought that a yak's chin-hair scarf looked like a gauze rag. And within his line of vision, Tiffany started taking up with "a man of the evening" by wrapping a yak around his neck.

Saturday nights rang in corporate political events under the guise of cocktail-dance parties. Smooth, young sophisticates blended in with the company hierarchy who kept a sharp eye on their competitive hopefuls. These were evenings for scouting time and playing out in futures versus failures when the CEOs made their final decisions for promotions. The contenders knew the routine: appear confident and in charge (even at social events), acquire, yet disguise, a certain level of ruthlessness in training for the desired position.

Some of the contenders artfully courted Bob Lauper and Associates. Others, honey-tongued, bowed and scraped.

It was at one of these company bashes that Tyler had failed miserably. Leaning against a faux marble pillar, he remembered the lyric from a Cole Porter song: "Down in the depths on the ninetieth floor."

He pressed a glass of bourbon to his lips and watched Tiffany aim her newly molded cleavage bursting to escape its red fabric so that every man in the ballroom would stare at her. Shifting his glance to the right, Tyler caught the look on Bob Lauper's face; it spoke pity and unsettling concern for a weakening member of the herd. Tyler tried for the bright, dignified pose of a man in control but couldn't hold it.

Gazing forlornly around the room, he noticed another woman standing off by herself, looking lonely despite a long-practiced air of importance. He knew her husband: a shrewd man, cunning, and a philanderer. The woman extended a silent invitation to Tyler, but he suddenly felt nauseous and ignored her.

Then he saw Tiffany slip out of a side door with that woman's husband. Tyler, feeling as though all this crap was nothing more than a big chunk in a stupid novel, began to laugh uncontrollably—a high-pitched, hysterical laugh. Everyone in the room turned to look at him. Bob Lauper quickly edged over, smoothly clutched Tyler's arm, and steered him into the corridor.

"What the hell's going on?" he whispered.

"It's all just a joke, isn't it, Bob?" Tyler gestured around the room. "This whole fucking thing is a big Goddamn joke, a stupid play."

"Come on, Ty. Don't screw up here. You've had too much to drink."

Lauper nodded at two large men standing next to the elevator with pagers in hand. "I want you to escort Mr. Burrell to his car," he said, "and check to see if he's able to drive."

Then he turned back to Tyler. "I'll see you tomorrow morning in my office. Go home now and get some rest."

The next morning, Tyler stuck his head in through the door of Lauper's office, still grinning, although he tried to look serious. When he noticed that Bob Lauper's lips made a thinner line than usual, he burst out laughing.

"What the hell's going on, Ty? This isn't like you. I know you're a little stressed about your wife, but believe me, there are plenty of other women out there. Just let me know if…"

Tyler's mouth clamped shut and he stopped grinning. Suddenly, he felt twelve years old again, witnessing another argument between his parents. His father had slammed the door screaming, "There are other women out there, Jenny. Plenty of them, all at my disposal."

Words flowed from Lauper's mouth into Tyler's ears like a series of dull sounds, like clumps of sod tossed about.

"You're valued here, Ty, an important part of our team. I don't have to tell you that we represent very big clients. They depend on us to clear up misconceptions that have a way of, you know, working the public into a frenzy. We want to avoid that. Be careful about revealing some things. Isn't that right?"

"I'm fine."

"You've been a part of our team all along, shown great promise here with T. Campbell, Pritchard & Longley. But lately, you've been under a lot of stress. We can't afford any slip-ups."

"I said I'm fine, sir."

"I'm sure you will be." Lauper placed an arm around Tyler's shoulders and gave him a quick hug. "Nevertheless, I think you'd benefit from a little time off. Go home. Relax."

IV

Tyler looked out through a slit in the cream-colored curtain. Half a block away was the same black BMW he'd seen two weeks ago—the day he'd been sent home from the firm like a misbehaving schoolboy. A dark figure sat behind the wheel. Once, when Tyler had left the house to run errands, he'd driven slowly past the parked car, trying to get a good look, but the man at the wheel had held up a large map, covering his face. Again and again, there was that car, near the grocery store, a block from the bank, just around the corner from the post office.

Tyler stretched out on his bed and read aloud from Fitzgerald's unfinished novel about a Hollywood producer. "You couldn't persuade a man like Mr. Schwartz, a failed producer, to lie down and look at the sky for a few months. Instead, he committed suicide."

"Well, that's not me," Tyler grumbled, checking his watch: nine o'clock. He turned to look out of the window once again, hoping to see his wife. She's not coming home, he thought. Not tonight. Probably never.

Tyler had grown tired of tracking Tiffany. A few months earlier, he'd cruised Rodeo Drive, trying to spot her by studying every flat stomach and perky rear end, each lifted face and flaxen mane. But he couldn't find his wife.

After several days, she came back to collect clothes and makeup. The two argued and then made up, promising each other to be more attentive toward one another. After a week, the lame excuses began again: marathon-shopping sprees, lunches with girlfriends who, after a little research, were actually vacationing on the *Côte d'Azur*. And what about those acting lessons with Ricardo? Sometimes, Tyler half-heartedly went looking for her in the evenings, hoping not to find her with him or any other man. As long as he had no evident proof of her infidelities, there might still be a chance.

He continued reading about *The Last Tycoon*, then backed up to chapter 5 and repeated a passage that he had underlined: "He saw the sands running out. At the moment everyone's back was toward him. Suddenly he brought up his hands from their placid position under the desk and threw them high in the air, so high that they seemed to leave his wrist—and then he caught them neatly as they were descending. After that he felt better. He was in control."

Tyler set the book down and undressed for bed, too tired to wash up or brush his teeth. Tomorrow he'd make some decisions: what to do, where to go, how to live.

The next morning, two weeks after Lauper had told him to take a rest, Tyler felt as if he'd slept for two hours instead of twelve. He went to the toilet, then to Tiffany's bedroom and discovered that she'd been there sometime during the night. The bed was still made, but the dresser drawers were open and bare. Bunches of hangers clustered together in her empty closet. The bathroom vanity was cleared of its jumble of makeup, face creams, blow dryers, hairspray, curling irons. A pale blue envelope with Ty's name written on it stood propped against a rosebud vase. He held it in his hand for a moment. No love letter, this. He stared at his name, the curlicue T, the loopy Y, and ran his thumb underneath the flap. The single blue sheet inside held four short lines: "I never meant to hurt you, Ty. I'm sorry. Our time together just ran out. I need something more. Tiffany."

Tyler read the words a second and a third time before dropping the page onto the cleared vanity. *Strange*, he thought, *I'm not upset or sad even. Just tired.* He went back to bed remembering the time, nearly a year ago, when he'd seen Tiffany in the supermarket produce section, laughing and dancing a silly rumba with some guy, wiggling along behind the cart to Muzak. She had spotted Tyler, and thinking that he hadn't noticed her, whispered in the guy's ear, then ducked behind the banana display like a child playing hide-and-go-seek.

Tyler had rushed out of the store and around the corner where he vomited onto a patch of ground littered with Styrofoam cups and cigarette butts.

That was the one and only time he let losing Tiffany sicken him. After that, he simply grew weary.

V

Lying in bed at two in the afternoon, Tyler stretched his arms toward the ceiling and then let them drop, straightened his wrists, studied his long, tapered fingers, and made a decision.

He got up, showered, and dressed. After breakfast, he packed his books, some clothes, and other essentials. The next day, he secured the house and locked his Mercedes in the garage. Trailing his luggage out the back door and through an alleyway, in case the black BMW was parked along a front street (although he hadn't seen it yet), he called a taxi to pick him up a block away. The driver dropped him off at a Chevrolet dealership where he bought a used Nissan, gray with a couple of dents.

Then Tyler reversed the Horace Greeley maxima and headed east, driving until he needed gas or food or a brief rest: San Bernardino, Kingman, Barstow. At each stop he filled the tank, jogged around the service station, bought sandwiches and coffee, and took short naps on the back seat of his car before rolling on to Gallup and Amarillo.

New Mexico: he hadn't returned to New Mexico since the year after his parents had died. Tyler would drive straight through McKinley County on Highway 40 as quickly as the law would allow. His parents' ranch, south of Gallup, near the Arizona state line, had been sold to the family of his father's competitor in the aggregate business. He had no desire to revisit the place. His education and comfortable life style had come from the trust set up for him by his Aunt Linda and Uncle Mitch who had raised him through his teen years. The comfortable life, he knew, could disappear at any time. But the education—never.

Tyler smiled at the memory of Aunt Linda's lecture: "A good education, Tyler, is something that no one can ever take from you. They can steal your money and they can grab your possessions, but they can never take what's up here," she said, tapping his temple.

When Tyler was young, he never knew who the "they" were. Now, twenty years later, he'd found out.

In Oklahoma City, he exchanged his Gucci loafers, flannel slacks, and cashmere sweater for a sweatshirt, blue jeans, and running shoes. He pulled into a truck stop and after stepping away from the urinal, looked at himself in the restroom mirror. *Not bad*, he thought. A little harried, and grisly with the beard, but otherwise, not bad. Feels good to be on the road.

But once he returned to his car with more takeout food and sat behind the wheel, considering his options, a wave of loneliness washed over him. He recalled the desperate look on the woman's face back in the ballroom in LA. He remembered seeing the back of her husband's suit and the flash of Tiffany's red dress as the two slipped out of the side door. Tyler slumped over the steering wheel and the horn began to honk.

Someone tapped on the window and shouted, "Hey, buddy! Are you okay?"

Tyler lifted his head and saw a burly truck driver leaning over, peering in, his gruff-looking face an inch from the window. Tyler sat back and ran his hands over his face.

"Yeah," he shouted back, "I'll be fine. Thanks."

The trucker nodded once then walked away. He turned and waved before climbing into his rig. Tyler waved back and started up his car.

Just outside of Joplin, Missouri, he pulled into a large truck stop. *I've got to make a choice here*, he thought. Either head to St. Louis or turn north.

Near the counter was a rack of state road maps. Tyler studied the large map of the United States above the display. "Let's see. There's Illinois, Kentucky, maybe the east coast. Or north toward Canada. Maybe Iowa. Or Minnesota." He pulled Iowa and Minnesota from their slots. "Who'd ever think of looking for me there? Godforsaken north."

The map of Minnesota looked interesting: Land of ten thousand lakes; state flower, a ladyslipper; state bird, common loon—a strange-looking bird with a dagger-like beak. There were pictures of men on machines flying over great dunes of snow, and people sitting on little stools in the middle of a lake, holding tiny sticks with threads, and staring into round holes cut in the ice; they were so bundled up, Tyler couldn't tell if they were male or female. There were rosy-cheeked children eating sap turned into maple syrup. Some were summer pictures: a man fishing from a canoe, alone on a placid lake, the Minneapolis sky-line behind him, and a branch loaded with apple blossoms in the foreground.

Tyler took his maps to the counter where an acne-faced young man stood behind the counter.

"What's the best way to get to Minnesota?"

"You gotta be joking," laughed the teen. "Why would anyone want to go there this time of year?"

"Oh, just thought I'd chill out for a while. No one would look for me there, would they?" Tyler furtively hunched his shoulders and cocked an eyebrow.

The cashier eyed Tyler suspiciously, and then his face turned red as he threw his head back and guffawed. "That's a good one, mister."

"So what's the best route?"

"Take 71 north of here, just off 44. Then pick up interstate 35 around Kansas City. Can't miss it."

"Thanks." As Tyler walked to the door, the cashier called out to him.

"Hey, man," he laughed, "stay cool."

"You, too, man," said Ty, grinning. For the first time in ages, he left a public place feeling relaxed.

Tyler had never been this far north before. He'd known snow, of course, and felt cold in the California-Nevada mountains where he and Tiffany had vacationed and skied. He'd heard stories about the massive snowfalls and the extreme cold near the Canadian border. Maybe a winter like that will keep me so busy surviving I won't have time to think about the mess back home. That's the place— Minnesota, here I come.

Tyler would turn thirty-six in October, one month away. He thought about how he might celebrate. Maybe rig up one of those little sticks with a thread. He laughed out loud, picturing himself hunched over a hole in the ice, dangling a string with what he assumed would be a hook at the end. *How soon does it freeze up there?* he wondered, beginning to shiver.

"Things couldn't get much worse," he muttered. "No family, no place to live, no job. Nowhere to go but up."

Tyler thought about the unsettling twist of events since the end of the Clinton administration, how quickly things had moved after the deregulation of the 1934 security laws that Clinton had vetoed, suffering a congressional override. Tyler had been quietly concerned about some of the high-level corporate executives who looked to T. Campbell for their legal and auditing services.

Trial lawyers and accountants were busier than ever. But they were also more somber and secretive than Tyler had ever seen them. It began to dawn on him that some accountants had started looking the other way when Enron and World Com made it worth their while. Cases were dismissed left and right. And Tyler watched, as his peer competitors grew incredibly rich, practically overnight. That's when his faith in T. Campbell and Bob Lauper became tested, starting with one of the many meetings that Lauper called.

"We're smart," he'd announced from the head of the long ebony table, "we're powerful, we're successful. We work to change the laws or we work around them." Lauper chuckled and said, "Don't quote me on that."

He directed his next comments at Tyler. "We owe it to our clients at Global Com to ward off predatory lawsuits. That's what they're paying us for and we're going to deliver."

On his legal pad, Tyler doodled and sketched stiff black lines.

"Now we've got a case that's going to trial," continued Lauper. "Our lawyers intend to work on the jury, explain how the prosecution is perpetuating the prejudice and hatred out there against corporate executives, a prejudice that targets execs from coast to coast.

"You've all worked long hours, done an admirable job. You know what remains to be done. Whatever it takes, we are ready!"

Lauper looked slowly around the table at each member of the team before ending the meeting.

As everyone else left the boardroom, Lauper took Tyler aside. "What's going on, Ty?"

"I'm concerned, Bob. From my assessment, the books just don't look right. We need to dig a little deeper."

"That's not the sort of thing we want to hear, Tyler. You've got to get with the game, son."

Tyler saw the determination in Lauper's eyes and in the set of his jaw.

"I'm sorry, Bob, I'm not sure I follow you on this."

"I'm pulling you off this case, Ty. I've got another deal I want you to work on, one that's a little less complex."

As Tyler drove home that night, the familiar lump rose up inside his throat. He popped a couple of antacids and waited for the feeling to go away. He'd been eating those tablets like candy lately—and now the Global Com case. After weeks of pouring over records, he'd been onto something. But Lauper hadn't wanted to hear it, had pulled him from the team. That would be the last time Tyler questioned the direction at T. Campbell, Pritchard & Longley.

VI

Now, driving along the interstate toward Kansas City, all he felt was an overwhelming nothingness. After two years of clamoring for Lauper's brass ring, it was a relief to feel exactly that—nothing.

There was a time when he had wanted children, but what kind of life would they have had? A workaholic for a father and an egocentric beauty queen for a mother. Whenever he brought the idea up to Tiffany, she reminded him of what a pregnancy would do to her figure.

"I'd like for us to start a family, Tiff," he'd said, after seeing friends with a new baby. Tiffany had never looked more tender and beautiful, the way she had held and caressed the infant, the way she looked up and smiled at Tyler.

"How about it, sweets?" he'd said as soon as they got home. He circled his hands around her waist and swayed seductively, "Let's start tonight."

"Ty, honey, we spent a lot of money to make me look this good. Why ruin it?" She slipped from his grasp, twirled, and shimmied off.

"C'mon, Tiff, I love you." Following her into the hallway, Tyler reached out to touch her face. "Wouldn't you like to have a baby? A family? That would complete us."

Tiffany slapped his hands away, "I said no! Now cut it out, Ty." She went to bed in the guestroom, which, from then on, became her room.

Eyes burning and thunder in his head, Tyler laid awake most of the night, feeling helpless and hopeless. He never brought up the subject again.

Blinking away the blur of oncoming headlights, Ty remembered the last time he had cried. He was ten, at home with his parents in New Mexico where they kept a few horses. Bella, the old brood mare, was twenty-six and inseparable from her two offspring, who were nearly twelve and fourteen. Tyler loved to watch the three of them run in the pastures, their manes and tails fanning out in the wind as they playfully nipped at each other.

Eventually, Bella became too sway-backed even to walk comfortably and the others slowed their pace in order to stay close by.

"She's in a lot of pain," his dad had said. "I've got to call Doc Simms. If he can't get here before the week is out, I'll have to shoot her. We can't put it off any longer. Once she goes down, she'll never get up again. It's time."

The vet wasn't able to come until the following week. When Tyler's dad led Bella away, the young mare and the gelding whinnied and tried to follow. But Tyler's dad locked them in the barn until it was over. Tyler stayed in the barn too, watching them rear up and pound at the walls and doors of their stalls when they heard Bella whinny from the field. Their eyes grew wide and frantic and they jumped when they heard the gunshot. All night long, they called out to her though they never got an answer.

Late in the night, Tyler went to his parents' room and crawled into bed with them. His dad was sound asleep, exuding the familiar odor of whiskey. Tyler's mother took her son into her arms, warning him not to awaken his father and patiently explaining that they had to do what was best for Bella. In a day or two, the others would stop looking for her. "They'll settle down and be fine," she said. "They have each other, sweetheart, just as we have each other."

But his mother had lied or else knew no better. Three days later, the mare and the gelding were still looking for Bella.

No, he hadn't cried since that night, when he was ten. Not even five years later when his parents died. He'd already cried for them the day Bella was killed. If death came to animals like that, he'd reasoned, it would come to people, too. And guns made it quick and easy.

Tyler had tucked a favorite figurine into his mother's casket— one of a pair—a little sorel mare. The shiny black stallion he kept for himself.

VII

It was almost dark as Tyler neared Kansas City. In the distance, just off Highway 71, he noticed the hypnotic ripple of neon lights: red for "Do," white for "Drop," and blue for "Inn." He was tired of driving and, on a whim, took the exit and drove toward the sign, pulling into the parking lot alongside a beat up pickup truck and a blue Chevy Bronco.

Inside the Do Drop Inn, the combined odor of cheap beer and urine hit Tyler full in the nose. He checked out the bar where piles of pull-tabs littered the floor.

"What'll it be, mister?" asked the young bartender, wiping a stringy, gray rag across the wooden bar. Yellowed Polaroid photos had been glued to the scarred surface and covered with epoxy. There were faces of happy, pie-eyed regulars, hoisting their beers in celebration of something or other.

"I'll have a bottle of Newcastle, please," said Tyler.

"Sorry, no can do. I've got Bud light and Shiners on tap. At's a good beer."

"Fine," said Tyler, "I'll have a Shiners. Make it a tall one."

The crack of a cue ball broke a new game in the far corner of the room where the blue haze of cigarette smoke drifted into the overhead light.

Two middle-aged women sat at the bar. The one next to Tyler turned and smiled, sweeping her coarse, bleached hair behind one shoulder with a flip of her hand.

"You must be new in town," she said. "Haven't seen you here before."

"I'm not from around here."

"Just passin' through?"

"Yes, that's right." Tyler nodded and smiled.

He had never seen such finely penciled eyebrows on a woman. The arch of them gave her a permanent look of surprise. And her hair was the texture and color of straw. When she spoke, her voice was low and gravely. She pulled a cigarette from a stained, beige leather case and turned back to the other woman.

"Like I was sayin', I've been a widow, now, for a hell of a long time." She glanced briefly at Tyler.

"What happened, Shari?" asked her new friend.

"We was on vacation to Lake Tahoe with friends—my God, that was fifteen years ago last month already—anyhow, the guys went out fishin' like they always done. Hell, that's all they ever did, fish and drink beer. Anyways, it got late. It was dark and real windy. We thought maybe they knocked off early, went to a bar to polish off a few more, you know. But then around midnight the cops knocked at our motel door. Said they found the rental boat drifting upside down and everything gone. They drowned—that's what happened. They drowned."

Shari glanced at Tyler to see if he was listening. He was looking at her with shock and pity when she started to giggle. "And you know what I said? I said, 'Jesus Christ, they've got the car keys.' That's what I said. 'They got the goddamn car keys!'" And she shrieked with laughter.

The new girlfriend and Tyler stared at Shari in stunned silence. Then Tyler turned away, stood up, finished his beer, and paid the bartender. As he reached the door, Shari called out, "Hey, wait a minute, mister."

Tyler paused and turned around.

"There was nothin' I could do about it," she said. "You understand? Nothin'!"

VIII

The stretch along Interstate 35 north toward Iowa was long. The constant glare of headlights, the hum of the engine, the stuffy car, and the residue of beer made Tyler sleepy. He thought about the woman back at the Do Drop Inn. She was right. There was a lesson to be learned from Shari. Her words were harsh, but she was right. There was nothing she could have done to save her husband. She'd likely joked about it so she wouldn't fall completely apart. How lonely she must feel.

While driving, Tyler began to drift off. It was comforting, soothing the way his mind went blank, like falling asleep on a beach, lying in the warm sand, listening to a low, rhythmic sound of waves.

Suddenly, he heard a shrill noise mixed with the long blast of a trumpet playing too loudly. He woke up in time to jerk his car back into the right lane and then glanced at the car traveling next to him. The man was laying on the horn and motioning. Tyler waved back gratefully before he realized that it was a squad car and the police officer was jabbing his finger at the air, pointing toward the edge of the Interstate. Tyler signaled and pulled over onto the shoulder. When he rolled down the window, a rush of cool air awakened him completely.

He watched from the side mirror as the highway patrolman opened his door and slowly got out of the squad car, one hand near his holster, the other beaming a flashlight on Tyler's license plate.

He flashed the light on Tyler's face and edged back a few inches.

"See your license, please."

Tyler reached for his wallet. The officer continued, "California, huh? Where you headed?"

"North," said Tyler.

"Obviously. What's your business?" asked the officer, aiming the light at Tyler's driver's license.

"I'm on vacation."

"See your proof of insurance please."

"Actually, I recently bought the car, Officer. I don't have the insurance packet. But here's proof of purchase and a temporary insurance card." Tyler pulled out a folder from the back seat and handed over the papers.

"You were weaving around pretty bad back there. You been drinking?"

"I just had a beer about a hundred miles back, Officer. I'm really okay. Just a little tired."

"Step out of your vehicle, please. Move over near the grass."

Tyler did as he was told.

"Stand straight with your feet together, close your eyes and place your right index finger on your nose…now your left."

Tyler fought the urge to laugh as he followed instructions. "Did I pass, Officer?" he asked, smiling.

"Now walk a straight line heel to toe."

"Really, is this necessary? I'm fine."

"Either follow instructions or come with me to headquarters. Which is it?"

"Understood," said Tyler, nodding his head soberly. He took a dozen smooth steps, heel to toe.

"I'd suggest, Mr. Burrell, that you take the first exit you see and find a motel for the night. I'd sure hate to find and pull you out of a wreck an hour up the interstate. Is that clear?"

"Yes, sir. Thank you, sir." Tyler got back into his car.

"Good luck to you," said the officer, touching the brim of his hat with two fingers. He climbed in behind the wheel of his squad car and sat there until Tyler was able to move back into traffic. As his left turn signal clicked away, Tyler wondered if the officer would have pulled him over again for failure to use the turn signal. I wonder if that's ever happened. He shook his head. *Definitely time to get off the road*, he thought, *taking the exit ramp*. The officer drove on by and with a quick note from his siren, bid Tyler good night.

IX

The next day, Ty crossed the Missouri state line into Iowa and stopped in Ames for a lunch of catfish.

"You'll have to take your time when you eat here, sir," said the host, proudly. "We fry on demand."

"I guess I can do that," said Tyler, reducing the urge to eat fast and move on.

"We're known miles around for our catfish dinners."

Tyler ate slowly and ordered up seconds, which he took with him to the car.

"Y'all come on back now, ya hear?" said the host.

After Clear Lake, Iowa, he crossed over into Minnesota, through Albert Lea, Owatonna, and Northfield. Off Interstate 35, he took the beltline west around the Twin Cities. Not wanting to face another city just yet, he stopped driving when he came to a little town called Medina. It was dark out and the next sign he saw was red neon. And it said "vacancy."

"At least it's not red, white, and blue," he said, making his turn into the parking lot.

He checked in, showered, shaved, and slept until noon the next day.

Before breakfast (served all day), Tyler picked up a copy of the local paper, and casually turned the pages while he devoured a stack of buttermilk pancakes. He skimmed the want ads until he reached the column listing rental properties. One particular ad grabbed his attention: *Cabin for sale, island location on Lake Minnetonka. Purchase or rent with option to buy.* There was a phone number.

Tyler crunched down the rest of his bacon, mopped up egg yolk with the last piece of pancake, and took a few more sips of strong hot coffee. He placed a generous tip next to his plate. As he left the cafe, the waitress smiled and winked at him. "Bye-bye now," she said.

From the motel lobby, Tyler dialed the number he found in the ad and arranged to meet the cabin owners at the end of Water Street in Excelsior. From there, they'd motorboat over to Manitou Island.

"How d'ya do? Name's Jaeger. Frank Jaeger. And this is my wife, Anna."

Tyler introduced himself and they shook hands. Frank's handshake was as numbing as a vise grip.

The elderly man was wiry with sparse gray hair that hung limp over his shirt collar. His arms were tan up to the elbows. Anna, slightly plump in navy Capri pants and matching top, smiled broadly. Except for his mother, Tyler had rarely seen such open faces and trusting eyes.

"Where you from, young fella?" asked Frank.

"Los Angeles. I've been on the road for a few days, deciding on a new location."

"Well now, you couldn't have picked a better area. This is a real quaint spot I'm about to show you. We've sure enjoyed living on the island, but Anna and I aren't as young as we used to be and the cold kinda gets to us now. I'll be seventy-eight next birthday. We're going down to Arizona now, spend this fall and winter, see if we like it there, maybe join the 'snow birds,' don't ya know."

He laughed then turned serious and leaned toward Tyler as if to share a secret. "This place has been real good to us and we're gonna miss it. But it's time we move on and turn it over to someone else who'll appreciate it as much as we do. I hope you like to fish."

"I'm sure I will," said Tyler.

"Well then, come aboard and we'll take you over to the island."

Frank and Anna led the way down Water Street in Excelsior to a small slip near the end of the municipal dock.

"Good thing this water level's up," said Anna, quickly stepping into the boat. "A lot easier to get in." She sat next to the ten-horse motor and pulled at the cord to get it started.

Frank steadied the craft for Tyler, who felt a little tipsy at first, then got in without help.

"I'll take the bow seat," said Frank, "and you can sit in the middle. Enjoy the view."

Anna steered the sixteen foot Alumacraft across Manitou Bay toward the larger of two islands.

Frank noticed how Tyler looked questioningly at Anna.

"We always take turns at the tiller. If anything happens to me, Anna knows what to do. Besides, she likes to take the boat out some days when I'm too busy to go."

The water was choppy and the boat's front end reared up and down with the waves. From a distance, Tyler could see two cottages on a hill. One was white with brick-red shingles and a large picture window reflecting the upper branches of a giant maple tree rooted just up from the shoreline. The other cabin, painted a grayish blue with black shingles, stood about fifty yards to the west. Two long docks stretched into the lake from the shore fronting each cabin.

"Ours is the white one," said Anna as she worked the boat through the waves and brought it up neatly alongside the dock. Frank caught the forward post. "Grab that middle one, Tyler."

Ty reached out for a post and missed, nearly falling overboard. He caught himself and tried again, this time hooking his fingers along the edge of the dock and slowly bringing the boat up against it. Anna got out and tied off the stern line while Frank lashed the bowline around a forward post.

"It gets a little gusty out here sometimes," he said, helping Tyler up onto the dock.

The small white boathouse, screened on all four sides, rose high atop its cement block foundation. Anna led the way up the steps made of flat boulders to the main property. Tyler stood on the hill and turned to admire the view. Gray waves were rolling in, slapping the boat against the white plastic fenders that hung from dock posts.

"It looks pretty rough out there. Can we make it back okay?" asked Tyler.

"Oh, sure. This is nothing," Frank assured him.

Tyler turned his attention to the yard filled with shrubs and large maple trees. There were oaks and clumps of birch and two huge pine trees that guarded either side of the cabin which had been freshly painted. A large picture window, with smaller windows on the right and a door to the left, reflected sky, lake, and tree branches. A nautical flag atop a pole cemented into the ground flapped like the sound of a bullwhip. Tyler slid his hands along the black wrought-iron railings as he followed Frank and Anna up to the door.

Inside the cabin, he smelled baking spices and fireplace ashes. The rooms glowed with the patina of aged knotty pine walls and ceilings. The furniture was a mix of wicker and wood, sturdy chairs and a table made of butternut. Cane poles, rods and reels, and a landing net stood in the corner of the main room nearest the door. A large dented, green metal tackle box with a silver handle kept the poles from sliding to the floor.

"The place needs some work," said Frank, "but it's a nice little spot for one or two people. Is it just yourself?"

"Yes, just me," Tyler replied.

"You might have some company," said Frank. "There's an old fellow by the name of Sam Other Day that lives over to the west. Everybody calls him by his first name, though. His grandfather was Dakota Indian. Sam was born and raised right here on the island and he knows everything there is to know about Lake Minnetonka. He's pretty smart, reads a lot. If he takes a shine to you, you're in good company. And if he doesn't—well, he'll just let you be. Isn't that right, Anna?" Frank laughed good-naturedly and turned to his wife for affirmation. Anna smiled and nodded.

"I'm sure I'll get on just fine," said Tyler.

Frank and Anna led him through the cabin as if they, themselves, were seeing it for the first time: the small living room with book cases on either side of a large stone fireplace opposite the big window; the bedroom, its ceiling and walls made of knotty pine, like a cozy cabin inside a ship; the small bathroom; the kitchen with a two-burner gas stove next to a white, cast iron sink. The table and chairs were painted orange and pale gold; sheer peach-colored curtains hung above the windows and the back door where one could peer out at thick woods.

"If you look carefully through those trees," said Anna, peeking between the curtain panels, "you can see the water on the other side of the island."

"I see it," said Tyler when it was his turn to look.

They went out the back way toward a pair of wooden doors built nearly flat to the ground and angled up to join the foundation.

"This'll get you into the crawl space," said Frank, lifting one door. He led Tyler down several steps. "I want to show you something." He aimed a flashlight toward an inside wall. "Come winter, a couple of these pipes might freeze, so we just keep this old hair dryer handy." Frank plugged the faded red appliance cord into one end of a long extension cord rigged next to the dirt wall, up through a hole in the floor and into the utility closet where there was an outlet. He pointed the dryer at some rusty water pipes to show Tyler the routine. "That usually thaws them out in a few minutes. You could wrap 'em with some good insulating tape. I just never got around to it."

"You mean it gets that cold here?" Tyler asked.

"This part of the country isn't for the faint of heart," said Frank. "Just build a good fire, drink an extra glass of wine, and you'll survive. Now, except for the pipes, everything else should be fine down here. It makes for a good root cellar if you ever raise a garden—or a storm cellar if need be."

"All right," replied Tyler slowly, wondering if he should have checked into a hotel in Minneapolis.

Anna called down, "I've left some of my canned tomatoes and apple sauce up here in the kitchen cupboard. Feel free to eat them up."

"Uh-huh. Yes, thank you, Anna." Bare bones around here, thought Tyler, but it might be fun.

"Have a seat," said Frank, once they had returned to the living room. "Anna, let's have a glass of that cream sherry we bought the other day."

"Good idea." Anna headed back to the kitchen while Frank settled into an overstuffed armchair in a way that showed it was his.

"This here's a nice, big fireplace," he said, "and you won't want for wood, obviously—got a big stack outside. There's a small furnace in the utility closet but you probably won't need to turn that on until December. That's what we generally do. Seems like the price of fuel gets higher every year."

"The cabin has some quirks and strange noises like a lot of places," said Anna, handing a glass of sherry to Tyler and one to her husband, "especially when it gets good and cold. You'll hear all sorts of creaks and groans, but don't let that scare you."

"And the lake," added Frank, "when the lake freezes over it'll start talkin' to ya. Sam can tell you stories. At night, when it's cold and quiet in the dead of winter, you'll be hearing loud reports from his ancestors."

"Frank, that's enough. You'll scare Tyler off with that kind of talk."

"Well, there's a lot of history about Minnetonka—legends that'll feed your imagination."

Tyler smiled and looked around the room, considering the work that needed to be done: insulation, wrapping pipes, gathering more wood for heat, minor repairs that Frank had pointed out. A few projects might be just the thing. He felt comfortable with these people, comfortable in this chair by the window. The surroundings, the warm cabin—it all seemed to welcome him, offer him calmness. Besides, he was curious to hear a lake that speaks.

"Where do I sign?" he asked.

"Wonderful, Tyler. Welcome to home port," said Frank, shaking Tyler's hand. He pointed at a spot above the lakeside door. "I made that myself." Tyler looked up to see a flat piece of driftwood with the words "Home Port" burned into it.

"The paperwork is back in the car."

"Just a minute," said Anna. And she went to the shelf near the fireplace and pulled out a book. "We'll leave this with you," she said, brushing her hand over a worn, faded blue volume. She handed it to Tyler as if it were a priceless treasure. "The author used to live in Wayzata before she died."

Tyler looked at the title: *Once Upon a Lake* by Thelma Jones.

"Thank you, Anna. I love to read."

"Take good care of it. They're hard to come by anymore...out of print."

Frank motored them back to the mainland. Tyler took special note of how the elderly man first turned the rich-lean gas-oil knob on the ten-horse Johnson, and then squeezed the black rubber bulb on the gas tank before he pulled the starter cord on the motor. It was just as Anna had done but Tyler had been too excited to pay much attention on the trip over.

"She starts right up. You don't have to pull your guts out like with some motors. Want to give 'er a try?" he asked, shutting the engine down.

"Sure." Tyler switched places with Frank. "If I mess up, you're still here to give me some pointers."

Tyler checked the arrow position on the knob and squeezed the tank bulb a couple of times, although it was already primed. He yanked the cord and the spark caught on his first pull.

"Good going, Tyler. We'll make a laker out of you yet." Frank reached over to pat him on the back. "Now put 'er in gear with that lever there. Once you're under way, just move the tiller in the opposite direction of where you want to go. There's a good chop out here today so you want to make sure we don't get broadsided."

Tyler held the boat steady into the waves. The municipal dock seemed to loom up rather quickly.

"Here, Frank, why don't you take over now."

"Naw, you can do it, Tyler. This part's a bit tricky, so you'll want to slow 'er way down. That's it…a little more! Oops, shut 'er down!" Frank quickly fended off so the bow wouldn't ram the dock full force. Anna grabbed a post.

"I'm sorry," said Tyler, "I hope I didn't damage your boat."

"That's okay. Just a little knick, no harm done. You'll soon get the hang of it. As Sam would say, 'The lake will always remind us of who's boss.'"

Tyler treated Anna and Frank to coffee and apple pie at The Anchor cafe on Water Street.

"Will you be leaving soon for Arizona?" he asked.

"We're gonna stay with our daughter over in Waconia for a couple of days, then we'll get underway, take plenty of time drivin' down."

Frank went over a few more instructions: "And be sure to take the dock out before the lake freezes over. Sam will show you how to do that. I'd take care of it by the end of October if I were you—at the latest—or you'll be singin' soprano."

"Very funny, Frank," said Anna.

"The waders are hanging in the boathouse. Even though you'll feel the cold coming through, they'll at least keep you dry. Just stack the planks and posts on the shore."

"I'm not sure what you're talking about, Frank."

"Well, Sam will show you."

Tyler took a deep breath. "Well, I guess this is it." And he picked up Frank's blue ballpoint pen that read Roy's Bait and Tackle. He paused and looked up at Frank and Anna. "Shouldn't we have these papers notarized?"

"A signature and a hand shake are good enough for me," said Frank. "That's how we do business around here."

Tyler nodded and signed the rental agreement with an option to buy. Frank folded the two copies, handed one to Tyler, and tucked the other into his pocket. Then he stood and gripped Tyler's hand with his own and gave it a good shake.

"You've got yourself a fine cabin there, son. Like to come out and go fishin' with you a time or two when we get back in the spring, if you don't mind."

"Of course, Frank. Any time. I'd like that."

Tyler paid for the pie and coffee then walked Frank and Anna to their car.

"It's been a pleasure to meet you two. I've really enjoyed the afternoon." He shook hands once more with Frank and hugged Anna.

"Well, good luck to ya now," said Frank. "Enjoy the lake and we'll see you some time in the spring." He turned to look back across the bay. "We're gonna miss the old place."

"I'll take good care of it, you can be sure of that," said Tyler. As he wished them good travels, they turned abruptly away.

X

Tyler loaded up on groceries, parked the car in one of the lots designated for islanders, and transferred his belongings to the boat for a half mile trip back to "his" island. Already, Beverly Hills, CA seemed long ago and far away, and he began to warm to this new adventure.

139

The water was less choppy than before and Tyler sat erect before the tiller. He tried to bring the boat up alongside the dock, neatly, the way Anna had maneuvered it, but his angle was off and the bow slightly rammed the end plank.

"At this rate, Frank and Anna won't have a boat or a dock left when they get back," he thought aloud. "I wonder if there's a knot-tying book in the cabin." He looped ropes around the dock posts the way he thought Anna and Frank had done it. The lines went limp, so he simply tied a couple of overhand knots and let it go at that.

Tyler stocked the cupboards and small Frigidaire with his purchases, hauled his bags into the bedroom, and rushed out to explore the island.

It was late afternoon, a warm and lazy September day when the bright sun began angling low along the horizon.

The island seemed to be about five acres, thick with pine trees, scrub oaks, and sugar maples. Cattails and swamp grass defined part of the shoreline. Along another stretch, boulders, small stones, and sandy beaches edged the clean, clear water. Tyler took off his shoes and socks, rolled up his jeans, and waded along the shore until the sand turned to mud where the lily pads and bulrushes grew. He looked out across the wide bay that suddenly rippled in spots with the puffs of low breezes. "Cats' paws," he whispered, remembering Richard Henry Dana's description in *Two Years Before the Mast*. "That's what the sailors called them—'Cats' paws.'"

Another island, much smaller than Manitou, rose to the east, within swimming distance. Through birch and box-elder trees, Tyler stepped over downed branches and made his way to the other side of his neighbor's cabin. In the middle of thick woods lay a clearing, which felt like a big room with trees for walls and a carpet of long prairie grass. The glade was very still and warm and in the center, like a strange, neglected altar, were the lopsided remains of a large boat, an ignoble pile, faded and crumbling, and resting on three stacks of cement blocks. It was an old wooden Chris Craft, about thirty feet long. Now it looked like a giant planter with weeds and wild flowers pushing through its cracks. Pieces of lapstriking lay strewn about the tall grass.

Tyler rapped his knuckles against the hull. It sounded solid. Then he stepped onto a cement block and peered over the gunwale, which immediately tore loose under his hand. Holding onto a stronger part of the railing, he balanced himself and gazed inside the clinker-built boat. Wads of stuffing poked up between the faded blue threads of cushions. Animal feces trailed along the decking. Dead leaves from many seasons huddled in every corner.

Tyler lowered himself from the block and walked around to the rear of the boat, reaching out to trace her name along the faded outline of broken letters: *Wakan Tanka*.

"Looking for something?" asked another man.

Tyler jumped. He hadn't heard anyone approach. He turned to see an old guy with long, white hair standing a few feet behind him.

"Oh, hello. Is this your boat?"

"Yep."

"Didn't mean to trespass. I was just curious."

"Uh-huh."

"What does this name mean—*Wakan Tanka*?"

"Great Spirit—from the Dakota language."

"The boat must have been beautiful in its day, cruising around the lake. What happened?"

"Who sent you here to ask questions?"

"Oh, I'm sorry. I'm your new neighbor, Tyler Burrell."

"Ah, yes. Frank and Anna said they would be taking off this winter. I'm Sam."

"Glad to meet you." Tyler sensed a mixture of smells as Sam shook hands with him: pipe tobacco, motor oil, and the acrid odor of an old man who works his days away, hard and long under a warm sun. "Frank and Anna told me you lived close by."

"Good folks. I'm gonna miss them."

"Yes, they are." Tyler knew that Sam was sizing him up, deciding if he would fit in on this island.

"Where you from?"

"Los Angeles. New Mexico before that. Horse country."

"Well, you're in God's country now. That's what I tell folks when they come here for a visit."

Sam seemed elderly, close to eighty, perhaps, with hair inexpertly cut in a Dutch boy style, like the picture on those paint cans, except shaggy and white, squared off on the sides below his ears, and hanging over the back of his sleeveless, ribbed undershirt. Bangs brushed his eyes, which were the color of ripe olives, and his skin that of a dry oak leaf. He had his own teeth, but one was chipped and the others worn down, stained the color of tobacco juice.

"That sure must have been some boat in its time," repeated Tyler.

"That she was—saw a lot of fish hauled up onto her decks."

As the two men became quiet, sounds of wild geese, along with the calling out of cicadas took over near the glade.

"Well, guess I'd better get back to the cabin and unpack." Tyler held out his hand. "Glad to have met you, Sam."

"Likewise. By the way, you've been staring at my hair."

"Guess so. It's pretty long; I've never seen such a style."

"Well, I get it cut twice a year. Once at Christmas time so I can see to open my presents, and once on the fourth of July so I can light my firecrackers."

Tyler laughed, shook hands once more, and started on a path that led toward his rental cabin. Turning to look back, he saw Sam reach out to touch the hull of his broken down craft.

They make quite a pair, he thought—that boat and Sam.

Tyler grabbed a cool beer from the refrigerator and went outside to sit on the stoop, just in time to watch the evening wrap itself around the long, wide bay. Houses and cabins on the opposite shore hid themselves among clusters of burnished trees touched by early autumn colors. It seemed to Tyler as if no one else existed in the world. He tried to imagine what his wife Tiffany, and Bob Lauper, and all of the others back in LA were doing at this moment. He wondered if anyone missed him. But he didn't feel like holding those thoughts for long, so he let them dissolve like the last changing shapes of clouds drifting above the lake before night set in.

Tyler picked up the pocket Solitaire game that he'd brought with him. Nearly every day, when he'd returned home from the office, he'd played a few games to relax and center himself. He had learned that term from Tiffany whose therapist had instructed her to "relax and center yourself." Playing Solitaire took his mind off everything else, thinking about which card to place where—not much of a challenge, but a pleasant little ritual. This time he opted for the Vegas hand and was on a roll, turning up good cards, one after another. The columns played out nicely, the suits stacked up, no reason not to win. But where's the jack of spades? Tyler pressed the On/Deal Draw button. Invalid. Game over. "So close," he muttered, "just when you think you're winning, the queen won't move without a king to place her on. And all you need is a jack to get that ten out. Then, 'invalid' and you run out of plays. Well, maybe next time."

Tyler relaxed and leaned his head against the iron railing. The breeze had subsided, leaving stillness that reminded him of when he was a child back at the ranch in New Mexico. There were evenings like this, quiet times, when the horses silenced for the night, and he and his mother relaxed with a puzzle or a book. All they could hear was the ticking of the clock. Sometimes his father joined them and they all three looked up to smile at one another. But those were the rare times, the few calm times when his father was sober. If memories of when he was not sober started creeping into Tyler's mind, Ty managed to slam the door on them before they edged in too far and caught hold.

Segments of his life in LA finally thrust themselves onto the stage set of his mind like short, rapid scenes from a movie: Tyler and Tiffany standing close together, watching seabirds from the pier at Santa Monica; Tyler and Tiffany wrapped in each other's arms on a picnic blanket at Echo Park; Tiffany squealing into the wind, alarmed and delighted, when a whale surfaced and swam near their sailboat, escorting them all the way to Santa Catalina Island.

Life had been good before the six- and seven-day work weeks, before Tiffany had got caught up with…her thing, before the mandatory parties of forced fun and laughter. Wave after wave of memories washed over Tyler, tossing his thoughts about like pebbles caught in the ebb and flow of a tide. He was worn out and felt as empty as a vacant shore.

All of a sudden, the loud quacking of ducks startled him. He watched them swimming in pairs near the dock: drakes and hens plus their grown up youngsters, dipping for morsels beneath the surface, with no concerns other than sticking together, finding enough to eat, and getting ready to fly south for the winter.

The next morning, Tyler awakened with *Once Upon a Lake* resting on his chest. He'd made it to page twenty-one before dozing off. It surprised him that he had slept so deeply, that he hadn't once turned over in his sleep.

He propped himself on an elbow to look out at the lake, remembering what he'd learned from those twenty pages: Minnetonka was "a romantic lake…fabulous and hidden…a great piece of water… lost in a great forest upon the prairie west of the fort." Tyler had read that people who explored this wilderness sometimes named places after poets and poems of the nineteenth century. Or they made up Indian names, such as Minnetonka, as "a sort of last rites ceremony for the dispossessed." Minnetonka = Great Water. Minnetrista, Minnehaha, Minnesota—everything to do with water. And the map of Lake Minnetonka showed it to be huge, with one bay after another: Gideon, Lafayette, Maxwell, and dozens more. And Tyler loved the meaning of "Excelsior"—originating from Latin: *still higher.*

A soft breeze brushed the pine tree just outside the open window. That sun, delaying its rise for a moment, launched an advance of pinks and lavenders cutting through a long gray cloud. The still lake reflected a brilliant sky. They could easily have changed places, the lake and the sky. Low growls of thunder rolled in from the cloud's distant tip and a burst of cool air filled the room and bounced the blinds against their window casings.

Tyler liked his bedroom; the walls and ceiling were covered with knotty pine that had darkened to a rich deep honey color, like the captain's quarters in an ancient ship. Two large front windows gave out onto the lake. A third window, off to the side, framed the tall Norway pine. On the wall, opposite the bed, hung a black and white picture of a very old sailor gripping his helm. That large, wooden helm supported the bent man whose weary eyes, turning white with blindness, still seemed steadfast. Destined never to give up this long watch, that old sailor would forever look out to sea.

Tyler stared at the sailor for a time, and then shifted his gaze back to the lake. The sky and water seemed on fire with shades of red and orange that filled the cabin with a strange energy. Then, just as suddenly, the sun reclaimed its own colors and took charge of the new day.

"'So dawn goes down today,'" Tyler recited as he stretched and yawned. He got up and padded into the kitchen to plug in the coffee pot. Then, with several slices of bread, he jogged down to the dock in his shorts to catch a full sunrise and feed the wildlife.

A large fish broke surface near where the boat tugged gently at its moorings. Screeching gulls vied for position atop the distant buoys after circling above an early morning fisherman who low-throttled his way off to another bay. Demure in their posture, several Canada geese and mallards started quacking and paddling away.

As soon as Tyler broke the bread into pieces and tossed them into the water, those ducks and geese skittered back across the surface and ate all of the crumbs.

After relaxing and soaking up the warm morning sunshine, he strolled back up toward the cabin humming a few notes from "*Chanson de Matin.*" Elgar must have composed that "Morning Song" with a place like this in mind, he thought; the lyrical phrases and trills were the painted prelude and fluttering light peeking over the treetops. And the determined, final chords announced the sun, which this morning cast a long, burning candle across the bay. Screaming gulls, barking mallards, and a leaping fish welcomed their new day. Tyler called back in response.

"Today," he announced to the lake and to all its noisy inhabitants, "I'm going to explore you. Get ready for me—Tyler Burrell!" And he laughed when the wild things seemed to talk back, especially those mallards who cackle-laughed en masse, as if they were thanking him for the bread.

Tyler was grateful for the boat, a necessity on an island. It ran well and guaranteed him certain independence, a chance to go beyond the confines of the island. He remembered a time, back in LA, when he felt that he could walk on water and poke at the heavens, right up there with the rest of the good old boys on the ninetieth floor. Now it was enough just to have a small boat.

He looked to the west but Sam was nowhere in sight, so he tidied up the kitchen, made his bed, and filled a cooler with snacks and sandwiches, water, and a couple of beers. He planned to be out all day and back before dark.

After loading up the boat and checking its gas level, Tyler casted the mooring lines and eased away from the pier, sitting up straight at the tiller. He felt confident, and wondered if Sam was watching to see how smoothly he could handle the boat.

He would take his time, spend the entire day as he pleased, maybe even beach the boat and explore some other areas. Just so I'm back before dark, he thought.

As he rounded a point, he realized that he had forgotten his map of the lake. Frank and Anna had warned him that a newcomer could easily get lost among its myriad bays and marshy inlets. Tyler thought of going back, but decided, instead, to navigate in his own way by paying attention to things that stood out: a small, red cottage with a sailboat in front, a tree hanging low over the water, a channel with an arched bridge, a huge house with acres of manicured lawn that sloped down to the shore.

He motored into bay after bay before realizing that he had forgotten exactly where the red cottage was. And there were several arched bridges and many low-hanging trees and dozens of mansions with great sweeps of weedless grass cascading all the way down to the water's edge.

Dusk arrived early. A thunderstorm, working itself into a frenzy, turned the afternoon into night. As thunderbolts crashed around Tyler he struggled to hold the boat, keeping its bow into the waves, as Frank had instructed. Instinct plus a close call told him not to get broadsided by the rolling water. Lightening cut the murky dark with its jagged threat.

Tyler hadn't realized just how big Lake Minnetonka was—so many bays and miles of shoreline, massive trees along every cove. He lost sight of shore except when the lightning flashed. Whenever he spotted a promontory, it was unrecognizable. He sensed the danger of skimming along the water during an electrical storm, hoping to be close to home. He wanted to avoid beaching the boat or tying off at a strange dock, then taking cover who knows where.

Instead, he held the throttle at medium speed, hunkered low and wet before the tiller, and squinted into the hard diagonal rain until he saw a bridge that seemed familiar. He motored under it, switched to neutral, and sat out the downpour. Sounds of his idling motor echoed under the cement arch while rain pelted down on either side. Lightning flashes lit up the surface where splashes of rain drops looked like a million silver minnows leaping up and down—a curious dance. Tyler breathed in the fresh smells of rain mixed with lake water and marsh plants. When the torrent let up, he left his shelter, rounded the next peninsula, and saw his island across the bay. The light in Sam's cabin was like a lighthouse beacon.

The storm passed as Tyler secured the boat. He heard Sam's low voice call out and saw him walking down to the shore.

"I've been watching for you, Ty. Figured you might run into trouble."

"Good God, I didn't realize how big this lake is!" Tyler tried to control his shaking and chattering teeth. "Forgot my map, but at least I made it back alive. Whew! It's beautiful out there."

"It can be tricky. We lose a few to drowning every year."

The two men walked up the steps to Tyler's cabin.

The rain had stopped. And the air, heavy with humidity, smelled of the earth. The island was quiet except for the faint rippling sounds of lake water lapping at the stones and the bloated drops plopping down from the maple leaves. Thin rivers flowed along the gutter above the cabin door and trickled from the downspout onto a muddy cut in the grass.

"You're welcome to come by for a drink after you've changed your clothes," said Sam.

"Thanks, I'd like that. I'll be over in a few minutes."

Taking a deep breath to calm his heightened senses, Tyler remembered the passage that he'd read in Thelma Jones's book. She had written about the Dakota Indians living in this area before any white man had ever arrived: "It was a hard life this Minnetonkan had, hard and precarious and therefore good. Dangers kept him honed to a fine edge of alertness, industry and self-command."

I've had a little taste of that today, he thought, *finding my way home in the storm.*

Learning more about his surroundings, and making it back alive, made Tyler feel more invigorated than he'd felt in a very long time.

He put on a dry T-shirt and jeans, rubbed a towel over his lengthening dark, curly hair, and glanced in a mirror that was tarnished with rust around its metal edges, noticing that the worry lines in his forehead seemed less pronounced. And for the first time in several years he saw something else: exhilaration brought about from this first day on the lake. Feeling more alive and energized, he grinned at himself in the mirror, saluted, and dashed over to knock at Sam's screen door.

"Come on in. I've mixed us a couple of Windsor and sevens." With swollen fingers and cracked nails etched in black, he handed Tyler a glass. "Hope you like whiskey."

"Looks good to me. Wow, that was incredible out there on the lake."

"Let's go sit outside while we can," Sam offered. "It won't be long before we'll have to stay indoors during sub-zero weather. Here, grab a cushion."

The two sat in lawn chairs that Sam had built out of thick, bent branches nailed together. Soft cushions from inside the cabin covered the seats and backs. A rhythm section of crickets pierced the quiet evening while a mallard's steady call sounded an alarm some distance away. Suddenly, an unusual and haunting voice called out from the middle of the lake.

"What was that?" asked Tyler. "Sounds like mournful yodeling followed by strange laughter."

"Nothing else on earth like it," said Sam. "That's a loon. Each one is usually alone. When you hear the cry of a loon, well, that's like getting a call from your best friend."

"It's kind of eerie. I've never heard a sound like it. Magical too."

"Most people aren't lucky enough to hear them much less see 'em. Folks have always got their television sets blaring."

"What are they like, Sam?"

"The loons? Well, like the other waterfowl, they pass through with the seasons. A few stay on a little longer. Not many, but some. Wait 'til you see one. That's a lucky day."

Sam twisted around in his chair to face Tyler. "Now I want to tell ya something, young fella. Don't take this lake for granted. I didn't see a life jacket in your boat when you got back."

"Whoops. Guess I was so eager to get going, I forgot to grab one."

"Watch the sky and the water when you're out there. Feel the air, check the tree tops for movement, and when the wind whips up, pay attention."

"I checked the weather report on TV this morning."

"Oh, you'll eventually figure out what your day will be like. Just stick your nose out the door, look around, listen, watch the birds, study the sky. That'll give you a weather report."

Tyler remembered the walls of rain that had suddenly closed in on him. He'd thought that they would stay off in the distance, leave him in the clear, let him motor yet into another bay and not get lost. He squared his shoulders. "I managed okay out there. It was unsettling at first, but nothing I couldn't handle."

He settled back comfortably in his chair of branches.

"Slick know-it-all from out west." Sam laughed. "This place'll take the swagger out of you, especially in winter."

Tyler crossed his arms, pretending insult. Then he laughed.

"Inlanders and city folk! They think they can come out here and take the lake by storm." Sam paused to chuckle at his own pun. "Well, it doesn't work that way."

"I understand," said Tyler.

"I'm not so sure you do. Not yet anyway."

Tyler looked at him full in the face. "You've got a lot of land here on the island. What do you think it's worth?"

"I don't care what it's worth. This is my home."

"I noticed some pretty impressive mansions around the lake."

"Those aren't what used to be typical homes. With each year, I'm seeing fewer and fewer cottages. Now, there are more and more monuments to wealth—or, as I call them, expensive storage units. I've had some smooth talkers stop by here from time to time, offering me big prices for my share of this island. It's not for sale. Besides, where would I go?"

Sam held up his arms and waved them in a broad sweep. "This was where my father learned to live—and his father before him. There aren't many like me left around these shores. I understand change, but change like this I will fight. The rich man comes to Lake Minnetonka only to destroy the home he has chosen in order to build a mansion. Then he levels the mansion to build a château. Then he beaches the canoe in favor of an "ocean liner." He is never satisfied. Soon, there will be no place for the heron, and other wildlife. Now, Tyler, do you understand?" he asked without pausing for an answer. "I actually feel sorry for these people. A lot of them are unable (or don't care) to learn how to live more simply, respect our natural world, stop using toxic yard chemicals, and care for animals."

The two men gazed out over the darkening lake and heard the loon call out a second time.

"Learn to respect all of this, Tyler, and what it has to offer. It's like riding a fine horse—you've got to work together, sense the power beneath and all around you."

"I understand."

"What do you do around here all day, Sam? How do you spend your time?"

"I manage to stay busy. I like to read and fish. Tie my own flies. There are some big bass right out there under that weeping willow." Sam pointed at the massive tree leaning over the water, its whip-like branches dangling just above the surface. "You don't have to go far to find walleyes, northern pike, crappies, and more. I like to cook, believe it or not—wild rice and fried fish, some garden vegetables. Then I spend part of the day splitting wood from leftover trees downed by beavers. I've just about got enough for winter. You know, Tyler, you've got a pretty nice fireplace over there yourself."

"Yes. Frank left a big stack of wood, but I'll be glad to add to it." Tyler thought for a moment. "Say, what about that old boat out back?"

"What about it?"

"You don't seem like the kind of guy to let a boat go like that—rotting and falling apart. It's looking like a giant planter."

"Still full of questions, eh?"

"Well, from the looks of it—high and dry on a heap of blocks in the middle of a woods where a boat doesn't belong—I'd say it's been out of its element for a number of years."

"Who's to say where anything belongs? Maybe I'm letting her go back to the earth. She turned into the shape of a boat for a long while. Now, I think it's time to let her rest and go back where she came from. Maybe that's why I named her *Wakan*. Every object in the world has a great spirit, and that is *Wakan Tanka*."

"But the hull is strong from what I could tell. Why not build her back up?"

"I've been tempted now and then. I've sure thought about it. Sometimes it's hard to see her go down slow like that. She was a good boat, that's for sure. Handled well."

"I'll bet she looked smart throughout the bays."

"I used to take a lot of folks out fishing back then, but I don't have the energy any more. Kinda lost heart after a time." Sam picked up a twig nestled in the grass and snapped it in two. "What about you, young fella? What's your story?"

"What do you mean 'lost heart'?"

"Well, it was a long time ago. Hard to talk about." Sam quietly watched the lake, then looked over at Tyler. "We lost one of our youngsters out here, fishing—a nephew. But he was like our own, since my wife and I had no children. He came with his folks, my sister and her husband, from Illinois—just a little guy, about six years old, full of energy. He slipped and fell overboard before anyone knew what had happened. By the time I got the boat turned around, he was gone—nothing left but his unzipped life jacket floating on the surface."

The crickets had quieted down, but the loon called out once more—a long and mournful cry. The full moon started its climb from behind the neighboring island.

"We dived in to search for him, but the water in that part of the bay was too deep and murky. The sheriff's patrol brought their divers out and got him to the surface within a couple of hours."

"I'm so sorry," Tyler whispered.

"I can't forget how his daddy cried and called out. My sister just stood by the railing, frozen, couldn't utter a sound. She eventually fell apart too. And so did I." Sam shook his head slowly, then finished his drink, stood up, and tossed the ice cubes into the lake.

In the middle of the bay that loon called out a third time before flapping his wings along the surface in order to generate a lift for flight.

"And you, young man, what did you leave back in Los Angeles?"

"Sunshine and a sea of Armani suits."

"Ah. I think I understand that remark. And do you have a family? Are your parents still living?"

"No, they're gone." Tyler stood and stretched then spotted a heron on Sam's dock, getting ready to fly toward its aerie for the night, at the end of Manitou.

Sam went up to his cabin, returned with two fishing rods, and carried them over to where Tyler was standing.

"Ever cast a line? Catch a fish?"

"Nope."

"Would you like to learn?"

"Yes, absolutely."

"Tomorrow morning at eight. I'll show you some good spots for pan fish. Who knows, we might even catch a walleye or a great northern."

He handed one of the fishing rods to Tyler. "Time to turn in. I know there's some fishing gear over at Frank's place, but take this with you, get the feel of it. I have all the tackle you'll need."

"Thanks, Sam." Tyler wrapped his hand around the grip and brought the rod up as if to cast. But the tip and line caught in a low-hanging branch. "Guess I'll need a lesson."

Sam untangled the line from a few maple leaves while Tyler reeled up the slack and secured the lure. Then they shook hands.

"Good night, Sam. And thanks for the drink."

"See you in the morning, around eight."

The full moon spread a wide, creamy swath across the middle of a bay that had not a ripple on it. The sky was filled with stars, constellations that Tyler had only seen in books: the Big Dipper, Orion's Belt, and Cassiopeia. They were all there for the looking. He figured that the night would be warm and dry, then felt a slight breeze picking up out of the southwest.

Tyler propped the fishing rod inside the cabin next to the door, undressed, and flopped into bed with the book that Anna had left for him.

According to Thelma Jones, the Mystery Lake People—Mdewakanton Dakota—displaced by the Ojibway around 1750, spent much time at Lake Minnetonka. "The lake…a place of special fruitfulness…a place where a man could experience the visions he yearned for almost more than anything else on earth…the sacred lake of the Dakota nation."

Among the white men who came later were "ailing professionals" who had counted on the fact that Minnesota had the best climate in the world for invalids.

"It looks like I came to the right place," said Tyler as he bookmarked that page before sleep took over, lowering the curtain on his first full day with the island.

XI

The storm began with heat lightning. Then distant, low thunder, like far off bombardments of war, rolled in over waves and shook the cabin. The storm's full force came down on the island with a blast that jolted Tyler upright.

"What the hell?"

Another blast was followed by strikes as if someone were pounding heavy sheet metal on the outside of the cabin wall. Tyler jumped out of bed and stood in the middle of the floor, uncertain what to do, where to take cover.

The vibrating window blinds reminded him of startled rattlesnakes he'd seen back in Arizona. Outside the open window, dry maple leaves hissed and huge waves slapped the little boat's hull, knocking her against the dock. Then the rain started to blow in and lightning strikes lit up that picture of the old sailor squinting into a gale.

As Tyler was about to run down into the crawl space beneath the cabin, the storm let up and passed as quickly as it had started. Relieved to have avoided the dank, cobwebby basement, Tyler peered from the window into the wet, black night and watched the silent flashes of lightning weaken in the distance. For the rest of the night he sat in Frank's chair, listening to the weather and reading from *Once Upon a Lake*, suddenly realizing that he didn't even miss television.

At first light of day Tyler went out to view the damage and check on the boat. The lines and fenders had held up, but hundreds of twigs and leafy branches lay strewn about the shore and yard.

Sam was already gathering the downed wood on his property.

"Quite a storm last night," Tyler called out. "We don't get 'em like that in California."

"Mornin', Tyler. You survived, I see. Mother nature was welcoming you. And she gave us a hand with our wood piles."

"I've got a lot of debris over here too."

"I figured something was brewing when I turned in for the night," said Sam.

"You felt it coming?"

"Sometimes that southwesterly breeds trouble. Say, Tyler, would you dig us a few worms? We'll need 'em for still-fishing this morning.

Tyler looked at Sam, speechless.

"You've got a shovel over there, right?"

Tyler didn't move.

"You've dug for worms before?"

"No, no I haven't. But I can figure it out."

"I'll be right over. Show you how."

Sam ducked into his shed and came out with an empty milk carton and a spade. Then he led Tyler to a shady spot on the far side of the cabin.

"It's best to dig where there's mulch or rocks to turn over, some-place damp." He knelt down to brush away dead leaves and twigs, then stood and forced the shovel downward with his left boot.

"Aren't you going to put on some gloves?" asked Tyler.

"Nope. Hardly ever use 'em. Too hard to pick up the crawlers with gloves on." He handed the spade over. "Here, you try it."

Tyler scraped away the rotted leaves and pushed the spade deep into the ground with his right sneaker, forcing his weight downward the way Sam had done. He lifted the shovel full of dirt, turned it over, and spotted two or three long worms tunneling fast.

"Grab 'em before they get away!" Sam got down on one knee to crumble the chunks of dirt, snatch up those freed worms, and drop them into the milk carton. "If you put plenty of dirt in here, a little water and mulch, they'll last quite a while."

Sam stood up and wiped his hands on the front his jeans. "I'll leave you to it then. We'll need a couple dozen. Meet you down at the dock in half an hour." Sam grinned and patted him on the back.

Tyler dug and dug and when one hole ran dry, he searched for new ground. At first, he picked the worms up gingerly, between his thumb and finger. Within minutes, he was down on his knees, break-ing up clods of earth, and grabbing gobs of worms that eventually tangled their way along the bottom of the carton. Tyler covered them with more dirt, a sprinkle of water, and a layer of moist leaves the way Sam had instructed. Then he set them next to his rod and reel, leaned back against a tree, and admired the clear blue sky and trace of clouds. He still had a quarter of an hour to gather and stack branches.

When it was time, he carried his gear over to Sam's dock, includ-ing an old Stanley thermos full of coffee, and a cooler he'd found in one of the closets. He filled it with sausage sandwiches, a couple of apples, and bottles of beer.

Sam was already in his small fishing boat, checking the gas lines and wedging his landing net and tackle box under the seats.

"All set?" he called. "Got the worms?"

Tyler grinned and held the carton up over his head. "A couple dozen right here!"

He handed them to Sam, along with the cooler and thermos. Then he cast off the lines and stepped aboard, fishing pole in hand.

"It's going to be a good day, Sam."

"Yup. A good day to be alive."

XII

The two men trolled through bays and inlets, around peninsulas and islands where the season's few remaining red-winged blackbirds *screeed* from low branches and reeds. Sam anchored in coves and at the edge of lily pads to still-fish for crappies and sunnies. Later on, Tyler practiced casting a bass lure toward cattails and under willow branches. Now and then Sam eased his boat toward the reeds and trees in order to rescue a lure when it hadn't quite made it into the water. On the runs between bays, Tyler learned how to troll, how far to thumb his line out to snag the bigger fish. When he caught a northern on the second try, he got as excited as a kid with new swim fins, feeling the rush of adrenalin as he played the fish in toward Sam's net.

"Take your time," coached Sam. "Don't horse him in too fast. Let him take some line out if that's what he wants to do."

Tyler cranked cautiously, then *whirrr*, out went the line again. Finally, the long, exhausted fish let Tyler raise him to the surface where Sam, ready with the net, scooped him up and into the boat.

"Great job, son! Would ya look at that beauty? I'd say this one's about an eight-pounder. We'll eat tonight."

Tyler beamed.

They threw nothing back except an uninjured perch that was too small to clean. Otherwise, Sam insisted on fishing to eat.

"If you only fish to release, then you shouldn't be out fishin'," he said. "Some of these fancy fellas in their fancy rigs cripple the smaller fish that don't come up to prize standard and turn 'em back to die. Hell, I'll bet plenty of those guys have never dirtied their hands cleaning one—probably don't even know what a fresh fish tastes like, except, perhaps, in a restaurant. But by God, they've got their trophies mounted on the wall for all to see."

Tyler's thought reverted back to Bob Lauper who had a stuffed sailfish hanging above the mantle in his trophy room. There he stood next to it with a drink in his hand, retelling how long it had fought and how hard Bob had worked to land and kill that "great silver prize, just as Ernest Hemingway did with a bunch of sailfish down in Florida."

Tyler liked still-fishing. After learning to thread a wiggly worm on his hook, there wasn't much else to do except sit back, watch the bobber, and wait for a tug on the line. He especially liked sitting still in the boat because it made for the best conversation, or quiet time.

"Times like this, I sure miss my wife," said Sam. "Catherine used to fish with me, sometimes caught more than I did for lunch or dinner. She was quite a gal." He cast his line between a drop-off and a stand of cattails. "We were married fifty-five years before she passed." He reeled up the slack.

"When was that, Sam?"

"Two winters ago come December." Sam reeled in his line and brought up a nice sunny. "How about you, Tyler? Ever married?"

"Yes, but not for long." Tyler kept an eye on the red and white bobber floating close to the reeds. "We're separated now, going through a divorce. I still think about her, though. About Tiffany."

"Nothing in life is easy," said Sam.

"That's for sure. Everything was terrific at the beginning. But she got caught up in glamour, money, and flirting with other men. I know now that I spent too many hours away from home, away from my wife, trying to fit into someone else's business plans and expectations. The break seemed to happen while we weren't looking. And then it was too late. She'd been seeing another man."

Tyler reeled in his line and cleared a weed from the hook. "I often wonder how she's doing, and it pulls at me. Sort of like that big boat of yours back there in the woods—how it must tug at you. Reminders of what happened. What might have been. How it will end."

"And California. Did you like it out there?"

"It's beautiful along the coast. Tiffany and I used to drive down to the lighthouse at Point Vicente and stop at every seaside town along the way. LA is exciting but since I've been here and away from it, even for this short time, I realize what it was that troubled me about that place."

"What was that?"

"The trees and grass, all that greenery—it didn't seem real. That must sound strange, but LA is like a giant movie set filled with props for another show—always another show, lush and green, waiting for the next crowd. As long as the young hopefuls pour in and keep it watered with their dreams and desires, it'll never go back to desert. You asked if I liked it there. Yes and no. But as soon as our divorce is final, my ties to the coast will be finished."

"And then what?"

"I may have found a new place to live. Right here! Got a lot to learn, though."

Sam smiled and nodded while Tyler reeled in a medium-sized fish. "You're doing fine, son…just fine."

"What's this one?"

"A perch. They make for good eating, as long as they're not wormy. But you can always cut those out when you're cleaning them, usually along the backbone."

A puff of wind skimmed along the still water, flipping lily pads and exposing their undersides.

"Wow," said Tyler, "they look like Can-can dancers on stage."

As the afternoon wore on, Sam talked about the first white men who happened upon the lake from Fort Snelling.

"There's a stream off to the east called Minnehaha Creek. Two young soldiers followed it all the way to Lake Minnetonka."

"Everything around here seems to be called Minne…something-or-other. What does Minnehaha mean?"

"Laughing waters. Those young soldiers canoed up the creek, west of the Falls, sometime in the 1800s. My granddad used to tell about the long stretches of prairie grass and knolls so thick with maples and ash that their branches grew into each other to form giant canopies. And then imagine finding that the stream opened into a big lake and then another and another—bay after bay. It must have seemed endless to those boys in their little canoe."

"I can vouch for that," said Tyler.

"Except there were no houses and docks in those days. They came upon the quiet settlements of Dakota Indians living in tepees. No mansions with clear-cut lawns back then! Those Native American settlers welcomed the soldiers once they figured they could trust them."

"It must have been a paradise before all of these massive buildings took over the lakeshore," said Tyler.

"It was. But something good will happen. Nature sometimes has a way of reclaiming whatever's been stolen from her. I don't know what it will be or when. Not in my lifetime. But soon, perhaps." Sam swatted his arm. "Don't forget, Ty, the natives also had to cope with these bloodthirsty mosquitoes."

"I guess nothing is perfect."

Just as Tyler threaded another worm, a pair of dragonflies landed on his fishing line, linked up together.

"Well, would you look at this couple," said Tyler. "They're going at it."

"A sign of luck, those blue dragons," said Sam, watching them hook up.

"Have you given any thought to *Wakan Tanka?*"

"Every day," replied Sam. "All that is sacred."

"How about your boat? I made a quick visit to the clearing this morning and looked her over. I'd be glad to help rebuild her, if you want to."

"I don't know, Ty. Seems to me there comes a time when you have to let go of a thing in order to hold onto yourself. I've got so I don't look at her much anymore, even though I know she's still out there in the woods. I guess it'll take a long time for her to go down— after I'm gone even. Maybe, if you want to cover her up against the snow when winter comes, just in case…but I don't know. Not sure what to do. I'll think about it."

"Then again, you may be right, Sam. It might be better to let her go."

The sun shone on the far side of the afternoon. Sam pointed out last spring's hatch of geese flying overhead, practicing their V formations.

"What about the rest of your family, Ty? Your parents."

"They died when I was a boy."

"What happened to them?"

Tyler glanced back at Sam and hesitated for a moment.

"My father got drunk one too many times. He had a bad temper and he loved his guns." Tyler paused and looked away. "He shot my mother then fired a shot at me. I ran. He missed. When the police drove me back to our ranch, we found both of my parents dead." As he spoke, he kept his eye on the bobber floating along the rippled surface of the lake.

Sam reached over to grip Tyler's forearm. "I'm sorry, son. I had no idea. I shouldn't have asked."

"I've never talked about it before."

The two men sat like that for a time—Sam with a firm hold on Tyler's arm while the younger man sat quietly in the gently rocking boat.

"There's a thought that keeps coming back to me, Sam. I've always wished that I could have put that shiny black stallion inside the casket next to my father, but I just couldn't do it."

"What was that?"

"A porcelain toy. I put one in for my mother. But my father? He didn't deserve it."

XIII

The fishing boat rocked hard in the wake of a closely passing speedboat—one almost too large for these bays and bridges. Instinctively, Sam and Tyler leaned toward the gunwales, balancing first the port side, then the starboard.

"Do you want to go back to shore?" asked Sam after the boat had settled.

"No, I'd like to fish awhile longer. Besides," said Tyler with a faint smile, "it's your turn to catch one."

Sam paid out another yard or two of anchor line, and then baited his hook. "You did what you had to do," he said.

"It was a long time ago, but you never get over something like that."

"No, you never do. But it helps to portion out your burden with a friend."

Tyler nodded, then cast his line next to a lily pad.

"I want to tell you a story, Ty. It's one that I haven't thought about for quite some time. Happened right out here in this bay. I was fishing late one afternoon, about six months after my wife passed away, when I saw a lake gull thrashing around in the water—unusual behavior in a gull, so I motored toward it. But each time I got close, he tried to paddle away. I say 'tried' because he was all tangled up in a large treble hook with a length of filament line trailing behind. One of the hooks was caught in the web of his foot and another in his beak so that each time he tried to swim away, his head went under water. He was about to drown. Finally, I was able to grab the line and haul him into the boat. I held him on my lap to work at getting the treble hook out, first from his beak, and then from his foot. It took a long time, yet he never fought it, never even budged. When he was free, I held him over the side of my boat, just above the water, like this, and turned him loose. That was a pretty sight, Tyler, when he looked up at me, spread his wings, and flew away."

XIV

The two men returned to Manitou Island before dusk. Sam set up a plank on shore, sharpened his filet knife on an oiled whetstone, and began cleaning their catch. Tyler watched how it was done.

"Aren't you going to use gloves?" he teased.

Sam laughed, held up his wiggling fingers, and turned the filet knife over to Tyler. "Here," he said, "you can clean these smaller fish while I go up to my kitchen for frying stuff."

Although it took twice as long for Tyler to clean the last few crappies, he felt pleased to have contributed for dinner.

Sam brought bread and butter, cornmeal and flour down from his cabin, dredged the filets in the mixture, added a sprinkling of salt, and arranged them in a big skillet balanced over pulsating red coals. Hot oil spit at the air.

"How do you know when the fish are done?"

"When they're brown and crispy on the outside," said Sam, sliding a spatula under the cluster of filets.

"Mmm, they smell delicious. I'm starving."

"These are almost ready. Hand me your plate." Sam piled on a half dozen golden pieces and opened the loaf of bread.

"Make sure to eat some buttered bread along with the fish in case you get a bone stuck in your throat."

"Where'd you learn to cook like this, Sam?"

"A case of necessity after Catherine passed away. I learned more about cooking during our fifty-five summers together than I realized. Can't make pies like she did, but I can fry fish. There's a trick to it though; you've got to start with hot oil and then turn 'em just once." Sam filled his own plate. "Go ahead, Ty, use your fingers. Eat 'em like popcorn."

"Best fish I've ever had."

After clean-up, Tyler tossed more logs on the fire, then sat back and watched that great blue heron at the end of his dock. The bird had just caught a fish and was working it down his long throat.

"There's one that doesn't need a boat," Tyler observed.

Sam smiled, filled his pipe, and lit it with a flaming stick from the fire pit. Sweet smoke curled into the air. "He fishes from my dock nearly every day. Sometimes, has better luck than I do."

From northwest to southwest, the sky above the trees turned as golden red as a pomegranate. Within minutes, the colors bleached, pulled down with the sun.

"'Nothing gold can stay,'" quoted Tyler, remembering the morning's sunrise.

Sam nodded. "'So dawn goes down today...' Have you ever noticed, Ty, how dawn goes down when the sun comes up?"

"You know Frost?"

"One of my favorites."

He and Tyler took turns reciting the rest of the poem:

"'Nature's first green is gold, Her hardest hue to hold.'"

"'Her early leaf's a flower; But only so an hour.'"

"'Then leaf subsides to leaf. So Eden sank to grief,...'"

"'So dawn goes down today. Nothing gold can stay.'"

Waves lapped softly against the shore as night came down. Tiny lights of fireflies scattered about among the darkened bushes. The great blue heron flew low over the water, toward its nest.

The few clouds hovering in the northeast sky dimmed. Suddenly, light from the waning moon gave shape to one particular cloud, which for a brief moment, looked like a canoe floating above the lake and trees, its paddles fluttering about like butterfly wings. Then, just as quickly as it had taken form, it was gone with the call of a loon and the flapping of wings as that great blue heron disappeared.

The shore fire, gone to coals, glowed with each breath of a fresh breeze.

"Reminds me of something Darwin wrote," said Sam, pointing at the red coals. "He claimed that the heart of a viper or a frog continues to pulsate long after it is taken from its body."

XV

During the autumn days that followed, Tyler made repairs in his cottage, wrapped water pipes, and stacked wood for winter fires. In the evening, he read books that he'd packed, written by Richard Henry Dana, F. Scott Fitzgerald, and John Steinbeck.

He boated into Excelsior and walked to the library to check out novels by new authors, books on remodeling, fishing, and knot-tying.

He also borrowed books from Sam.

As a result of his frequent trips across the bay and into town, he got to know the locals, including a man named Jimmy, who, decades ago, had been struck dumb and silent after a house fire killed his parents. Eventually, he became a non-stop talker who spent every day of the week strolling up and down Main Street, wandering through stores, and spending time inside the bakery and drug store where, every day, he was given free eats and drinks.

It pleased Tyler to see that everyone in town looked after Jimmy and cared for him.

And then there was a guy named Mike who had so many DUIs that he became destined for a life of dependence on his bicycle, which some thought should be traded in for a tricycle, especially after closing time at the VFW.

Then there was Gloria Spencer, a middle-aged woman who worked part time at the Water Street Art Gallery. She loved to speak French and talked about her travels to faraway places, including Italy, France, and Ireland. Soon, she would be traveling to Sicily.

One afternoon, at the Anchor Cafe, Tyler picked up a copy of the *Minneapolis Star and Tribune*. He turned to the business section and read: Los Angeles accounting firms under investigation for fraud. The paper listed several firms, including T. Campbell, Pritchard & Longley. He took a deep breath, glad to have left that firm, folded the paper and tucked it into the corner of his booth. Then he slowly finished his pie and coffee before strolling back to the boat.

XVI

Tyler celebrated his thirty-sixth birthday fishing and exploring Lake Minnetonka with Sam. They packed their lunches and spent the entire day on the water, watching the wildlife signal a change of seasons, including the perfect formation of long-necked Canada geese working their way south. The lead goose, strong and confident, broke through the cold wind, high up in the sky.

By late October, a different kind of chill grabbed at the evenings. Gone were the black coots (Sam called them hell-divers) that swam clear down to the lake bottom. And fewer were those large geese whose honking had provided early morning wake up calls.

The ground was thick with golden yellow leaves, dropped from Norway maples and Lombardy poplars. Covering the deck were maple tree spinners, like tiny helicopters; they were pairs of seeds, two hooked up together, attached to long, papery blades that made them spin, whirl, dance, and sail with the wind.

Mist hung above the lake as the water turned itself over, dropping its cool, dense top layer to mix with the warmer water below, while the wind and waves stirred in the rich oxygen needed by the fish. Sam explained it best: "The lake water remembers the summer and takes a dive to seek out warmth along the bottom."

Late one night in early November, shortly before the snow fell, a fire blazed in the clearing. Sam's propped up boat whose threadbare cushions, hull, bow, stern, and scraps of curved lap-striking, hidden in the brittle grass, burned. The cement blocks, relieved of their burden, stood free. Among the ashes, a small piece of the boat's transom remained intact with a faint outline of the word *Wakan*.

Before falling asleep, Tyler read a poem written by Wendell Berry: "The Peace of Wild Things":

"I go and lie down where the wood drake
rests in his beauty on the water, and the great heron feeds.
I come into the peace of wild things
who do not tax their lives with forethought
of grief. I come into the presence of still water.
And I feel above me the day-blind stars
waiting with their light. For a time
I rest in the grace of the world, and am free."

At daybreak came the familiar staccato call of the loon, followed by a strange laughing sound. Tyler trained his binoculars on the single, dark bird halfway across the steely bay. Its glossy, emerald green head with a dagger beak curved out of the quicksilver water. That loon darted a look in every direction, then raised its white and black checkerboard body, dived and disappeared only to surface far away and laugh once more.

Strange Tales on a Body of Water

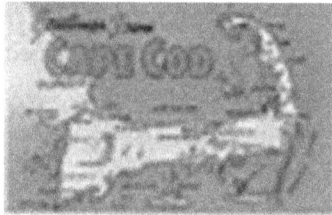

Gathered in a small cove on Mashnee Island, near the entrance to Cape Cod, Gloria Spencer and her cousin Wayne, along with a group of locals, relaxed around a bonfire, feasting on quahogs and Atlantic bay scallops, roasted corn dripping with butter, cranberries, and cold bottles of beer.

The sun had ended its day's job an hour earlier, leaving everyone happy-go-lucky in the dimming light. And Gloria was pleased to be learning new words like "quahogs," called clams back home in Minnesota.

A short distance away, a young woman was riding her horse up and down the shoreline. Occasionally, she'd jump off and jog, then hop back on to gallop once again.

"Around Labor Day," said Wayne, "a mild haze settles over Buzzards Bay. And you know what? Water remembers the summer as cool air begins mixing with warm currents."

And that's precisely what happened that night—a mild haze, along with some strange stories shared around the bonfire. Strange tales, especially one about a horse.

STONE WALL AND OTHER STORIES

Invited east for a visit, Gloria became just as impressed with this area as she had been during her travels to Europe. She and her cousin, who worked at the post office in Bourne, had already gulped down a lobster stew with an ocean view, and explored the mighty arm of Cape Cod, which flexed from Woods Hole to Chatham, and Sagamore to Provincetown. She loved its life-like description: *"Cape Cod is the bared and bended arm of Massachusetts; the shoulder at Buzzard's Bay, the elbow at Cape Mallebarre, the wrist at Truro, and the sandy fist at Provincetown."*

Patches of tan sea grasses waved freely all along the "arm," undisturbed after the crowds of tourists had left shortly after Labor Day, leaving the winding roads, sand dunes, and miles of green for the locals to enjoy.

Marvelous smells poured in from the salty air: a briny scent off the cool breeze, a whiff of iodine, and the odor from stranded shell-fish: oysters, clams, mussels, cockles.

"Cape Cod Bay is bathing its biceps," said Wayne, "and Nantucket Sound is flowing beneath."

Seawater kept checking most edges of the causeway; they were strewn with shells dropped by gulls from heights gauged to weaken and crack them open. Then those birds dove down to peck out the flesh.

"Gulls have some interesting brains," said Gloria.

Occasionally, jeep and car tires crunched the shells, reducing them to tiny snippets. Over time, they would break down like grains of sand and flow from the causeway back into the sea.

Flames from the bonfire heeled and reached upward as the wind began gusting off Buzzard's Bay. Glowing coals in the roasting pit pulsated next to the long tarp piled with food.

Several friends of locals also joined the shore party to celebrate the end of summer. One girl rode her horse along the water's edge. Another watched a large osprey (hawk) and several cormorants flying back and forth above the waves, diving for fish. Several beachcomb-ers collected a variety of edible shellfish, and then swam next to a sea turtle.

Sometimes, sounding like a long, single note from a contrabass saxophone, the foghorn hummed into the air from Buzzards Bay.

Next to Gloria, Wayne and two friends of his strolled along the sand dunes, then settled down against a large boulder, watching all that was going on, including a sailboat easing along the middle of Buzzards Bay.

Russ, a born and bred easterner, was slender, a soft-talker, and pale as an endive. "Not long ago," he said, "a huge sailboat had gone down in a storm off Nantucket. It had sailed too close to shore, searching for safe harbor, snagged a shoal and broke up, beaten by the wind and giant waves. Everybody drowned, except one man who remained lashed to the mast with lines."

Gloria wondered how anyone could survive tied up like that, jerking and pounding against a large mast for hours in a storm, all night long.

"Out of a crew of eight, he was the only survivor. At daybreak, an old woman came out of her house to rescue him. And that man, let me tell you, still feels guilty to this day."

"Why?"

"That's a typical feeling of single survivors."

"Who was it? Did you know him?"

"It was my brother."

On the opposite side of the bonfire, a teenager was hammering live clams on a flat rock.

"He seems," said Russ, "to take great satisfaction in smashing them way too hard. One after another, destroying meat and shells that are ricocheting all over the place."

"Obviously," said Wayne, "he's not doing it for eating."

Like footlights on a stage, the firelight enhanced a diabolical glee that spread across the young man's face as he raised one arm high above his head, with a large stone clutched in his fist. Then, sadistically, he smashed the rock down on large gray and white shellfish that exploded into tiny pieces, landing among dozens of others.

Jack, a recent transplant from Wisconsin, was burly, tall, and rather moody. "Hey!" he called out. "Knock it off! That's disgusting."

"You talkin' to me?"

"Yeah, cut it out, I'm tellin' ya."

"Well, shit, the gulls do it out on the causeway. No difference."

"Hey, asshole, if you want to roast and eat 'em or eat 'em raw, that's one thing. But what you're doin' isn't funny."

Jack gathered himself up tall in front of the boulder and started approaching the teenager who quickly tossed his rock down among the debris he had created and shuffled off to join others near the bay's edge.

"He's the kind of guy," said Gloria, "who'd go out of his way to run over a raccoon that's trying to cross the road."

Russ, who had just finished telling his story about the shipwreck, nodded in agreement.

Nearby, the chestnut horse with a lighter mane and tail seemed happy being led along the shallow water by its owner.

Wayne stepped over to his cooler and pulled out bottles of beer—one for each. Then he waved at the young woman who hopped on her horse.

Jack, watching the rider and her Sorrel trotting along the shore, was quiet for a moment. That horse reminded him of one that he'd saved years ago. Finally, he took a long pull from his fresh beer, glanced at his friends and said, "I'd like to tell you about something that happened back in Wisconsin a long time ago."

"Yup, your turn," said Gloria, smiling at him and taking a sip from her bottle of beer, eager to hear another story.

"I used to live near Green Bay—grew up on a cattle farm, not far from our long lake that fingers off Lake Michigan. I had a fishing boat and caught a lot of pike while trolling around the bay in fall, summer, and spring. Built a fish house and shoved that onto the ice as soon as it was safe enough for winter fishing. You had to be careful, though.

"When I was twenty-five, I met a woman named Ursula who had moved into the area from someplace in the east. Her parents had bought up acreage near our farm and decided to raise horses. I thought Ursula was pretty cute so I started hanging around, helping with chores on their place. We went out a few times—to movies, dances, picnics.

"Eventually, I felt uncomfortable with the way she handled animals, especially horses. She used to slap them for no reason while we watered and fed them. She could get pretty rough with people too. For instance, when we were having a couple of malts, or frappés, as we say here in the east, she'd get mad about something, take a swing at me and stalk out of the café. A lot of my friends were in there and saw what she was doing. They'd frown and shake their heads.

"What really got to me, though, was the way she treated her horses."

Jack stopped talking for a minute, as if to make sure he could choose the right words to describe what had happened.

"Ursula often took perverse pleasure when she rode, jerking on the bearing reins as hard as she could, driving the bit up into their tender mouths. Those reins hurt the horses' tongues and jaws and gave them neck aches.

"She whacked their flanks and made them bleed by digging in her sharp spurs to get them to race across the clover and hay fields, mindless of gopher holes and stones that could trip a horse and bring him down, possibly breaking his legs."

Hearing Jack describe such evil treatment of horses reminded Gloria of the famous book she had read at age fifteen: *Black Beauty* by Anna Sewell. She felt her eyes water up.

"I finally had to stop seeing Ursula," he said. "She was too much of a bad thing for me to watch and deal with.

"Five years later, in December, when we had a series of freezes and thaws on the lakes, I saw her leading a beautiful chestnut along the shore of our bay. I watched them for quite a while, assuming that Ursula had become much kinder to animals. What a fine sight that was, seeing the young sorrel quarter horse glowing copper-red in the winter sun. There was a fresh layer of snow outlining the bare branches of oak and maple trees and the giant pines pointing at the broad expanse of white bay.

"Ursula looked great in her jeans and boots. She was wearing a black turtleneck sweater and a red down vest. Because her horse had no saddle, I guessed that she had really broke him good if she could ride such a young one on bareback covered with a white comforter.

"She stopped and looked out over the lake, then back at her horse, coaxing him out onto the ice. He was reluctant, so she whacked his flank.

"In a flash she mounted and urged the sorrel onto the ice and snow, assuming that it was thick enough. He balked, digging his hooves into the frozen pebbles along the shore, rearing slightly, nostrils flaring. His eyes were wide and wild. I could see all of that from where I stood, as if it were a bullfight—human against animal.

"Ursula kept kicking him and slapping his neck, keeping his head straight with the double lead she had attached to his halter, clutched in her fists. She was obviously going to have it her way."

"Did you rush over to help?" asked Gloria, still thinking about *Black Beauty.*

"I did. I ran toward them, screaming at Ursula to stop. But she had managed to get the horse out about thirty yards on the tricky ice and snow. Just as she turned toward me, crazy with laughter, they went down, crashing through a spot of thin ice."

Gloria, Wayne, and Russ sat up straight, staring at Jack with deep concern.

"I was about twenty yards from where they stepped out onto the lake," he said. "What I watched and how I ran toward them seemed like the slow motion you see when a movie projector loses its power and the film goes down to a fraction of its normal speed, until a frame freezes and then goes out.

"All I could see for a moment were sun glints, falling chestnuts, a crunching white comforter studded with shards, the black hole gasping with bits of red like giant apples bobbing seismically, then slower, and gently sinking from sight into that quiet black hole.

"The horse, with a scream-whinny, snowy and blood colored froth flying from his mouth and nose, fetlocks stabbing at the cold air in somersaults that seemed both amazing and awful, finally became whole, kneeling on the ice like a downed statue. His struggle was over, his energy depleted.

"After feeling suspended, as if held by strings like a marionette whose legs run in midair, going nowhere, I finally managed to pick my way across those several yards with a snow prod, in order to reach for the horse's lead and coax him up. I couldn't believe he hadn't broken a leg or gone under for good. We were damn lucky that he and I hadn't sunk down together on our way back to shore.

"Divers came running out and went down to search for Ursula, whose family eventually blamed me for her death. They said that I hadn't acted responsibly, and wondered why I'd concentrated mainly on saving the horse.

"For a long time after that, it all seemed like fog covering my brain. People made me wonder why I couldn't save Ursula. I left Wisconsin and came here to live."

"Do you still feel that way?" asked Russ.

"No. There's no longer a fog that picks at me. I did what I could do back then."

"Here's the question," said Russ. "Would we save an unkind human or an exquisite animal if we can only save one of them?"

"I know why you chose the horse over that woman," said Wayne. "I would have done the same thing."

"Have you ever read *Black Beauty*?" asked Gloria.

"Yes," said Jack, smiling for the first time, "when I was a young boy. My grandmother gave me a copy for my birthday."

"I'll bet that helped you figure out what to do. Remember how Darkie narrates the entire story? It's an animal autobiography ending with this beautiful line that I've never forgotten: '*I feel my strength and spirits all coming back again…My troubles are all over, and I am at home; and often before I am quite awake, I fancy I am still in the orchard at Birtwick, standing with my old friends under the apple trees.*'"

"And I," said Jack, "will always remember those lines, along with these from poet James Wright: '*I have come a long way/To surrender my shadow/To the shadow of a horse.*'"

Beneath a full moon, Gloria, Wayne, Russ, and Jack grinned and nodded at each other, then eased back against the boulders.

Gazing out at Buzzards Bay, they were glad to see that the young man who had been hammering too many live clams was gone.

From a distance, the young woman who had been riding up and down the shoreline was now walking alongside her horse. She stopped for a moment to wrap her arms around his neck and give him a hug and a kiss on the cheek. The horse gazed at her, nodded his head, touched her shoulder, and off they strolled, back to wherever they came from.

Omertà

"I am worried about you, Gloria. Promise me you'll keep a low profile. And for God's sake, be careful what you say. Do not—I repeat—*do not* utter in public the words Mafia, *Cosa Nostra*, or *Il Padrino*."

"Or 'an offer you can't refuse?'" Gloria tossed her head back and guffawed, attracting brief attention from their fellow diners on the sidewalk in front of Brit's Pub.

"Oh, Charlie," she said, "you're such an alarmist."

Relaxing as best she could against the metal back of her chair, Gloria sipped a Newcastle straight from its chilled amber bottle, glanced at a nearby planter filled with the pansies and petunias of early May, and turned her face to the sunshine.

Spring had finally announced itself in Minneapolis. Gloria Spencer and Charlie Finelli, friends since elementary school, fell quiet for a moment, absorbing the long-awaited shift in the weather that prompted clusters of pasty-faced pedestrians to take to the streets with easy gaits, unbundled, no more squinty eyes narrowed against the sleet and snow that had pelted them into April.

"Did you hear what I just said, Gloria? Look at me! This is serious!" Charlie leaned forward. A wedge of white T-shirt peeked out from beneath his trademark French blue dress shirt, open at the throat.

For a second, Gloria focused on the tight pattern of his fancy sky blue and black suspenders.

"Charlie, you're such a drama queen. You've been watching "The Godfather" again, haven't you?"

"No, sweetie, I'm just concerned about you. It's not good for a single woman to travel alone in a place like that." He fingered his shirt collar tabs to make sure they were still buttoned down.

"I won't be alone. Kathy's going with me."

"Ah, yes, our friend the pants-chaser. Perfect. *Two* single women wandering through Sicily. No problem."

"Don't forget, I went to Ireland alone and had a fabulous time."

"You could send a child to the Emerald Isle and not worry. Except for the priests."

"Not all priests are like that!"

"Way too many *are* like that. Anyhow, I can't imagine why you decided on Sicily."

"Why not? I've always wanted to see Mount Etna. And the very idea of crossing the Strait of Messina makes it all so exotic. You must agree, those words conjure up a beautiful image: 'Crossing the Strait of Messina.' I'm so excited. It's going to be unforgettable!"

"It's going to be dangerous, my dear."

"Oh, stop it. Why can't people just say, 'Bon voyage! Have fun!' the way they used to?"

"You mean *buon viaggio.*" Charlie peered at Gloria over purple half-readers, sat back, and hooked his thumbs behind his suspenders. "I have to watch it too, you know."

"At least you have more choices. As a man."

"Oh, poor!"

Gloria envied Charlie his double cachet in the world. Not only did he have the unquestioned entry into male-dominated places, like pool halls and roustabout bars reminiscent of "On The Waterfront," but he was also capable of seeing things from a female perspective. Upon occasion, however, Gloria found his pontifications annoying. Although he was smart and sensitive and a good friend, she found his condescending manner irritating.

"You and Kathy have no idea what you'll be getting yourselves into," said Charlie.

"Have you ever been to Sicily?"

"Certainly not! It has never been on my list of vacation spots. Naturally, I wouldn't mind viewing Mount Etna and tasting the food. Aside from that, I'm certain of what I speak."

"You always think you know so much. Well, I've studied up on that part of the world, so stop worrying. I'm not one of those naïve travelers running around in a baseball cap, snapping a wad of chewing gum, and broadcasting my plans in public. All I know is I can't stay home for long before I need to pack a bag and go someplace exciting, away from bland, boring suburban architecture. Kathy and I have purchased our tickets, we're going to Sicily, and that's that."

Charlie's iron chair scraped loudly against the sidewalk as he scooted backward. "I can just picture you two getting launched from Italy's toe," he snorted with a kick of his shiny black loafer. "A regular Fascist boot in the butt. Well, good luck, girls! That's all I can say."

"If I followed your advice, I'd take to my rocking chair with an afghan tucked around my knees and watch travelogues narrated by some cocky young guy skipping happily through the latest popular country. Oh, the world is *so* safe for men!"

"There you go, again. Men! Always the men! We're getting off topic here."

"Read the papers. Listen to the news. Who ends up in shelters, needing protection? It's not the men, damn it!"

"Must you swear, Gloria? You're more articulate than that."

"How do you say 'asshole' in Italian?" Gloria sneered. "You're just jealous that I'm taking an exciting trip abroad and you're not."

"Well, you *would* be safer in the company of a man. But go ahead. Get yourself robbed. Or killed…or worse."

Intentional or not, Charlie had nearly succeeded in sabotaging Gloria's carefree excitement. Worse things? What was worse than getting killed? She didn't want to imagine anything remotely connected with the horrific likes of the Marquis de Sade.

And there was that singular story she'd heard about an attractive American woman visiting the stalls of Marrakech with her fiancé. They were standing shoulder-to-shoulder, admiring Moroccan wares, when the unthinkable happened. He'd looked away for a second and when he turned back, she was gone. Just like that! The man was frantic, racing around, wild with fright, screaming her name. He stayed on for another week or two searching for her, day and night, begging the police to help find her. But they told him it was no use, impossible to locate a woman of that description. She had most likely been stolen away and dragged deep into the Kasbah, vanishing in the small dark alleyways of the medina. And why? Because she was blond with creamy white skin. The rest could only be imagined.

Well, at least Gloria didn't have to worry about the blond part. Or the creamy white complexion.

She did have to consider the fact that the world had changed, had become a fearful place after 9-11, her country on edge with weekly advisories about the levels of danger Americans should expect, the news blasting out codes orange and yellow with red constantly hovering in the background. Vice President Cheney practically salivated into the microphones during his frequent televised news conferences—stern, in charge, acting more like the president than the president himself.

Well-meaning friends and family advised Gloria about the dangers of flying and rampant anti-Americanism abroad. They talked about the latest reports of terrorism and torture, some of it political and sanctioned by their own government. Charlie told her of unspeakable things happening in remote places, like beheadings and the harvesting of human organs.

"Now see here," she'd replied, "I won't be hitch-hiking around Pakistan or wandering the streets of Marrakech or traveling by train through the remote hinterlands of India any time soon."

Gloria wished she could feel as nonchalant about travel as she did twenty years earlier, when wishes and plans were as free and easy as she was then—when *bon voyage* parties were laced with simple celebrations, little gifts and glad envy, and everyone gobbled up gooey squares of chocolate cake decorated with a ship or an airplane made of icing, and shouted those wonderful French words: "*BON VOYAGE!*"

"Charlie, I refuse to stay at home just because times have changed. Or because there's no man in my life."

"Me, too, Glo."

They laughed and downed their last drops of ale.

Snug in their small black rental car, Gloria Spencer and Kathy Watson waited in line at the docks of *Reggio di Calabria*, passing the time reading aloud to one another from guidebooks.

"Oh-oh," said Kathy, "listen to this: 'Calabria's grim capital is worth braving only for the *Museo Nazionale*.'"

"That's absurd," said Gloria. "In my opinion, some travel writers come across as too judgmental. They have a negative experience somewhere and end up writing a jaded article. I wish we had time to stick around *Calabria* for a few days. I'm sure there's a great deal more to see besides the museum."

Gloria paged through her volume. "Here, listen to this about Sicily: 'Although subjugation, together with poverty and the Mafia, have crippled the island, they have rarely cowed its population. As a result you will find Sicilians some of the most singular and most hospitable of Italians.'"

"Now that's what I like to hear," said Kathy, tossing her book onto the back seat. "Sicily, here we come!"

Fifth in line with several more vehicles behind them, the two women watched for the ferryboat, as yet nowhere in sight.

"I'm really hungry," said Kathy, reaching for her handbag. "How about you?"

"Well, yes, but we don't dare leave now."

"Who knows when we'll get a chance to eat? I'll be right back." Kathy got out of the car, slammed the door, and took off down the rubble-strewn street in her platform sandals and skin tight white pants.

Gloria rested her head against the seatback and watched for the ferryboat. After a while, she spotted it in the distance.

Oh my God, she thought, *what if Kathy doesn't make it back in time.*

The passing minutes seemed like hours and still no Kathy. Nearby, a scrawny dog searched the gutters for something to eat then slinked away the moment some swarthy-looking type threw a stone at it. Startled when the same man paused to peer in at her through the windshield, Gloria quickly checked the door locks. *I'd better have a Plan B*, she thought. *What if Kathy gets lost and we miss the boat? What if she doesn't come back? What if…? Oh, here we go*, she whispered, *off to a great start. I can just hear Charlie's imperious "I told you so."*

Then, suddenly, there was Kathy, grinning and rapping at the passenger window, balancing a large flat package and two cans of soda.

Oh, the relief. And the wonderful mouth-watering smells that filled the inside of their car. And how the gastric juices kicked in as Gloria chugged her lukewarm Orange Fanta and munched on a scrumptious wedge of pizza loaded with the tastiest pepperoni, sausage, olives, and cheese she had ever devoured.

"*Formaggio*," said Gloria, smacking her oily lips. "Let us never forget the word for cheese."

"Here's to the best *formaggio* in the world." Kathy clinked her soda can against Gloria's. "And the best pizza!"

"And here's to a great trip!" The women clinked their cans a second time.

They'd made it to Calabria, Italy's toe, without feeling the hard boot Charlie had warned them about. They'd bought round-trip passage to Sicily and would soon board the ferryboat, which had just entered the harbor. Their guidebooks repeated Charlie's instructions not to speak of the Mafia. His alarm surfaced in her mind as soon as Kathy left to find food then faded into the background with her return. Now, with a stomach full of delicious pizza and Orange Fanta, the very idea of two women being dragged into a dangerous Sicilian underworld made her laugh. Nevertheless, she and Kathy had devised a secret code in case they spied men who looked the part or seemed in any way threatening: They'd refer to Charlie's cat: There's Charlie's cat, they would say. That guy moves like Charlie's cat.

Charlie had named his cat Marlon.

The boat ride, like a fantasy in the planning, was only minutes away. Gloria shook off her concerns and thought about the sights they would visit: Mount Etna, a stratovolcano capable of some of the most explosive eruptions in human history; the ancient mosaics and Greek ruins of *Agrigento*; the lovely coastal village of *Cefalù*. She couldn't wait to wander barefoot along the beaches, talk with the locals, and taste foods vastly different from the usual hot dishes or roast beef, mashed potatoes, and gravy she'd grown up on and now prepared for herself. According to their research, she and Kathy would soon be sampling delicacies foreign to most Midwestern palates: eggplant *caponata, pasta con le sarde,* and *cassata,* a cake like no other, according to its description—"a cake," she whispered to Kathy, "fit, not only for Charlie's cat, but for the *capo de tutti capi.*" She felt little gushers of saliva drizzle down the insides of her cheeks—cheeks that would soon be bulging with some of the most delectable food in the world. The very idea of bulging cheeks reminded her of Marlon Brando.

The noisy, towering ferryboat loomed toward them and bumped against massive dock fenders. A young crew, reminiscent of the youthful Al Pacino and Sylvester Stallone, called out to one another in that passionate cadence unique to the Italian language. They leaped onto the dock and scrambled to lash heavy ropes around capstans the size of a man's torso. The fortified ramp, rigged with train tracks, lowered amidst a scream of gears until it meshed with the landing. Cars and trucks lumbered off first, followed by pedestrians and those wheeling bicycles.

Within minutes of the unloading, one crewmember signaled to the waiting vehicles and individuals to board, motioning drivers forward, softly slapping car hoods. He winked and smiled at Gloria and Kathy, which made them feel like young women as they found their parking spot aboard the dipping, trembling ferryboat. After a hollow, ear-splitting blast of the horn, the men raised the grinding ramp and hauled in their lines. The diesel engine grumbled into reverse and the boat shuddered away from the dock.

As soon as they were under way, Gloria and Kathy hopped out of their car and double-checked the locks. Then, eager as children at play, they pranced up the narrow, clanging iron steps to the top deck where they squeezed in among other passengers already pressed against the railings for a view of the city they were leaving behind— *Reggio di Calabria* with its wharves and tacky shacks along the waterfront, its sandy-colored buildings with shops, palm tree-lined piazzas, and a tall stone building with the narrow windows of a fortress rising from a mountain of stone, sculpted and towering above the shore, a lookout over the green-blue sea.

Although the late afternoon sun beat down hot and fierce, the air cooled as soon as the boat chugged into open water. They were finally crossing the Strait of Messina with the Ionian Sea on port side and the Mediterranean on starboard.

"Look," said Kathy, pointing out a saturnine type on the other side of the deck. The man, whose skin was the color of ripe olives, hid his dark, penetrating eyes beneath the brim of his hat. "That could be Charlie's cat."

"Hmm, you're right."

"*Turistas*?" asked a woman standing next to them.

"Yes, *si*," answered Gloria.

"English? I speak a little English."

"American," said Kathy.

"Ah, USA. Bush." The woman scowled. "Terrible. Many killed in your awful wars." She paused for a second, then smiled and bowed her head to one side. "Ah, but you are on holiday. Welcome to *Sicilia*. *Buona vacanza*."

She shook their hands, clearly grateful to meet likeable Americans—Americans not intent on making demands while away from home, showing off their wealth, ruling the world. She pointed out approaching sights as they neared Messina, recommended other towns to visit and foods to taste: mussels, sardines, pasta with eggplant, fresh basil, *mozzarella* and tomato sauce, custardy *panna cotta*, and an ice cream cake called *cassata*.

"Oh, there is much to experience here in *Sicilia*," she exclaimed.

Gloria glared at Kathy when she asked about the Mafia.

"Yes, of course they have roots here," said the woman, her eyes shading over, "but not for a long time have they caused trouble."

With that, she wished them good travels and hurried away.

"I thought we agreed not to mention Charlie's cat," Gloria scolded.

"She seemed so nice. I didn't think it would hurt."

"Well, we'd better be more careful."

The day wrapped around them like a warm, blue blanket. Friendly clouds passed over the *Duomo* and pastel buildings of Messina, a town anchored by rings of green shrubs, chestnut trees, and giant bougainvillea—deep purple, red, and fuchsia. Rows of colored fishing boats tugged gently at their moorings. From out at sea, distance was kind to Sicily's emerging coastline. At closer proximity, Messina's waterfront warehouses stood battered and rusty, having suffered through earthquakes and World War II bombing raids.

Some of the buildings near the docks had a sinister feel about them. The closer she got, the more Gloria imagined dangers lurking around shadowy corners, behind a dark door, in the basement of an obscure watering hole. She pictured the glint of a knife blade slamming down on the sinewy hand of a frightened man, pinning him to the bar while a long, thin piano wire tightened around his bare neck.

Shivering, Gloria gripped the deck railing as the ferryboat entered the harbor.

"Are you seasick?" asked Kathy. "You look awful."

"No, just Charlie's cat slinking around in my imagination."

One by one, the passengers clamored down the narrow metal stairway to the main deck of the ferryboat, which slowed, reversed engines, and bumped against the enormous dock at Messina.

It took some minutes for the hands to secure the lines and orchestrate the unloading of vehicles. When it was their turn, Gloria and Kathy inched their car down the ramp and eased it through a seedy part of the city in search of highway A18 in the direction of *Taormina.*

They would explore Messina on their way back.

Smells from the harbor poured in through the open windows of their car: saltwater, boat fuel, fish—and not all of it fresh. Boats of every size and color, metal boats and wooden boats, painted blue and yellow and red, sat dry-docked on huge wooden sawhorses, or bobbed rhythmically in the water while barefooted men in T-shirts and rolled up pants hosed down their decks. The rusty orange colors of waterfront warehouses in sunlight gradually turned brown, like old blood, with the approach of evening.

Soon the buildings of Messina receded in the rearview mirror. After the long drive down Italy's boot and the hours spent waiting to cross the Strait, Gloria and Kathy decided to stop at *Santa Teresa di Riva,* the first town en route to *Taormina.*

"Nothing about *Santa Teresa* in here," said Kathy, studying one of their guidebooks. "But it does say that *Taormina* is Sicily's most beautiful town and that D. H. Lawrence wrote *Lady Chatterley's Lover* while he lived there."

"Fun! I'm eager to see the place," said Gloria. "I should read his book again. It's been a long time."

"And I'd like to find myself a handsome gamekeeper," said Kathy. "Preferably one with a nice…"

"Not if I see him first!" Gloria laughed and eased into the curve of their last stretch before *Santa Teresa.*

At the edge of town, next to the roadway, a young man stepped out of an isolated telephone booth, still tethered to the phone, talking loudly, and waving his arms around in broad gestures.

"Not enough room inside the booth to make his point," said Gloria turning into the small parking lot of the only hotel in the tiny town. "That's what I love about the Neapolitans."

A man who appeared to be in his thirties, sober and sockless in scuffed, black leather shoes, and a stained peach-colored shirt over shrunken black pants, met Gloria and Kathy as they stepped out of their car. He kicked at a skinny dog whose only transgression was to pass in front of him, then sauntered up to the women, one hand outstretched, palm up.

"Why did you kick that dog?" asked Gloria, frowning.

The man shrugged. "Keys," he said, pointing to himself. "I park for you."

"No!" said Gloria, clutching the car keys. She motioned for Kathy to follow and quickly walked toward the hotel. As she neared the door, she tripped over a large stone poking through the hard yellow clay.

Kathy grabbed her arm to keep her from falling. "I don't like the feel of this place already," she grumbled.

"Neither do I," said Gloria, glancing back at the grim-faced man, who followed them inside.

Except for a rickety card table and a lazy fan, the room stood empty, with no desk or counter for check-in. A high ceiling made the room feel hollow and larger than it was. Half a dozen men of various ages sat in a cluster on folding chairs, smoking strong cigarettes, whiling away the end of their day. They fell silent as soon as the two women entered and crossed the tiled floor. Gloria imagined how she and Kathy must have appeared, an unexpected highlight, perhaps: two foreign-looking women, herself dressed modestly in slacks and a turquoise blouse, but Kathy in a tank top, Capri pants, and platform sandals. The men stared at them hard and long.

One of the men, younger than the rest, seemed to be in charge. He stood up, but before he could speak, the guy from the parking lot drew him aside and whispered in his ear. The manager nodded.

"*Buonasera, signoras.* You are with the others? The party?" he asked, approaching the women.

"No," said Gloria, shaking her head. "No party."

"Let's get out of here," said Kathy. "I don't like the way they're looking at us."

"Remember what the guidebook said? About how to dress around here?"

"It's hot out!"

As they turned to leave, the manager called out, "*Scusi, signoras.* I have one room left."

"That's all right," said Gloria. "We changed our minds."

"This is the only hotel in *Santa Teresa.* Nothing more for a long way."

The two women hesitated.

"You are welcome to stay here. But first," said the manager, indicating his disgruntled friend, "you give your keys to Gianni."

"No, we prefer to keep them with us," said Gloria. "We'll park the car in a different spot if there's a problem."

"You don't understand. Gianni watches your car for you. That's his job."

184

Gloria glanced at Kathy, silently asking if they should stay or drive away. Suddenly, Charlie's voice whispered in her imagination: *You're afraid, aren't you? Afraid you'll never get out of there alive. Or worse, worse, worse.*

Gloria took a deep breath and handed the keys to Gianni. The manager smiled and reached for the battered clipboard lying on an empty chair.

"Well," Kathy muttered, "that's the last we'll see of our car. Now what?"

"I don't know. Maybe that's how they run things around here. At least we have witnesses."

"Oh, sure. Didn't see a thing."

"Kathy, if we're going to be scared all the time, we might as well turn right around and go home."

"Passports, please," requested the manager, a friendly smile lighting his dark eyes.

Nice-looking, thought Gloria. Straight white teeth, clear olive complexion, trimmed black hair, long and full in the back. Sexy guy. She turned to smile at Kathy who was likely noticing the same attributes.

"He couldn't possibly allow anything bad to happen here, do you think?" asked Gloria.

Kathy shrugged her shoulders. "He seems okay."

After checking them in (signatures on a scrap of paper torn from a tablet), the manager said he would hold their passports overnight for safekeeping.

"No, thank you," said Gloria, snatching them back. "We'll need them for when we go out this evening."

He handed Gloria the key to their room.

"I have a bad feeling about this place. And I know you do, too," said Kathy, trailing Gloria up some steps and down a dimly lit hallway, each carrying a suitcase.

"You're right. But there's nowhere else to stay, unless you want to drive in the dark to who knows where."

"I say we should turn around first thing in the morning and get back on the ferry."

"Unless something disastrous happens, Kathy, I'm not about to let Charlie win this one."

"All right. I just hope nothing happens—nothing bad, that is."

The small room, clean at first glance, was decorated with blue flowered wallpaper, a chest of drawers, two beat-up chairs, a small scuffed nightstand, and a tall window that looked down onto the *piazza*.

"Uh-oh. No bathroom," said Kathy, opening the only other door to find a tiny closet with one bent wire hanger dangling from a short rod. "It must be at the other end of the hallway."

"We can handle the inconvenience for one night," said Gloria.

Although it was only nine o'clock, the two were exhausted from driving and from the stress of all this wonder. Charlie had nearly won the first round. His words stayed with Gloria, causing her nerve to all but disappear, leaving her too tired and afraid to explore Santa Teresa at night.

"At least we have a room," said Kathy, circling about. "Let's keep each other upbeat about this."

"Right! We're just tired and hungry."

"I'm sure tomorrow will be better."

"Yes, Scarlet. 'After all, tomorrow is another day.'"

Gloria had traveled enough to know that fresh new mornings, plus a good breakfast, usually erased the doubts and fears of a previous night.

After making an excursion to the toilet at the far end of the hallway and dressing for bed, Gloria rooted through her luggage for something to eat.

"Looks like saltine crackers and chocolate bars for dinner tonight."

"I could go for a cold beer about now," said Kathy.

"Or a martini," added Gloria. "Wish they had room service."

"I'll bet they'd be more than happy to provide room service. Wonder what kind of a party the manager was talking about. Did you see the way those old guys ogled us?"

"You, you mean. Don't you feel flattered?" Gloria chuckled and ran her fingers through her dark auburn hair, yawned and stretched. "I'm turning in. Just you wait, Kath. Tomorrow we'll have a blast."

She flipped back the covers and noticed stains and strands of black hair on the sheets and pillowcases.

"Oh, yuck! This is disgusting!"

"Should we call housekeeping?" asked Kathy, examining her own bedding.

Gloria laughed. "Now what do you think? Honestly!"

They yanked the covers back over the beds, spread out the beach towels they'd packed in their luggage, and replaced the pillowcases with T-shirts. Then they tried to sleep.

Instead, they lay awake, wondering what might be crawling around inside the mattresses, worried about their car and their keys, and what lay in store for them the next morning. Ear plugs and sour-smelling pillows packed around their heads did nothing to block out the nocturnal noises emanating from other rooms: loud moaning, rhythmic bouncing of metal bed frames against thin walls, shrieks of ecstasy. Someone tapped at their door at 3:00 a.m. then tried the latch. Gloria got up and tiptoed across the floor to check the flimsy lock.

"Kathy," she whispered, "help me shove this chest of drawers against the door."

"Why are we tiptoeing, when everyone else in the hotel is rocking the place? I'm sure they can hear this thing scraping across the floor."

"Score another one for Charlie," muttered Gloria as she pushed at the piece of furniture. "I can just hear him! 'TO THE BARRICADES!'"

They'd barely drifted off to sleep when the phone rang, promising not to stop until someone answered. Gloria groped for the receiver, muttered a tentative hello, then slammed the receiver down.

"Oh my God! That was revolting!"

"What? Who was it?"

"Some guy trying to sound French: 'Aiee waant tooo maake looove weeth youuu.' Jesus help us!"

"I suppose you could take it as a compliment." Kathy giggled. But it wasn't her usual good-natured giggle.

After shoving the nightstand and a second chair against the growing heap of furniture hugging the door, the two lay awake, listening intently to the sounds of the night, longing for daybreak.

At first light, they jumped from their beds, quickly dressed, rearranged the furniture, and wadded up their towels and T-shirts, which they poked into separate pockets of their luggage.

Gloria circled around the room once then rushed off to the lavatory. "Remind me to pack sheets and pillowcases next time we travel to a place like this," she called out.

While Kathy took her turn in the bathroom, peeking first around the corners ("I'll scream if necessary," she whispered), Gloria raised the shades, opened the window wide, and peered onto the street from their second-story room. The sun was already cooking everything in sight, radiating off the sea and cobble stone street. The butcher shop window glinted like a mirror (or a giant razor blade), reflecting rays intense enough to burn through paper.

Directly below, a vendor arranged bins of pistachios and pans heaped with glistening green, black, gold, and brown olives. Next to these, mounds of fruit rose up in brightly colored pyramids, as the merchant began the meticulous stacking of citrus, apples, melons, grapes, artichokes, and dates still hooked to their long stalks.

Across the street, the butcher climbed up on a stool and, from window case hooks, suspended dressed chickens and rabbits with feathers and fur still clinging to their heads. Slabs of veal, pork, and lamb hung next to them. A dog with protruding ribs paused at the open door, then cringed and loped off down the street, chased away by the butcher.

Gloria felt sorry for the animal and was about to turn her back on the scene when she spotted a figure standing at one corner of the street. Dressed as if for a funeral, the tall man emerged from the shadows, slender in a long black coat. He adjusted his black fedora, glanced around, and started with confidence across the square—in Gloria's direction.

Odd clothing for such hot weather, she thought. *Oh, Charlie would love this. See, see? I told you! Mafia! Shhhhh.*

She stood on tiptoe, keeping the man in her sights as he approached the market directly beneath her window. He picked an orange from the top of a pyramid and bit off a large chunk of skin, which he spit onto the stone pavers. While glancing over his shoulder at the butcher, he squeezed the fruit in one muscular hand and let the juice drip onto the stones before sucking at the flesh. The fruit vendor stopped arranging his wares and, with a slight nod, stood off to one side. The tall man tossed the half-eaten orange into the street and slowly approached the vendor. Something exchanged hands and was quickly pocketed by the man in black.

Gloria couldn't wait to tell Kathy. Talk about a scene straight out of the movies. She had a sense that something else was about to happen. The man in black touched the brim of his hat then sauntered across the street to the meat market. All this time, the butcher had been watching, fidgeting, pretending to adjust the meat hanging in his showcase window.

As the dark man approached him, the butcher backed away as if to look around the shop for protection, for a weapon perhaps. Empty-handed, he stepped outside, the look on his face changing from fear to anger, and began arguing with the tall man, who stood calm and silent. After some minutes, the man in black began gesticulating very slowly, like a priest bestowing a blessing.

Mesmerized, Gloria watched the hypnotic movements of his arms and hands—smooth and sinister. Then, with the deadly aim of a cobra, the man in black triggered a switchblade stiletto and thrust it into the butcher's chest. Red blossomed across his white apron as he dropped with a loud grunt to the stones, a look of shock in his eyes—eyes that stayed wide-open.

Stifling a scream, Gloria jerked away from the window and fell back onto the bed, her heart pounding. Trembling, she stared at a cut of the blue flowered wallpaper that butted up against the nicked window frame. Her mind raced. Light-headed, she sensed tiny stars creeping around the edges of her vision.

Had he seen her? She had to be sure. On hands and knees, Gloria crept back to the window just in time to see the man in black wipe the bloody knife on the butcher's own apron, sheathe it inside his coat, and walk away as though he'd just been browsing at the hanging meat.

The merchant, collapsed in a heap, legs twitching, gasped and clutched at the air. Then he lay still.

Gloria, stunned and too frightened to scream or run for help, could only watch as the murderer returned to the corner, where he was quickly joined by a younger man in a white shirt, neck scarf, and khakis. As if they could feel her eyes on them, the two men looked up. Straight at her. Horrified and riveted, Gloria gripped the windowsill, frozen and wide-eyed. The man in black smiled up at her, a disturbing smile, doffed his hat, and placed his right hand over his heart. In those few seconds before recoiling, Gloria mapped his face: the long, curved nose; thick, meaty lips; his hair shiny black. But it was the eyes that got to her—dark, piercing eyes under arched brows—intelligent eyes, which, even from this distance, Gloria knew also memorized her face.

Kathy's return startled Gloria.

"Pack up! Fast!" she said in a hoarse whisper. "We've got to get out of here!"

"You look like you've seen a ghost. What happened?"

"A murder! Right down there!" Gloria pointed at the window.

"Oh my God!" Kathy started for the window, but Gloria stopped her.

"No! Don't look! They've already seen me! They know what I look like."

The two scurried about the room, throwing even the cracker and candy bar wrappers into their luggage and hustling out the door.

Because no one was in the reception area, they tossed the room keys on a folding chair and raced outside where Gianni stood leaning against the wall next to the door, half asleep on his feet.

"Must have been some party last night," said Kathy, traipsing after Gloria as she rushed around the parking lot, looking for their car.

"Did you see?" asked Gianni, following them with their car keys, pointing toward the *piazza* side of the hotel. "Everybody is there."

"No, we didn't see a thing!" Gloria shot back.

She thanked Gianni for watching their car and gave him twenty euros in exchange for the car keys, with the vague notion that a big tip might bring them luck, keep them alive if matters came to that.

Gloria jumped in behind the wheel and, with Kathy barely inside, sped away, leaving Gianni clutching his tip, looking confused.

She turned onto the highway, unsure what to do or where to go, wondering how she'd ended up driving instead of Kathy who was supposed to have a turn at the wheel. Just keep going, she thought, put some kilometers between us and *Santa Teresa*, get back to the ferry. This is the right direction. Or is it?

As she was spilling the details of the murder, she saw a sign for *Taormina*. Perhaps there they could get lost among the crowds and obscure streets until they were clear-headed enough to make a decision. Certainly the man in black couldn't find them there. Or could he?

"Look out!" shouted Kathy, her hands braced on the dash.

Gloria had veered onto the soft shoulder of the highway and overcorrected, nearly rolling the car. Both screamed as she struggled with the wheel.

"Jesus Christ, are you trying to get us killed? Slow down for heaven's sake."

"Well, I'm sorry! I'm doing the best I can!"

"Pull over. You'd better let me drive."

"Fine." Gloria let out an exasperated breath, feeling angry and frightened. Her eyes burning with tears, she looked up at the rear-view mirror.

"Oh my God, there's a car coming up on us fast."

She shielded the left side of her face with her hand and tried to hold the wheel steady.

Whoosh! The car whizzed by.

"Couldn't see who it was," said Kathy. "They were going too fast."

Gloria pulled off the road onto a grassy offshoot, a path that had once led to a small field, but was now overgrown with weeds. She sat clutching the wheel for a moment before switching seats with Kathy.

"Maybe we should head back to the ferry," she said, her legs like noodles beneath her as she got out of the car to trade places. "I don't know what to do. I just feel like going home."

"Well, we can't stick around here," said Kathy. "I know I was all for leaving last night, but now I think we should keep driving for a while until we can figure things out."

"I hate to give up, but I'm just shaking. It was so awful."

"You say that man spotted you?" asked Kathy, backing the car onto the highway and heading west.

"Yes! He and another guy stared at me with these strange looks, as though I were next. Oh, Kathy, what if...?"

"No, no! Don't even go there! He didn't see me or our car."

"I wouldn't think so, but who knows? There'll be informants, you know, from the hotel. Someone might even have bugged this car."

"I never thought about that. If what Gianni said was true, that everybody had gone to check on what happened, then that guy would have no idea where you went or that there were two of us."

"I hope you're right. But those types are so slick. They have connections everywhere. All he has to do is phone ahead. And Gianni might have pointed out the direction we took. Unless..."

"Unless what?" asked Kathy.

"Unless the twenty euros I gave him meant anything."

"Ha! Don't bet on it. They'll just offer him a thousand."

Gloria turned around to see another car fast approaching. Shiny and black, it came up on them like a hellhound. As soon as she spotted the two men inside, she ducked down low in her seat.

"Are they passing?" she asked.

"No." Kathy tightened her hands on the wheel, her eyes flicking to the mirror. "They're right alongside us."

"Oh no!" Gloria slid to the floor.

"Did you bring that little thing of mace? You know, on your key ring?"

"A lot of good that'll do," Gloria whispered from the floor, her elbow propped on the seat. "A spritz of mace against the mob."

"They're rolling down the window! But only part way. I can see someone peering out at us."

Kathy's face paled as she tried to shake them, first slowing down, then speeding up. But the other car hung tight.

"What the hell?"

Gloria pulled the neck of her shirt over her nose and mouth and brushed her hair down to her eyes. Then she edged upward enough to see the passenger roll his window all the way down and make some curious gesture. She quickly ducked down to the floor again.

"God!" Kathy squeaked. "They're acting so weird."

"What do they look like?"

"Can't tell. They're wearing dark glasses and smiling in a creepy way. What if…? Maybe they're just flirting with us. Oh, no! He's reaching down for something. I think they have a gun!"

"Oh, Kathy, I never thought I'd die in Sicily. We're done for."

"Wait a minute. Hold on."

"What are they doing?"

"He's waving something out the window. It looks like a passport."

"That's crazy." Gloria stayed crouched on the floor of the car. "Can you get a good look at him?"

"Not really…oh, wait a minute! It's Gianni!" Kathy waved back. "What's he doing out here?"

"Who's the driver?" asked Gloria.

"Can't tell. Doesn't look familiar. They want us to pull over."

Gianni got out of his car and, with passport in hand, approached the women.

"*Signora*," he smiled, stooping to peer in, "you will need this."

"Oh my God," muttered Gloria, brushing her hair back in place and sitting upright. "I must have left it on the nightstand."

"They find it on floor," said Gianni.

"Thank you. *Grazie*," she said, nearly blinded by the hot sun hovering just above Gianni's right shoulder. "That was very kind of you."

"*Prego*. Where you are going today?"

"We...we haven't decided," answered Kathy.

"Those men in the *piazza* at *Santa Teresa*. You saw?"

"No, no!" Gloria said, her voice too loud. "I told you. I saw nothing! No one!"

Gianni leaned closer, dropped his voice. "Benedetto Valentini. Watch out for him. He is from *Napoli*. Very, how you say, famous."

"Yes, yes, thank you." Next to Kathy, Gloria subtly waived her hand forward, indicating that they should hit the road now. "Goodbye."

"*Ciao*," said Gianni. "Enjoy your holiday."

"Good thing you gave him those twenty euros," said Kathy, pulling back onto the highway.

"That was close," exclaimed Gloria, kissing her passport. "I can't believe I left this." She tucked it into her purse.

"My friend Gloria, experienced traveler *par excellence*."

"I just saw a murder, for heaven's sake!"

"Did you see the driver? He was really good looking."

"Is that all you can think about at a time like this?"

The two drove along in silence, continually checking the rearview mirrors. A few trucks and cars streamed past them from each direction, nothing suspicious. And no one was parked alongside the highway lying in wait.

"I say we keep going," said Kathy. "Follow our itinerary. Besides, as you said earlier, we can't let Charlie win this one."

Gloria felt as though she were in a locker room before a big game while Kathy repeated with gusto, "We can't let Charlie win this one!"

"Right!" chimed Gloria, at last. "We're gonna beat Charlie! And Marlon—scat!"

"Okay, that's settled. Now, I'm hungry."

"Me, too. We've had nothing decent to eat since you went for pizza yesterday afternoon."

The memory of those thick cheesy slices made Gloria's stomach rumble. Saliva trickled along the insides of her cheeks. She fished a package of almonds from the glove compartment and a plastic bottle of warm water from under the seat.

"Here," she said, "at least we won't starve to death."

Just outside Taormina's city limits, Kathy slowed down as they approached an animal lying at the edge of the road—a scrawny dead puppy surrounded by scavenging birds.

"Oh my God, not another one," said Gloria. "Sicily sure doesn't take care of its dogs."

"You've just witnessed a murder and you're worried about a dead dog?"

"I happen to love animals!"

"So do I, but…"

"I'm beginning to realize this isn't a good place to visit if you care about animals. Or life in general, the way we're used to looking at it."

Gloria's tiny reserve of renewed confidence drained away with the images of the butcher lying in the street, bleeding, clawing at the air. And now this dead puppy. She thought about her own dog, Beau, left in a kennel back home and wondered if he was all right.

For the time being, Gloria and Kathy were alone on the road with only the sounds of their car's droning engine and tires rolling along hot tar. Soon the smoking, snow-etched cone of Mt. Etna shone magnificently against a deep blue sky.

"Oh, would you look at that!" said Kathy. "It is beautiful."

Gloria sat up straight, trying to regain her enthusiasm for this place. "I can't believe we're actually here. Ever since studying about Mount Etna in grade school, I've always wanted to see it firsthand."

"Me too, Glo. Now here we are!"

"I just wish our introduction to this island had been more auspicious."

Gloria rested her head against the seat back and took a deep breath. Gazing at the mountain through half closed eyes, she thought of her very first trip to Europe, when she was twenty-two, and how she and her girlfriends had spread their sleep sheets at night on a beach near *Pisa* because they'd run out of money and couldn't afford a hotel. They hadn't known fear then. There'd been no problems, except for a few sand flea bites. And in the morning, the four girls stopped at a gas station to wash up, brush their teeth, and shave their legs in the sink. The owner had to pound on the restroom door because they were taking too long. Gloria thought of the interesting people they'd met, the strangers who'd become their friends. It was a time when people trusted one another, when most Americans believed Roosevelt: "The only thing we have to fear is fear itself."

Now this perfect mountain loomed before her. At the very top, Etna's crater wasn't the only smoldering spot. Steam poured from fissures along the high slopes. Even from a distance, they could see the eerie landscapes of ancient lava flows; their narrow fields running black ribbons through live vegetation that had managed to seed itself after the burns. The lower areas were lush with vineyards, citrus and olive groves.

"I can't wait to drive up there," said Gloria, cheered by the idea of an agreeable adventure far from the morning's crime scene.

"Maybe we should find a hotel first," said Kathy, "then grab a bite and wander around town."

"Are you tired after spending last night at the brothel?" asked Gloria, forcing a chuckle.

"Yes, I am. Oh, that was something else, having to build a barricade. They should have given us a discount for our trouble."

"I'm going on adrenaline," said Gloria, "but I know it won't last. I can feel a crash just around the corner."

"Same, but not like you. I can't imagine what it must have been like to witness a murder."

"I just can't shake it—that man plunging a switchblade into the butcher. And that white apron bleeding red in a flash, like a giant hibiscus. If only I could have helped in some way."

"There was nothing you could have done, Gloria. You said so yourself. Best to keep still. Like that line from a film: "Knife wounds at a block party and no one saw a thing." In this country it makes sense to hold your tongue if you want to stay alive. You didn't see a thing. By tomorrow everything will seem brighter and we can spend the whole day exploring Etna."

"A nice, long hike in the snow." Gloria shivered. "It'll be refreshing! Like back home in Minnesota. Oh, that sounds so good right now—'back home in Minnesota.'"

Kathy pulled over at the edge of town. Together, they studied the guidebook section for hotels then drove down *Via Dionisio Prim*, the street which would take them to the Hotel Continental.

The night was hot, and the city of *Taormina* throbbed with music and mobs of gaily-dressed people. Delicious smells emanated from glitzy pizzerias and restaurants. Disco music pounded a monotonous rhythm on the streets. Glad for the thousand diversions in the middle of all this bustling life, Gloria tried to shut out the possibility that around some corner lurked the man in black. By ten o'clock, she figured they were going to be all right, and was especially relieved after hunkering down in the security of their hotel room.

"You know, Kathy," she said, dressing for bed, "I've been thinking hard about that murder scene. There was something really strange about the whole thing."

"Try to forget it, Glo. There's nothing we can do about a Mafia hit. Don't let it ruin our vacation."

"I know, but I can't help mulling it over. There was something odd, almost staged about it—not that I've witnessed a murder before, but it was so unreal, like the reenactment of some Sicilian ritual. You know, like "'Gunfight at OK Corral.'" Gloria shuddered. "Oh, but there was so much blood. On second thought, maybe we should have gone to the police—for protection, if nothing else."

"Are you kidding? Not after Venice. Remember Venice? The police are still after you for those parking violations. And that story about Paris? You would never get home. You'd end up like that woman your hairdresser told you about. Remember? The one detained in

Paris indefinitely because some guy she'd hooked up with was found murdered, drowned in the river?"

"Ah, *Paris*! Can't think of any other city I'd rather be detained in—especially now."

"Welcome!" said Kathy, as if narrating from a travel brochure. "Come spend a night in the dungeon. The river Seine and Notre Dame cathedral as seen through the bars of your very own cold, damp, rat-infested cell. This could be you pacing back and forth, gripping rusty bars until your fingers bleed, screaming, *Je suis innocente!*"

"And you could be the woman in the iron mask!" chimed Gloria.

"Oh my God. Can you imagine having to wear an iron mask for the rest of your life? Arghh!"

"No. I'm too tired. Let's get some sleep."

But Gloria could only close her eyes for a few minutes at a time. All night long she flopped about while her brain played tricks on her. There she was smack-dab in the middle of that sun-filled *piazza*, surrounded by a dozen pyramids of fruit that began tumbling to the ground in a violent earthquake while World War II aircraft dropped bombs all over the island. Just steps away, the tall man in black stood over an innocent butcher—the silent thrust of a stiletto and that blossom of blood sprouting over the butcher's white apron like a Georgia O'Keefe painting.

Finally, in the early hours just before daybreak, Gloria fell into a deep and heavy sleep.

The next morning, while waiting in the lobby for Kathy to meet her for breakfast, Gloria flipped through a rack of postcards and chose one with a splendid view of Mount Etna. On the back, she wrote, "Dear Charlie, Have I got a story for you! As ever, Gloria." Somehow, having written those few simple words made her feel better, more in control.

She requested an envelope at the desk, sealed the postcard inside, paid the postage, and left it for mailing. Then she wandered into a small, darkened room off the lobby. Against the far wall, in the shadows, stood an old upright piano with a single piece of sheet music propped against its rail: *Il Padrino 2*.

Why on earth, she wondered, would anyone leave the theme from *Godfather II* in plain view? One of the guidebooks even jokingly suggested that tourists also keep *omertà*—the Mafia code of silence—while traveling in these regions. "*Omertà*: A rule or code," said the guidebook, "that prohibits speaking or divulging information about certain activities to the police, especially the activities of a criminal organization. From the Italian word, 'humility.'"

Charlie's cat!

Gloria's first inclination was to rush from the room, get away from this bad omen. Why would anyone display that particular song here, much less play it? Or sing it? She stopped and looked back at the music. Curious. No, by God, she'd sit down, play the notes, and sing the words, daring that man in black.

But the guidebook had also said that the "old image...is a thing of the past, that Mafia bosses are now slick-suited *supremos* (with politicians in their pockets), involved in every dubious trade from arms to heroin." Then why was that man in Santa Teresa dressed so stereotypically?

Gloria sat down at the piano. Soon the plaintive song in A minor filled the room. As she sang, she sensed someone behind her, near the doorway. Probably Kathy or the desk clerk. She didn't turn around, but instead, gave herself over to the sublime and menacing music, hoping that whoever might be listening would enjoy her performance. With a flourish, she sustained an arpeggio on the last chord just as Kathy came bounding in.

"Ready for breakfast? I'm starving!"

"Me too," replied Gloria, getting up from the piano bench.

"Who was that man standing in the doorway?" asked Kathy.

"I don't know. The desk clerk maybe?"

"No. Whoever it was, he seemed to be enjoying your music, which, by the way, was beautiful. Very haunting. But then he just slipped away."

"What'd he look like?"

"I don't know. Tall. Thin. Rather distinguished looking."

"Uh-oh. What was he wearing?"

"A dark suit. Probably just another guest in the hotel. He left before I could get a good look at him."

Gloria breathed a long sigh and scowled.

"You've got to stop worrying. I've never seen you like this."

"I know. I've never been at such loose ends on a trip before. I hate feeling this way. Fortunately, the killer never saw you."

Kathy crossed her arms, looked up at the ceiling, and sighed loudly. "I was hoping we could have some fun today."

"You're right," said Gloria. "We spent a lot of money to get here. I refuse to let Charlie and Marlon spoil it for us."

They laughed and sat down together at a small table near the reception area. Soon they were sipping strong coffee and devouring slabs of warm bread heaped with red berry jam.

Fortified, they left for Mount Etna.

"It says here," said Kathy, reading from her guidebook, "that as far back as the eighth century, the Arabs used ice from this mountain to make *gelato*."

"No wonder Italian ice cream tastes so good. They've had twelve centuries to perfect it. By the way, did you bring warm clothes? We don't want to freeze to death up there."

Driving through pumice fields, Gloria and Kathy marveled at the huts and shelters people had built from chunks of cooled lava. Soon the day turned windy with rushing clouds that occasionally made room for small patches of blue with a ray of sunshine peeking through. As they continued upward, along the narrow road, they saw that Etna's summit was having a wild time of it with high winds, racing clouds, and swirling snow. By the time they reached the tree line, the wind had turned into a gale. The parking lot was empty.

"According to the guidebook, we should allow for three hours to hike to the summit," said Kathy.

"Well, are we just going to sit here," asked Gloria, "or are we going to face the blizzard?"

They pushed open their doors, took three steps, and stood for a minute in the cold while the horizontal snow pelted their faces.

"Sure we aren't on Mt. Everest?" shouted Kathy over the gale.

"Or back home in Minnesota!" cried Gloria.

"Okay, I've had enough. Back to sea level."

"So much for our three-hour hike."

They jumped back into their car, cranked up the heater, and opened the windows in order to feel the gradual change in temperature on the way down, from the peak to the high hills to the lower mountain. Soon the orange groves, vineyards, and olive trees began to fill out the flat land. Stone hedges outlined green and umber fields where flying clouds chased their own shadows. Flocks of sheep slowly crossed the road in front of the car.

Kathy spied a pastry shop in the little town of *Milo*. "Let's celebrate our almost-got-there-for-a-hike," she said. And they bought *cannoli* and a large round loaf of bread.

"I think we should have a nice big dinner tonight," said Gloria, leaning against the car, licking whipped cream from her fingers. "Celebrate our survival!"

"Sounds good to me."

Out of nowhere, an emaciated dog approached, eyes large and wary. He stopped a short distance away and stared at the women. Gloria tore off a big chunk of the bread she was eating and tossed it to the animal.

"I wonder how any of them make it," said Kathy, shaking her head. "Left to fend for themselves, at the mercy of mankind."

"And many a man not so kind," Gloria said, troubled as she watched the scrawny dog snatch the piece of bread and slink away with it. She hated this uneasy feeling, this loss of ebullience, her usual sense of well-being whether sightseeing or at home. Even before Charlie had warned her about traveling alone, about the dangers of the world, especially for women, a nugget of fear had lodged within her, a fear that was impossible to dislodge since that murder in Santa Teresa. Never in her life did she think she'd ever witness such a thing.

The notion of powerful types imposing their will on others enraged Gloria. Kathy too. They'd had plenty of conversations about it: anyone in the way or perceived as a threat, could be eliminated in some creative way: a fall from a top floor hotel window, a live burial, deep-sixed wearing concrete boots, a brain scramble with an ice pick through the ear. "Illustrious corpses" was how the guidebook described Italian magistrate Giovane Falcone and Judge Paolo Borsellino after their assassinations in 1992, by a roadside bomb and a car bomb.

A line from the Our Father came to Gloria: "Thy kingdom come. Thy will be done." *Il Padrino*. She guessed that was how a Mafia Godfather considered himself—a kind of God Almighty.

That evening, Gloria and Kathy decided to dine in style at the San Domenico Palace hotel, a former monastery overlooking the sea. The next day, they would head for Agrigento's archeological site, the valley of Greek temples, then motor on to Cefalù. Kathy suggested taking a detour to the village of *Corlione*, but Gloria replied that surely she was joking. "I, for one," she said, "have had enough of Godfather for a lifetime."

"Well, I'm in search of 'temptations,'" said Kathy, laughing and repeating the translation for the word "information" on a tourism website she'd checked on the hotel's computer: "Click for the latest temptations," it read.

The hotel restaurant, not yet crowded at eight o'clock, was luxurious, decked out in deep lavender with ruched window dressings in burgundy and lavender stripes. A dozen tables, covered with heavy ecru linen, glowed under dim lights. The chairs, cushioned in a plush burgundy, promised comfort. The room was filled with the kitchen smells of fish sautéed in olive oil, roasting lamb, spices, breads, and strong coffee.

Each had worn her best outfit: Kathy in a rose-colored dress and heels to match; Gloria in the silver spandex off-one-shoulder top she'd worn in Paris on an earlier trip, but with a long black skirt instead of capri pants. Black heels made her feel taller, more confident. She smiled, remembering the sound of Parisian women click-clacking down the cobblestone streets on their stiletto heels.

The two women had just opened their menus and begun sipping from crystal water glasses when in came a small entourage. They couldn't see who was in the middle, someone very important they guessed. Two men were eventually seated across the room while the rest, mostly women, clustered around their table.

"Would you look at those groupies," said Kathy. "Such a fuss. One of those women just kissed that man's hand, as if he were the Pope."

Gloria was about to comment when she got a good look and turned ashen. "Kathy. It's…"

But Kathy already knew from the look on Gloria's face.

Just then, the man in black held up a hand to part the several remaining women next to his table. Catching sight of Gloria, he held her stare for a long moment, made a comment to his friend, pointed, and slowly stood, the blank look on his face replaced by what seemed a menacing smile.

Grabbing Kathy by the arm, Gloria jumped up and ran. The tablecloth, caught in the clasp of her purse, trailed after them. The breadbasket, plates, water glasses, and silverware crashed to the floor. Gloria yanked at the cloth to release it as she and Kathy rushed into the hall and down the steps.

"Wait!" yelled Kathy. "I can't…I can't run in these shoes."

"Take them off!" shouted Gloria half running, half skipping as she tugged at her own heels.

They ran until they got to their hotel room and locked themselves inside, panting.

"Don't turn on the lights!" Gloria fell onto the bed and tried to catch her breath.

"We're on street level. That window," said Kathy. "They can see us!"

Both rolled off the beds and onto the carpet. Gloria imagined gunfire blasting through the windows.

They reached up for pillows and blankets, then lay down next to their packed suitcases, trembling, anxious for daybreak and the first ferryboat out of Messina.

Slouched low in the car, they waited in line, disguised in high-collar jackets, sunglasses, and long scarves wrapped around their heads. Gloria held a handkerchief against her nose and mouth as if she had the sniffles. From behind these getups, they peeked from the car window. Finally, it was their turn to board. They bumped up the ramp and onto the train ferry, then waited inside the locked car until the crew raised the platform and cast off the lines. As soon as the boat chugged into open water, Gloria and Kathy, feeling safe at last, crept from their car, inched up the steps to the top deck, and edged toward the railing where, just three days earlier, primed for their exciting Sicilian adventure, they stood, breathing in the fresh air, thrilled to be crossing the Strait of Messina.

This time, a young man with an expensive-looking camera stood next to them, commenting with a knowing smile on the commotion across the deck, near the opposite railing.

"Silly women," he said. "They scramble for his autograph, fight for his attentions. See how shamelessly they flirt with him? It is quite annoying, but I must admit, he is *primo.*"

Gloria and Kathy stared wild-eyed at the familiar tall man. Instead of black clothing, the murderer wore khakis and a loose-fitting white shirt. His face was unmistakable.

"Would you like to meet the most famous actor in all of Italy?" asked the young man with the camera. "He has just finished shooting a major scene in *Santa Teresa*. His name is Benedetto Valentini."

The Forest of Broceliande

After all her years of travel, Gloria Spencer decided to take one more trip—this time, in search for The Fountain of Youth.

Loving the language, she returned to France, rented a blue Renault, and drove to Brittany—the province of *La Bretagne*. In order to research chivalry and courtly love, along with the time of King Arthur and Knights of the Round Table, she visited Viviane's castle near *Comper* and planned to explore the enchanted forest.

Gloria rolled down her window, felt the warm air, and inhaled grassy smells of farms and cooking in small villages. Massive clusters of hot pink hydrangeas, called "hortensias" in French, fronted beige and gray Breton stone buildings. Red and white geraniums flowed from window boxes.

"Fairy tale towns," she sang while driving near streams and a lake, into the castle parking lot. Yellow coneflowers and mums grew next to stone walls. Near a huge boulder, close to the pond, blossoming hawthorns waved at the sky.

Gloria entered the castle.

"Centuries ago," announced a speaker, "the *chevaliers* helped those in distress, showed mercy toward the weak, protected women and children. The knights were honorable, loyal, brave, just, and courteous."

"However," said another, "there were plenty of exceptions. And the large pond next to us, the pond of *Comper*, is related to Viviane, the Lady of the Lake. Hidden deep under the water, she lives in a crystal palace, built by Merlin."

Gloria wondered if anything similar to that had ever happened back home in the land of 10,000 lakes.

Another memorable item came out of a twenty-minute film documentary—an interview with John Boorman at his home in Ireland. "Ex Calibur" was based on the Arthur legends, including a magic sword and the importance of trees in the world and how they tie in with the harmony and wholesomeness within oneself. This reminded Gloria of how her elderly friend Jacqueline, who lived on a farm in Minnesota, adamantly expressed her need to be surrounded by trees.

"We must harmonize with nature," she'd said, "and stop the destruction of rain forests."

Determined to locate that Fountain of Youth, deep in the heart of Broceliande, King Arthur's enchanted forest, Gloria left the castle, hopped into her rental car, and began following several signs, handwritten and posted. After driving off the primary and secondary paved highways, she ended up on increasingly narrow roads and meager trails that eventually made her feel lost.

Instead of being frightened, she remembered what the speaker had said back at Viviane's castle, including "The road to nowhere and the road to everywhere," along with all she'd read about chivalry and these magic places in the woods: "The valley of no return; the forest of *Paimpont*." And she recalled her earlier travels and romances in life, wondering if, some day, she might meet a courtly one, should another *chevalier* turn up soon.

Gloria laughed, remembering how one of her friends had described some of the men she'd met: "nimpy-nosed, tinny-toothed, jut-jawed, wet willy." And "duck-butted, jelly-ribbed."

How on earth could that woman make up such words?

Thank goodness, she thought, there'd been a shift of the cave man stereotypes dragging women off by their hair, to men who pleased the lady fair by doing their every bidding.

Now, however, in the twenty-first century, Gloria wondered what had brought more heartbreak back into the world. So many women were putting up with cheating, physical and verbal abuse. Fortunately, these were not a part of her life.

Although she was lost, those were Gloria's thoughts while inching along. Through the opened car windows, she listened to mockingbirds and green-yellow leaves flitting softly in the breeze. She spotted a raccoon, several squirrels, and a large tortoise tiptoeing toward a pond.

"Here we all are together, along these paths of the *Paimpont* woods," she said, grinning at the wildlife. "This is where Merlin, Lancelot, Guinevere, and Lady of the Lake lived for a spell, away from England."

Suddenly, she spotted a hand-written, weather-beaten sign that read "*Fontaine de Jouvence par ici.*"

"The Fountain of Youth!" shouted Gloria, driving onto a narrow, weedy trail that eventually filled up and ended with branches and small shrubs. There were no further directions or signs—no other tourists and no one to ask if this, indeed, was *the* spot.

"I guess I'm on my own," she said, "deep in the woods of Broceliande."

Gloria got out of the car and decided that traipsing by herself, she would accept some little spot that took her fancy. After strolling a short distance, she was thrilled to find a large pond where that tortoise she'd seen was swimming along the edge. At one end, an historic set of huge rocks reminded her of many places and things during years of travel, including the poem she'd read back at the castle: "The Myth of Sisyphus." Ceaselessly carrying a huge bolder, hefting it on his back, and pushing it to the top of a mountain—for eternity—and seeing it roll down again and again, he does not realize that he may let go of it at any time. Then he can head home and live out the rest of his life, reaching a state of acceptance.

This summer afternoon, Gloria, finding a magic place and accepting much of what she'd learned throughout her travels, rolled up her slacks, sat down on a large, flat stone, swished her legs around in the water, and spent time listening to the birds.

As Harper Lee had written, "Mockingbirds don't do one thing but sing their hearts out for us."

"I love your music," sang Gloria, gazing up into the trees, feeling younger than she had in a long time. One of the mockingbirds glanced down at her and kept on singing.

While relaxing in the woods Gloria remembered her long ago travels to Ireland, Italy, and Paris. While skiing in Colorado, she'd met her future husband who was no longer living. Most recently, she'd visited her cousin in Massachusetts, and traveled to Sicily where she witnessed strange, unusual activities.

Suddenly, a rabbit hopped along one side of the pond and onto a rock. It sat there for a moment staring at Gloria, reminding her of a similar experience on the island of Inishmaan.

All those stones upon the Aran Islands, located off the west coast of Ireland, across the mouth of Galway Bay, had been lifted, carried, and stacked up among the fields by men, women, and children. So many stones! So much hefting. Beautifully lined up, they delineate private property. And those who tried to beat back the sea with their fists—ah, Gloria would never forget how it felt to approach and lie down on her stomach at the edge of a three-hundred-foot cliff overlooking the sea that never rests along those islands. Atlantic waters crash against the rocks, supplying inescapable, uncontrollable sounds of Aran.

"Bread and water," whispered Gloria, remembering the English translation for Irish Aran and loving the fact that those islands were able to keep one step ahead of an ever-encroaching civilization.

She remembered a man from Inishmaan saying, "Electricity, when it comes, is certain to darken the memories of the past as much as it will brighten the houses of the future."

"So I bundled me heart," sang Gloria, waving at the mockingbirds, "and I roamed the world free, to the east with the lark, to the west with the sea...Look, look, look to the rainbow, follow it over the hill and stream...Follow the fellow who follows a dream."

The people and animals, along with each country, city and unique countryside flowed through her open mind, along with the love of foreign languages and unique lifestyles. And then there were more songs like "Finian's Rainbow":

"You Must Believe in Spring": "'Just as a tree is sure/Its leaves will reappear/It knows it's emptiness/Is just the time of year…'"

"*L'Amore Ha Detto Addio*"—'Love Said Goodbye' in *The Godfather*.

"I found out how were things in *Glocca Morra*," she whispered. "And I was sure to fall in love with Old Cape Cod where they'd ask 'Would you like some coffee? Regular or black?'

"*O Sole Mio*—My Sun—it's now or never. Now, in this far-away forest," said Gloria, "I can hear a cuckoo. And these lovely mockingbirds."

Each night, in Massachusetts, after visiting with her cousin, she fell asleep to the fog horn in Buzzard's Bay—even one music-type note, she thought, can wash away the dust of everyday life.

And she began to feel younger and younger.

Sitting among tall trees, these forest songbirds reminded Gloria of a poem by Emily Dickinson: "Hope is the thing with feathers/That perches on the soul/And sings a song without words/And never stops at all."

Finally, her thoughts about home popped up: the 10,000 lakes, four seasons and snowy winters, farmland, woods, pets, and wildlife.

And then there was that kind man she'd met and visited with a couple of times—Tyler, who had left California and decided to live in a tiny cottage on Lake Minnetonka.

Gloria looked forward to seeing him again.

Homeward-bound, she returned her rental car, purchased a train ticket, and traveled back to the airport near Paris. Relaxing on board the railway coach, she remembered what had happened to her several years ago, trying to find a specific train that would be leaving in minutes for her destination. She had too much luggage back then and didn't know which track to run to. After a young man lead her in the right direction, she ran and ran, trailing her large suitcase and hauling a heavy backpack, hoping to enter the first door that was about to close along with the others. Unable to breathe properly, she tossed the luggage inside, squeezed herself through the double door as it slammed shut, and the train began to roll. Out of breath Gloria flopped onto the floor next to her luggage, and couldn't move.

Suddenly, a man rushed over with a bottle of water and kneeled down next to her. As soon as she was able to breathe properly and stand up, he led her to an empty seat, carrying the suitcase and backpack, making sure she had recovered and could sip some water.

Gloria never forgot what it felt like back then, to receive that kind of help from a stranger. And now, after having visited *Broceliande* and studying history, chivalry and kindness toward women, she compared that man to Sir Galahad, one of the greatest of all Medieval Knights.

Close to home, Gloria stared through a window from inside the airplane, watching its shape grow larger and larger along the runway, until it and its shadow met at touchdown.

About the Author

Connie Claire (Peterson) Szarke, novelist, poet, short story writer, presenter, and classical pianist, lives on a bay west of the Twin Cities. Her trilogy novels, *Delicate Armor, A Stone for Amer,* and *Lady in the Moon, A Novel in Stories,* have earned Nominee Awards, Midwest Book Award finalist, MIPA (Midwest Independent Publishers Association) finalist, and Winner of The Jeanette Fair Memorial Award Tau State.

As a former high school French teacher and lifelong pianist, Szarke's links with music, European culture, history, and the arts provide her with literary, historical, semi-autobiographical fiction.

Born and raised in Southwestern Minnesota, the prairie land, farms, small towns, woods, lakes, and wildlife also influence her writing.

Her presentation for various organizations is entitled "Elements of Fiction."

CPSIA information can be obtained
at www.ICGtesting.com
Printed in the USA
FSHW010545200320
68241FS